NORDIC VISIONS

THE BEST OF NORDIC SPECULATIVE FICTION

NORDIC VISIONS

THE BEST OF NORDIC SPECULATIVE FICTION

EDITED BY
MARGRÉT HELGADÓTTIR

SOLARIS

First published 2023 by Solaris
an imprint of Rebellion Publishing Ltd,
Riverside House, Osney Mead,
Oxford, OX2 0ES, UK

www.solarisbooks.com

ISBN: 978-1-83786-029-6

10 9 8 7 6 5 4 3 2 1

A CIP catalogue record for this book is available from the
British Library.

Designed & typeset by Rebellion Publishing

Printed in Denmark

CONTENTS

Introduction   7

SWEDEN
She, John Ajvide Lindqvist   15
Lost and Found, Maria Haskins   47
Sing, Karin Tidbeck   69

DENMARK
The False Fisherman, Kaspar Colling Nielsen   91
Heather Country, Jakob Drud   99
The Traveller Girl, Lene Kaaberbøl   117

THE FAROE ISLANDS
The Abyss, Rakel Helmsdal   139

ICELAND
The Dreamgiver, Johann Thorsson   147
Hamraborg Babylon, Alexander Dan Vilhjálmsson   153

NORWAY
As You Wish, Tor Åge Bringsværd   173
The Cormorant, Tone Almhjell   195
The Day Jonas Shadowed His Dad, Thore Hansen   223
A Lion Roars in Longyearbyen, Margrét Helgadóttir   235

FINLAND
A Bird Does Not Sing Because It Has an Answer,
   Johanna Sinisalo   261
Elegy for a Young Elk, Hannu Rajaniemi   277
The Wings that Slice the Sky, Emmi Itäranta   301

Contributor Bios   329

INTRODUCTION

I HAVE EDITED anthologies of stories from all over the world—an experience that has taught me how important it is to include all voices in speculative fiction, which can enrich and broaden this literature immensely. Not only do they show us the multitude of cultures and ways of life, but also challenge us to think outside the box, to step off the usual path. Maybe it even makes us view world events, historical or futuristic, differently. With luck, it creates new possibilities in our minds. All these things, in my view, increase the quality of speculative fiction, and, more importantly, make this literature relevant.

Being slightly biased—I'm a native of the Nordic region—I have long wished to show off the region, as I think there is a special feeling in tales from these countries, tales rarely translated to English, tales that I believe readers would enjoy.

I am thrilled to present to you an anthology of short stories by some of the best contemporary authors hailing from Sweden, Norway, Denmark, Finland, Iceland, and the Faroe Islands. These collected stories will give you a glimpse of the speculative literary scene in this part of the world. Thanks so much to the wonderful people of Rebellion Publishing for making this possible!

THE WORLD TENDS to speak of the Nordic countries as a unit. Yes, the way of looking at life is quite similar, be it democratic values, ethics, politics, the emphasis on equality and security for all, and the strong idea of society as a caregiver from birth to death. Yes, there is established co-operation through the Nordic Council of Ministers (governmental) and the Nordic Council (parliament). There exist numerous agreements and legislation between the countries, such as the Nordic Passport Control Agreement. Yes, the languages are much alike—setting aside the countless dialects. Scandinavians (Swedes, Norwegians, Danes) can mostly speak with each other regardless of language, and Norway and Iceland have the same language roots.

But there are so many differences inside the region too; something you will notice when you meet the people—stretching from the reserved Finnish people in the east to the confident and fearless Icelanders in the west. And in between, you have the three Scandinavian countries—Denmark, Norway and Sweden. All old Viking kingdoms, yet the people might seem to be poles apart—the Danish said to be the relaxed 'Italians of the North', the Norwegians said to be too direct, too honest, too nature-loving, and the Swedes said to be well-dressed, distant, politically correct.

As you see, the stereotypes flourish, also among the people in the Nordic countries themselves, and the characteristics I gave you above *do* exist but are of course highly speculative and generalised, as I am sure most inhabitants of the North will tell you, though most regard themselves with an ironic and amused eye.

Today we also include the Faroe Islands, Greenland, and the Åland Islands when we speak of the Nordic region. Norway also includes islands such as the Svalbard archipelago. The Nordic region is thus geographically huge—and with a varied nature, not to mention weather. Something that perhaps could also explain some of the differences between the Northerners in how they view life.

There are voices I have sadly not managed to include. The Nordic region has several indigenous and First Nations peoples, such as the Inuits in Greenland and the Sámi peoples of Norway, Sweden, and Finland. Today, the region also has huge immigration from other parts of the world and 'the Nordic' is changing. I hope these short stories I have collected, nevertheless, will bring you some idea of Nordic voices, reflected through speculative glasses.

So, WHAT IS the Nordic literary voice? Most people know of the classics (such as Henrik Ibsen, Karen Blixen, H.C. Andersen), or have heard about Norwegian, Icelandic, and Danish crime fiction, Pippi Longstocking's adventures, or the quirky Moomin tales. You might even have heard about the Icelandic sagas or the Finnish epic poetry *Kalevala*.

Storytelling has been a major force in these countries for thousands of years, and I think there is a particular sense of dark humour, a pact with nature, and a view of the world you cannot find in other places. Maybe it is the cold winters, the closeness to the Atlantic Ocean, and the Arctic. Maybe it's the huge old forests or the deep fjords. Maybe it's because we have been so isolated.

Contemplating Nordic writing, one tends to think about the dark noir element in the region's crime fiction, with its psychological depths and inner journeys, stark realism, and strong characters. The darkness is indeed a characteristic also of Nordic speculative fiction. Today, a growing number of Nordic authors write the darkest dystopian science fiction or terrifying horror. They are concerned with social criticism and themes of loneliness and rootlessness, as well as the human impact on the wilderness.

Several writers from the Nordic countries tell tales lyrically and with few words—maybe it is because the Nordic languages are small in word range, which means each word can have several meanings, so it is crucial which ones you choose. Often the tales are told quietly, almost chanted, bearing strong resemblance to stories told around camp fires, legends, fables, and folk tales. Many authors have elements of Nordic folklore (trolls, elves, grey people, shapeshifters) in their stories, or Norse mythology, or threads from *Edda* or *Kalevala*—and it is not uncommon to include these in a tale of modern life.

In my opinion, the Nordic writing style that touches the speculative genres often plays with the weird and surreal. It can sometimes be difficult to place writing by Nordic speculative authors strongly within particular genres because many of them like to mix elements from different genres and maybe even create a style of their own.

Several stories in this anthology portray dark and/or bizarre post-apocalyptic futures. You'll find terrifying and fantastic tales about shapeshifters, ghosts, and creatures in the night. The importance of the deep ocean or the freedom of the vast sky recurs. Exploration (and exploitation) of other worlds is the theme in many of the stories, be it finding unknown worlds under our feet, or space travel and colonisation of space. I'm also very pleased to have a story which is a wonderful take on the epic *Kalevala*. I have also, for the first time, included a story I wrote, to provide an example of Nordic tales from the Arctic area.

SWEDEN IS SAID to have the oldest tradition of science fiction in the Nordic countries—fandom and fanzines emerged as early as the 1950s. A few genre cons and fan clubs were established in the other Nordic countries in later decades, and you'll even find studies at university level and the academic Nordic journal *Fafnir*. But in general, there seems to be a lack of a solid speculative fiction scene in most of the Nordic countries, and most countries have only a small group of established authors within the genres. And few are translated. Genre fiction has increased in popularity in the last decades and several Nordic authors have had success, also internationally— such as Norwegians Siri Pettersen and Maja Lunde, Swede John Ajvide Lindqvist, Icelandic Sjón, and Fin Hannu Rajaniemi, to name a few. But if you wish to read speculative short stories from these countries, say for instance by a Norwegian science fiction writer or an Icelandic fantasy short story writer, you'll struggle to find authors published in English. Which, I think, is a pity.

There aren't many speculative anthologies in English from the Nordic countries—there are only a very few theme-based anthologies from Sweden and Finland. Recently an anthology of Norwegian science fiction stories has also been published, though not yet in English.

I'm thus very pleased to have many stories translated for this anthology. Thanks so much to all the translators that have contributed, and also to the authors who took it upon themselves to translate their own stories for this book.

I hope that this anthology will help bring some of the best contemporary speculative writers from the Nordic countries to a wider audience. Enjoy!

Margrét

Editorial note: where the stories in this anthology are reprinted from a previous publication, the original spelling has been preserved at the authors' request.

SWEDEN

SHE

John Ajvide Lindqvist
Translated by Marlaine Delargy

'A haunting is dependent on a series of highly unlikely coincidences, hence the rarity of such occurrences.'

Nathan Wahlqvist

SHE IS RUNNING through the forest. The ground is a shimmering blue mosaic of moonlight filtered between bare branches. Wet oak leaves are crushed beneath the thick soles of her shoes, and her hands smell of petrol. In the distance she can hear the sound of voices shouting orders, dogs barking. Her seventeen-year-old heart is like jelly, splashing and squelching with every pounding beat. She runs.

The First Night

THE FIRST NIGHT in our new house—we couldn't wait!
Over the past few months, barely an evening had gone

by when we hadn't crept in with our torches to see how far the builders had got during the day. We wandered around the empty, half-finished rooms and imagined what our future lives would be like in these spaces, then we returned to our neighbours' summer cottage, which they had kindly allowed us to use during the seven-month construction project.

The original plan had been to carry out a major renovation. Replace the windows, improve the insulation, add an extension to the upper floor. However, when the builders opened up the walls it turned out that the house was in such poor condition that the only solution was to tear the whole thing down and start again. We looked at our finances, spoke to the bank and discovered that it would be just possible if we used what was left of my inheritance from my paternal grandfather.

It would never have worked with Swedish builders. I might as well admit it right away: we used a Polish construction company that did the same job for a third of the price. Cash in hand, of course. It's not something I'm proud of, but otherwise, there would have been no house. They also imported some cheaper materials from Poland.

Enough about that. We swallowed our shame at cheating the Swedish state out of money and watched our solidly built house take shape with every day that passed, and now our first night had arrived at last.

The removal truck with our stored furniture and other possessions wasn't due to arrive until the following day, but Alice and I were so eager to start on the next phase of our lives that we decided to spend the night on a mattress in our future bedroom. In a rush of optimism, we made passionate love, and after snuggling up together for a few minutes, Alice fell asleep while I lay awake, listening.

Every house has its own sounds and aromas, its own breathing and atmosphere. Ours had yet to find its individuality, and smelled mainly of newness. Paint, wallpaper paste, new wood. My heart gave a little leap as I thought that Alice and I would be the ones to give this house its particular character through the lives we lived.

And maybe there would be a third person too. We were both thirty-five and had worked hard so that we could afford to build the house—cash in hand, admittedly— and now we were ready to have a child. We had been trying for a year, without success. We were intending to give it another six months before seeking help.

It felt almost presumptuous when we asked the architect to add another bedroom, as if we were tempting fate by imagining that we were capable of creating the person who would sleep there. But we crossed ourselves, tossed salt over our shoulders and spat three times—only mentally, of course—then showed him where we wanted the room to be.

Okay, so I wasn't entirely free of superstition. When we were inspecting our new house earlier in the day, we ended up in the empty room where a putative child would one day live. Just *standing* in there made me feel as if we were nurturing unreasonable expectations, and I knocked three times on the door frame. Alice looked at me and pulled a face. Then she knocked too.

Little one…

When we started talking about having a baby a year ago, it felt… all right. Reasonable. People are meant to have kids, and maybe it was time now. That kind of thing. As the months went by and nothing happened, that reasonableness became a hope that became a longing that eventually became a *hunger*. Even though I wasn't the one who would be carrying the foetus, I had a baby-shaped hole inside my body. A whimpering and squeaking that only the patter of tiny feet would be able to drown out.

Little one...

I had gone so far as to visualise the child in detail and at so many different ages that I was now experiencing a sense of grief over something I had lost. I thought, *Little one*, and felt sorry for the uncreated child and its non-existence.

I turned over and looked at the clock on the floor next to the mattress. 02:07. The alarm was set for seven, when I would get ready for another day as a case worker with social services. I had meetings booked with a couple of really tricky clients, and I wanted to have a clear head. Debt consolidation might not be the sexiest job in the world, but someone has to do it.

I tensed every muscle in my body as tightly as I could, then slowly relaxed. Something softened within me, and a gas lighter than air seeped into my joints as I drifted up towards sleep. Suddenly my legs jerked, I inhaled sharply and opened my eyes.

At first I thought it was the kind of jolt that sometimes comes when you're falling asleep, but no. I'd heard a noise. A bang. From above. From the loft. That was what made me react.

The loft? This afternoon we climbed up there to check it out. It was unheated, with exposed beams, and all it contained was a small pile of sawdust that the builders had forgotten to sweep up. Not a single thing that could fall over and make the noise I'd just heard.

Taking care not to wake Alice, I eased myself off the mattress, stood and pulled on my dressing gown. The oiled floorboards were cool against the soles of my feet. We had considered installing underfloor heating in the bedroom, but at that point the budget had dug in its heels and said No. Maybe one day.

I padded over to the door, which didn't make a sound when it opened. I stepped out onto the landing and closed the door behind me. Directly ahead were the stairs leading down and to my right a corridor that ran past the longed-for child's room to the bathroom. Halfway along the ceiling was the loft hatch. I looked up. Blinked. Looked again.

Where I should have seen the white surface of the hatch, instead I saw a black square. The moonlight coming in through the window was enough to pick out the contours of the corridor in pale blue, and I could even distinguish the wallpaper's floral pattern, but it wasn't enough to illuminate the loft. There was nothing to see but blackness because the hatch was open.

I can't deny that I felt uneasy. I thought back to the afternoon. The loft probably wasn't going to be used for anything except storage, so we had chosen the simplest solution due to budgetary constraints. A plain, square hatch that opened inwards, then the loft could be accessed with a stepladder.

I racked my brain for a logical explanation, something that could cause such pressure from below that the hatch flew open, or alternatively something in the loft pulling on the ring we'd requested so that no one could get shut in. To be honest, there was only one reasonable explanation. My throat felt dry and tight as I whispered: "Hello? Is anyone there?"

Just saying those words sent a shiver down my spine, and in my mind, I searched the house for a weapon. My toolbox was downstairs, there was a hammer in it. What kind of person had hidden in the loft? Maybe one of the tradesmen had fallen asleep and… no, there hadn't been anyone up there in the afternoon, so someone must have sneaked in and…

"Hello?" I croaked. "Come down from there!"

Against all my instincts I was about to take a step towards the hatch when I heard a scraping sound from above and then… I died. I can't describe it any other way. I was so terrified that my heart stopped, everything went black before my eyes, and I really do believe that I was dead for a few seconds.

The first thing that appeared in the hole was two dark lumps, then everything happened very fast. A woman plummeted straight down through the opening, feet first. I caught sight of a pair of thick trousers tied at the waist with a piece of string, and a torn check shirt. Long black hair fluttered around a pale face.

A few inches before the woman's feet reached the floor, the movement stopped abruptly. Her head jerked forward and her hair fell over her face, and at the same time, I heard a sort of wet, dull crack like breaking ice. Only now did I notice the rough rope around her neck, stretching up into that dark square in the ceiling.

I fell towards the stairs and only managed to save myself from tumbling straight down by grabbing hold of the banister. I squeezed my eyes tight shut as a dark red swirl eddied around my brain and made me feel sick.

I didn't see that. It didn't happen.

I was dreaming. I was hallucinating. I'd had a bleed on the brain. I lowered my head and tried to take deep breaths, but my compressed lungs could manage only shallow panting. I held my breath. And then I heard it. The muted creaking of fibres rubbing against one another. A quiet dripping.

I didn't dare open my eyes completely, I just squinted along the corridor. The woman hung there, a few inches off the floor, her body slowly swinging from side to side as the rope complained about her weight. I clung to the banister as if it were my lifeline, keeping me on the right side of insanity. I had never been so frightened, and was incapable of a single rational thought.

Suddenly a flash of lightning passed through my mind as the reptilian brain, or possibly the child's brain, took over. I hurled my body at the bedroom door, opened it then closed it behind me. When I had double-locked it, my legs gave way beneath me. I crawled over to the mattress, wriggled onto it and pulled the covers over my head.

I lay there motionless with my eyes wide open, holding my breath. It must have been my imagination, but I thought I could still hear the dripping. Something was dripping from *her* out there. I thought back to the pale face I had glimpsed before it was covered by her hair.

She had been young. Only a girl. And now she was hanging dead, here in our newly built house. In our life.

SHE CAN'T GO *any further. Weeks and months of malnutrition have eroded all the energy reserves in her body. She crawls into a hollow beneath a fallen tree, rests her face on the ground. Cold, wet leaves cool her fevered cheek and dampen her shirt and trousers. She has nothing left. Even the hatred that has kept her going lately seems to have ebbed away. She is nothing more than a bag of bones and internal organs waiting to be obliterated. The barking is getting closer.*

The Second Night

I DIDN'T SLEEP a wink during the first night in our new house. After half an hour I got too sweaty under the covers and tentatively poked my head out, ready to pull it back in if the girl turned out to be standing next to the bed.

The child's brain, like I said. But there was no one there, and both the creaking and the dripping outside the door had stopped.

Is it over?

I couldn't believe what my eyes had seen, and yet I still didn't have the nerve to go out onto the landing to check. If she really was still hanging there, what would I do? My thoughts were scurrying around like a flock of hens frightened by a fox, trapped inside my head. I rubbed my eyes hard and tried to pull myself together.

As I saw it, in my agitated state of mind, there were three alternatives: 1) I'd had an incredibly detailed hallucination, 2) a young woman had actually hanged herself from the loft in our house, or 3) I'd seen a ghost.

None of these alternatives were appealing. I'd never had a hallucination in my entire life. The idea that a young woman had managed to sneak up into our loft and then hang herself was just too absurd. And a ghost? They were supposed to haunt old houses with a terrible past, weren't they? Ours was brand spanking new and had no history whatsoever.

Okay, so the house that had stood on this spot had been here for just over a hundred years, but we'd lived in it for eight years without the slightest hint of supernatural phenomena. It didn't make sense.

So what did that leave?

In the end, it was only the hallucination that seemed possible, however weird it might be. Maybe I'd dropped off momentarily and had a nightmare that lasted seconds? But surely I'd stood on the landing for longer than that, looking up at the opening? Oh well, time functions differently in dreams.

That had to be the explanation. A terrifying image had been hurled at my defenceless inner retina, and my mind had reacted to an illusion. That's what must have happened. I still didn't get out of bed, though; I lay awake staring at the ceiling with the covers drawn up to my chin. Alice snored gently and trustingly beside me.

It was the beginning of April, and at about six o'clock the dawn came creeping. By ten to seven it was almost full daylight. I reached out and switched off the alarm. During the night I had wriggled out of my dressing gown; I got up and put it on again.

With my arms folded across my chest, I stood perfectly still, staring at the door. My heart began to beat faster. *If* the improbable was possible and there really was a dead girl hanging out there, what would I do? I didn't know, but I *definitely* wasn't going to leave the discovery to Alice. I had to check.

With sweaty fingers, I turned the key and placed my hand on the door handle. My head pounded, and I realised I'd been holding my breath ever since I got up. I slowly exhaled and pushed open the door. It opened to the right, which meant it obscured my view of the corridor.

In the same childish spirit as I'd dealt with everything else last night and this morning, I stuck my head around the edge of the door, presumably so that I would be able to pull it back quickly if I saw... But sunlight poured in through the window, illuminating an empty corridor. I let out the air I had left in my lungs in a huge sigh of relief. Alternative number two—a girl had actually hanged herself—could be ruled out.

I still padded cautiously towards the hatch, which was now closed. I examined the floor immediately beneath it, looking for traces of whatever had been dripping. Nothing. Only prime Polish oak floorboards, without so much as a scratch or the tiniest mark. I looked up at the hatch and considered fetching a ladder, but no, I wasn't quite there yet.

I went back into the bedroom, kissed Alice's bare shoulder and told her it was time to wake up. She gazed at me in some confusion, took in my dressing gown and said: "Morning. You're up already?"

"Yes, I didn't sleep too well."

"Oh dear." Her eyes narrowed as she remembered, and her lips curved into a sensual smile. "Thanks for last night."

"Thank *you*."

Alice looked into my eyes, which presumably weren't at their best after all those sleepless hours, and asked: "Didn't you get any sleep?"

"No. I think I might call in sick."

"Poor you. Why couldn't you sleep? I mean usually, after we've…"

"I don't know, but maybe it's for the best. I can be here for the removal men, start unpacking."

I had no intention of sharing my nightmare with Alice, partly because I didn't want her to worry about my mental health, and partly because I didn't want to scare her. The image of the loft hatch and the hanged girl was suggestive to say the least, and Alice might be frightened if she needed to pass beneath the hatch to go to the bathroom during the night. Better to say nothing.

I called work then went back to bed while Alice showered and got ready to set off for Rådmansö School, where she was a teacher. At seven forty-five she came into the bedroom and stroked my cheek. "Are you sure you'll be okay?"

"I'm never okay without you, but I can fake it."

"In that case, I'll do the same. See you later—love you."

"Love you."

I heard her footsteps descending the stairs, the front door opening and closing, the car starting up. We usually drove to work together, but now I lay there following her in my thoughts. A warm feeling spread through my chest as I contemplated the fact that the woman who was driving away would come back to me, over and over again. That this was what she wanted. I was the luckiest man in the world.

There was only *one* piece of grit in my shoe, *one* fly in the ointment.

Before I had time to weigh up the pros and cons, I got dressed, fetched a torch and the stepladder, carried it over to the hatch. Even though the corridor was in bright daylight and last night's ghosts had been chased away, a viscous sense of dread ran through my blood, creating an internal tremor. I climbed five steps, gritted my teeth and pushed the hatch open.

It flipped over and hit the floor, making exactly the same sound as I had heard last night. I took a deep breath, swallowed and stuck my head up through the aperture. Nothing, absolutely nothing, apart from the little pile of sawdust. I climbed the two remaining steps so that I could heave myself up and into the loft.

It was chillier than the rest of the house, and the smell

of fresh wood was strong. I shone the light of my torch into every dark corner beneath the pitched roof. Empty, empty. One of the beams ran across the opening in such a way that meant it *would* be possible to fasten a rope around it, then fall to one's death.

I felt a bit ridiculous, but I decided to do a thorough job. With the help of the torch, I inspected every square inch of the beam, searching for the tiniest sign of friction damage, the smallest trace of fibre that could bear witness to the rope used by someone hellbent on suicide. Nothing. The beam was as undamaged and spotless as the floorboards down below. I nodded to myself.

Okay. Time to let this go.

I climbed down, closed the hatch and put the ladder away. Enough. We had a new life in a new house to tackle, and nightmares and hallucinations were not going to be part of the inventory.

The previous evening we had made do with takeaway pizza because the kitchen wasn't set up. I set to work unpacking the three boxes of equipment we had taken to the neighbours' cottage and brought back. When I'd finished I made a start on our clothes. I became fully absorbed in the task and barely gave the dead girl a thought. She belonged to the past, and an imaginary past at that.

At noon the removal truck arrived, and there was even less time to speculate on the paranormal. I lifted, carried, unpacked, flattened boxes. Both Alice and I read a great deal, so our library alone filled twenty heavy boxes. Words have *weight*. I was looking forward to the two of us spending several evenings sorting our books and placing them on the built-in bookcases in the living room.

Everything had been carried indoors and the truck

had left by the time Alice got home shortly after four. We worked side by side putting our lives back together, prepared a simple meal, then carried on emptying boxes until eleven. We fell into bed and barely managed to say good night before we fell asleep.

Annoyingly, I slept for half an hour then opened my eyes, wide awake. This happened sometimes, and I knew that it was going to be very hard to get back to sleep. I got up, went down to the kitchen and warmed some milk. I drank it while reading the crime novel I was currently enjoying. At one thirty I went back to bed. Yes, I did glance over at the hatch before I opened the bedroom door, but there was nothing to see.

And yet still sleep refused to come. I lay there in the semi-darkness staring at the second hand as it crawled around the clock face until two. Then a number flashed inside my head: *02:07*. That was the time it had been when I looked at the clock last night, just before *it* happened.

No chance of sleep now. I lay on my side with my fists clenched between my thighs, staring at the minute hand as if it were a hypnotist's pendulum. 02:05, 02:06, 02:07... When the hand slipped over to 02:08 it was as if a balloon inflated to bursting point inside my chest slowly began to let out its contents with a soft hiss.

Oh God, the things we...

BAM! I heard the bang as the hatch flew open, it felt as if a shudder passed through the entire house, through floors and walls, up through the frame of our bed and into my body. I let out a strangled cough and began to shake, drew my knees up towards my chest and dug my fingernails into the palms of my hands.

No, no, please, don't let it... don't let her...

I lay in quivering expectation for perhaps seven, eight seconds when a rattling noise came from the loft, followed by the sound of rope fibres creaking and stretching, then almost simultaneously the crack of cervical vertebrae breaking. And then the dripping, the dripping.

No sleep tonight either.

THEY GRAB HOLD of one of her boots and drag her out. They beat her black and blue with the butts of their rifles and let the dogs bite her wherever they can. They spit and piss on her, call her a Jewish whore and an arsonist. As she lies sprawled on the ground with her limbs broken and battered, the soldiers begin to discuss the best method of execution for the bitch who had burned down their barracks. They agree that it would be fun to make her dance for them. Someone fetches a rope and throws it over a thick, straight branch. They fasten a noose around her neck, then two men hoist her up. Her feet twitch and jerk in an entertaining dance while the soldiers clap their hands, keeping time.

The Third Night

I MUST HAVE somehow managed to nod off for a couple of hours because I was woken by the alarm. I felt sick and groggy from the lack of sleep. When Alice saw my face, she said: "Sweetheart, whatever's wrong? You look terrible."

I was overcome by a powerful urge to tell her what made it impossible for me to sleep, but I wanted to make at least *one* real attempt to put an end to the haunting before I confided in her, so I said: "I just think maybe I'm not used to the new house. You know I struggle with change."

"I do…"—Alice glanced over at the chair where I'd left my clothes—"speaking of change… Those corduroy trousers that you've had for two years…"

"Please. Not now."

Alice looked a little put out, but took my wretched appearance into account and dropped the subject. It wasn't as if I wore those trousers to work. Well, not very often. Alice made a start on her morning routine while I stayed in bed with grit inside my eyelids.

During the night I had become increasingly convinced that we were dealing with a haunting. Admittedly I couldn't rule out the idea that my tense anticipation as the clock approached 02:08 might have made me conjure up an audio hallucination, but I couldn't do anything about that. And I was determined to *do something*.

Alice went off to work after saying goodbye and kissing me on the forehead. I closed my eyes and tried to sleep for an hour or two, but my body was in a state of readiness, and my fingers itched to get started. Or maybe the lack of sleep was physically making my fingers itch. I got up and pulled on the offending trousers.

The sky was grey outside the window, the branches on the trees were still bare, and a soft drizzle was falling, spattering the glass. I sighed. Everything felt so desolate. We had looked forward so much to moving into our new house, and to the warmth we would create there. Now it felt as if the house was our enemy and wished us anything but well.

I was so dizzy that I had to hold onto the banister as I went down to the kitchen to get the cordless drill and screwdriver out of my toolbox. After I'd gone back upstairs and carried the stepladder over to the hatch, I had to sit and rest for a while. I felt as if I was eighty years old, about to burst into tears. When I felt the tears fill my eyes I gave myself a metaphorical slap and said: "Pull yourself together and get this sorted!"

I nodded and placed a thin drill bit in the chuck, then climbed the ladder. There was a frame around the perimeter of the hatch, and I drilled three holes in each side, except the one with the hinges. Then I drove nine screws through the frame and into the hatch itself. I pushed the hatch as hard as I could with my hand; it didn't move even a fraction of an inch. I had no idea whether ordinary screws were capable of impeding a ghost, but I had to give it a try.

I went back to bed, but couldn't settle. I grabbed my laptop and looked up hauntings and ghosts online. I found mostly links to novels or personal accounts of dark spirits, things moving of their own accord, glimpses of the dead. There was nothing with the detailed, brutal character that was plaguing our house, and no solutions.

What do the dead want of the living?

Back on the landing, it struck me that if Alice and I had a child, we would have to fit a gate at the top of the stairs. But there was no child in sight, and besides: could I allow our child to have the door of its room directly below the hatch? Even if the screws helped, I would know that *she* was up there at night, waiting to plummet to her death.

What do the dead want of the living?

In a fit of madness I yelled down the corridor: "Leave us in peace, do you hear me? We haven't done anything to you! What do you want from us?"

No response, fortunately. No rasping little voice explaining what I was guilty of and why I would never be allowed to sleep again. Although in a way I might have preferred it—the opportunity to reason, to argue my case rather than mutely awaiting the horrors of the night. If they came. I knocked on the banister three times and hoped for the best. Then I went back to unpacking.

On Friday Alice came home from work with two bottles of wine—something of a tradition. We didn't often get around to opening the second bottle, but it had to be there *just in case* we got the feeling and wanted to drift into the mist together.

We spent a while unpacking some of the last few boxes that didn't contain books. When we'd finished, Alice put her hands on her hips and nodded towards the pile of flattened cardboard in the corner of the room. "What shall we do with that? I was thinking we could put it in the loft."

"The wardrobe would be better."

"The *wardrobe*? There's no room! And surely that's what a loft is for?"

"I haven't got the energy right now, I feel…"

"Who said *you* have to do it?"

Before I could say anything else Alice was running up the stairs, then I heard her moving the stepladder. That's what she was like. If she got the idea of doing something, then it had to happen right away. She hated it when I said: "Why don't we give it some thought?" She often teased me about my inability to make a decision.

She swore to herself, and I went and sat on the sofa. My head felt as if it was full of cotton wool, and I hadn't a clue what I was going to say to explain my actions. I lowered my head as she came down the stairs. The first thing she said was exactly what I'd expected: "Have you screwed the loft hatch shut?"

"Mm."

"Why, for God's sake?"

Suddenly the word was simply there, and a second later it was out of my mouth. "Draught."

"Draught?"

"Yes, there was a draught coming from the loft, so I had to insulate the hatch."

"By screwing it shut?"

"Mm. It worked."

I was a genius. When it came to things that could make life in a house unbearable, mice were at the top of Alice's list, and draughts at number two. Spurred on by my own brilliance, I ventured to add: "Actually, I thought I heard a mouse up there too."

"Shit, have we got mice already?"

"Seems that way."

If only you knew what we've really got, sweetheart.

Alice was convinced, and we agreed that for the time being, we would store the flattened boxes in the room we didn't dare refer to as anything other than 'the small bedroom'. No over-confidence, no tempting fate.

After dinner, we relaxed on the sofa with a glass of red. Alice did most of the talking because the wine I'd had with the meal had made me dull and lethargic, but I did my best to keep up with her stories from school. I even managed the odd comment on her ideas for decorating the house.

At about ten o'clock she said: "You seem exhausted. Do you want to go to bed?"

"If that's okay with you?"

"Of course. I'll just finish my drink."

I was finding it hard to stay awake. My brain felt like an office block where the lights were being switched off one by one until the only glow came from the caretaker's room. Alice and I had our own word for this condition: *zonkered*. To be honest, I was completely zonkered. I hardly even had the energy to worry about the night to come.

When we'd got undressed and gone to bed, Alice's index finger felt its way across my chest, bent like a question mark: *Do you want to?* I drew her close, kissed her forehead and said: "Good night." Alice let out the faintest sigh, brushed my shoulder with her lips and said: "Good night." We had been together for twelve years and had our signals. I just wanted to sleep, sleep, sleep. Not to think, not to worry, not to make love, not to be afraid. Sleep. After only a minute or so I did exactly that.

I was woken by Alice getting out of bed. Her naked body was blue in the moonlight as she moved towards the door, like something out of *Avatar*. I mumbled: "Where are you going?"

"Toilet. The wine."

I glanced at the clock. 02:04. As Alice reached for the door handle, I said: "No, wait."

"I need to pee."

"Yes, but could you wait… five minutes?"

"Why?"

"Please, Alice. I'm begging you."

Alice pulled a face, placed her hand on the lower part of her belly and came over to the bed. "Joel, what's wrong?"

Alice only used my name in that way when she was annoyed or puzzled; maybe this was a combination of both. "Something's… been happening at night. At about this time."

"What kind of something?"

"Just… something." It was now 02:05. "In three minutes. But I'm hoping it won't happen tonight."

"I don't understand. What are you talking about?"

"I don't want to… I promise I'll tell you after, if it doesn't happen tonight. And I don't think it will."

Alice sat down on the bed, her hand still on her stomach. She sat in silence for a minute or so, then asked: "Is that why you haven't been able to sleep?"

"Yes."

Her eyes narrowed as she looked at me. "Does this have anything to do with the loft?"

"Yes."

"How…" Alice stiffened and listened. I glanced at the clock. 02:08. From the loft came a determined, long-drawn-out knocking. Alice's eyes opened wide. "What the hell…"

The knocking grew louder, followed by the sound of splintering wood, then the bang as the hatch hit the floor. Alice covered her mouth with her hands and stared at me in horror. Between her fingers she whispered: "Sweetheart, what…"

The rattle, the fall, the rope pulled taut, the neck being broken with a crack that made Alice jump and let out a little whimper. Then the dry creaking. And the dripping. Alice was still staring at me wide-eyed, shaking her head.

"It's a girl," I whispered hoarsely, "hanging herself. From the loft. Every night."

"Ev—every night?"

"Yes. It must be some kind of… you know."

"So you mean..."—Alice glanced at the door—"... she's hanging out there? Now?"

"Yes. Presumably. She's gone by morning."

Alice's eyes darted from side to side as she tried to absorb what I'd told her. Then her gaze landed on me. "This isn't a joke, is it?"

I couldn't help sounding slightly hurt. "Would I joke about something like this?"

"No, you wouldn't. Sorry. But..."—she broke off, blinked—"I want to see."

"It's horrible. The first time it happened I was so scared that I felt as if... I'd died."

"You saw her do it?"

I nodded. I would never be free of the image of the skinny girl plummeting through the hole or the sound of her neck breaking. The impressions were so deeply imprinted on my brain that it was probably deformed forever, conditioned to see the world in a new and darker way. As Alice moved to stand up, I put my hand on her arm. "Do you have to?"

"I think so. Otherwise, I'll just lie here imagining the worst."

"That might be better."

"No. Not for me."

As I said, that was the kind of person Alice was. Tackle problems right away, whatever they might be. I also sensed that there was another reason for her comparatively casual approach: she didn't believe me, despite everything. I didn't challenge her. It was easier to assume that I was crazy or joking than to take my words seriously.

And what did I know? Maybe the apparition had already faded while we'd been talking. Part of me hoped so, another part hoped not. I clenched my fists and chewed on my knuckles as Alice pulled on her dressing gown and walked towards the door. She glanced at me one last time, frowning when she saw how anxious I was. Then she pushed down the handle.

Despite her scepticism, there was a fragile caution in her movements as she took a couple of steps then turned her head to the right. She stiffened and gasped in such a theatrical way that I thought *she* was the one teasing *me* now. There was nothing to see, but she was acting as if there was.

But Alice remained where she was, motionless, her mouth hanging open as she stared down the corridor. Her right hand clutched the fabric of her dressing gown.

"What is it?" I whispered. "What can you see?"

I listened hard and I could just hear the faint creaking of the rope, along with Alice's shuddering breaths. A few seconds passed, then she uncurled her right hand and made a vague gesture in the direction of the corridor.

"Her finger," she said in an unsteady voice. "What's happened to her finger?"

"Which finger?"

"Her index finger. It's missing. Her hand is bleeding. Dripping."

IT IS ABSOLUTELY *incredible, and none of the soldiers have ever seen anything like it. It seems the noose hasn't completely cut off the girl's air supply, maybe it's to do with her scrawny frame and low weight, but somehow she manages to grab hold of the rope above her head. She begins to climb.*

The soldiers look at one another and their rhythmic clapping changes to applause as the girl hauls herself upwards, a couple of inches at a time. It is an astonishing achievement, and by a little Jewish whore! What a will to live, what spirit! The girl heaves herself all the way up to the point where the rope is secured, then she raises one hand and grasps the branch.

Enough. A couple of the soldiers raise their guns and compete in aiming for the girl's hands. A young soldier by the name of Martin, with the most innocent blue eyes, is the one who succeeds. His first shot merely splinters the tree bark, but the second scores a direct hit on the girl's index finger.

The finger is torn off and tumbles down into the night, hitting the ground just before the girl screams and loses her grip. Her body falls until its descent is stopped by the rope, which tightens around her throat and breaks her neck. The body jerks, then becomes slack. A quiet creaking can be heard as blood drips onto wet oak leaves.

The Fourth Night

THE FOLLOWING DAY Alice also called in sick. We had spent the night whispering, holding onto each other in terror, and eventually managed a couple of hours of shallow sleep towards dawn. We shuffled around the house with blank expressions as if we too had turned into ghosts, mechanically unpacking the last of the boxes.

The result of the night's discussions was that we had no idea what to do. We realised that it would be impossible to stay here if things carried on like this, but then what? If we sold the house we would suffer a loss that our finances couldn't take, plus our consciences wouldn't allow us to hand over a haunted house to some poor unsuspecting family.

But we couldn't stay. Or could we? Would it be possible to steel ourselves, get used to the fact that our house had this… quirk? Wear earplugs in bed and hope it would pass in time? Would it pass? What the hell had we done to deserve this? Questions like this had preoccupied us during the night, and we couldn't find any answers.

What do the dead want of the living?

"Maybe she's trying to tell us something," Alice had suggested. "Show us something. Isn't that usually the case?"

"I have no idea what is *usually the case*," I had replied. "I think that's only in films."

"But what does she want? Why is she doing this?"

"Perhaps there is no reason. Perhaps it's just happening."

"But why? Why?"

That was the key question, and we didn't have an answer.

One thing was clear after last night: *she* was neither an illusion nor a hallucination. When Alice and I crept into the corridor in the morning, we found the hatch closed, but all around the frame were cracks and holes left by the screws, which had been ripped from the wood with what must have been considerable force. Physical obstacles did not hinder the haunting.

Towards lunchtime, after we had listlessly munched our way through a bowl of muesli with yoghurt, Alice said: "Right, I'm going to say something really stupid."

"Good. Say something really stupid."

"We're both agreed that this is completely crazy, right? The fact that we not only have a ghost in our newly built house, but a ghost with superhuman strength?"

"You saw for yourself…"

"Yes. I saw. I heard. I accept. It's not that. But…"—Alice held up her index finger and wagged it, as she did when she wanted to underline something—"… if we accept this supernatural event, or whatever you want to call it, then maybe we can pin our hopes on another."

"Such as?"

"The power of three. This has happened for three nights in a row. Maybe last night was the final time."

"Doesn't sound very convincing."

"I know, but have you got a better idea?"

I hadn't. We kept talking and decided to give it one more night, hoping that *she* was subject to the magic power of the number three. If not, I had no intention of staying in this house for much longer. The neighbours' cottage was still empty, and I was sure we could carry on borrowing it while we… what? Employed some sort of spiritual cleanser, an exorcist, took part in a reality TV programme?

I was so tired and downhearted that the latter option sounded moderately appealing. The way things were at the moment it would actually be nice to have a film crew here, documenting the impossible and confirming that Alice and I were not in fact halfway to the nuthouse.

The only thing left to unpack was a box of assorted bric-a-brac in the bedroom, plus the boxes of books occupying a considerable amount of floor space in the living room. The very sight of them made me feel weary, but I gritted my teeth and we got on with it.

Sorting the books, which should have been thoroughly

enjoyable, now became a silent and methodical task, with Alice and I each lost in our thoughts. The thing in the loft lay above our heads like a thick, suffocating cloud, making our shoulders slump as we moved between boxes and shelves.

I made a cheese omelette with salad for dinner, but neither of us had much of an appetite. We ate half, then remained seated at the table. We glanced shyly at each other, ventured a smile. Alice reached across and placed her hand on mine.

"Joel—we can fix this, can't we?"

I turned my hand over so that our palms met, and gently squeezed her fingers. "Of course we can. It's just that…"

"Go on. Say it."

"It feels so weird. We're used to… I guess we're spoiled, but if you have a problem, there's always someone you can call. If the drains are blocked, if there's a fire, if you've got damp in the house, if you're sick… There's always *someone* you can call. But this…"

Alice nodded. "We either take care of it ourselves, or head for the loony bin."

"Exactly. And what I don't understand… When I looked online, checked out a few films, there was *nothing* anywhere near the… magnitude of this. There's the odd creaking noise, a door opens, someone senses a presence. It's all crap compared with what's going on here. Why aren't there more examples?"

Alice frowned. She ran her index finger over her lips, then said: "I once read… Hang on, I saw it when I was unpacking." She got up from the table and went into the living room. After a minute or so she was back with a book. She showed me the cover: Nathan Wahlqvist,

The Unquiet Soul. She flicked through the pages and found what she was looking for. She cleared her throat and read aloud: "A haunting is dependent on a series of highly unlikely coincidences, hence the rarity of such occurrences."

"Okay... If we assume that's true, then what are the 'unlikely coincidences' that are making this happen in our house?"

Alice shook her head. "Nathan doesn't have anything to say about that."

"I thought as much. At the moment I can see only one possible solution."

Alice raised her eyebrows in surprise. "Can you?"

"Yes. We open the second bottle of wine."

During the afternoon we had managed to unpack all of our books, and it was a consolation in the midst of our misery to sit on the sofa with a glass of wine and contemplate the wall of words that was ours. A decent bookcase does something to a room, standing there like a manifestation of stories experienced, thoughts set down, time lived through. A little monument to intellectual activity, and in addition an excellent way of dampening the sound in a room, providing a much pleasanter atmosphere. In our opinion.

We started reminiscing about various books, and the hours passed as we topped up our glasses. Somewhere inside me, there was a taut string the whole time, but at least it didn't vibrate as long as we kept the conversation going. The wine relaxed my muscles, but unfortunately, it ran out at about eleven o'clock. We toasted each other with the last drops, and Alice said: "Here's to the power of three."

I nodded. "The power of three."

We went to bed, and I was only a little disappointed when Alice's questing finger didn't come creeping. I didn't dare make any moves myself, because that taut string made me unsure of my capabilities. If things went wrong, it had to be on her initiative. And so, we lay there. After a few minutes, I heard Alice's breathing change; incredibly, she had fallen asleep. She's always been good at sleeping, regardless of the circumstances.

I stayed put for a while feeling more and more wide-awake, my limbs getting stiffer, so in the end I got up, put on my dressing gown and stood in the middle of the room, wondering what to do. My gaze fell on the very last box, the one filled with all kinds of bits and pieces. Why not?

I carried it down to the kitchen so that I wouldn't disturb Alice, and started laying things out on the table. There were bundles of hockey cards from my childhood, a couple of ashtrays from the time when Alice and I still smoked, a root shaped like a crocodile that we'd found on a walk, old certificates and commendations from competitions that had been important back then, and were now more or less forgotten.

I found my father's diaries, which he'd kept until the day he died in a car crash just after I'd left home. They contained mainly notes about the weather, with the odd cryptic abbreviation that meant nothing to me. I flicked through school yearbooks and looked at a few photographs from before I was born. The hours passed.

Right at the bottom of the box, I found a photo of my paternal grandfather taken a couple of years before he died, only six months before my father. That was why I thought of the money we'd used to build the house as the inheritance from my grandfather. The money had simply passed through my father's hands for a short time before it came to me.

There was nothing in Grandfather's face to suggest that he would soon die. His jawline was strong, his white hair was thick, and there was something innocent about the expression in those sparkling blue eyes as if he still regarded the world with an element of surprise. It was hard to understand, but on his deathbed, he had confessed to my father that he had fought in the war as a young man, on the side of the Germans. There wasn't much more discussion on the matter, because he drew his last breath soon afterwards.

I lifted out the cigar box that my father had found among Grandfather's belongings. Although the old man had said that he regretted his actions during the war, he had saved what you might call his badges of honour from those days. I found a folded diploma, written in German and issued to Martin Stenwall, plus a medal adorned with the swastika.

I knew that Nazi memorabilia could sell for considerable sums of money, but as I had no intention of profiting further from my grandfather's misdeeds, the cigar box and its contents went straight into the bin. Why had I saved it?

I glanced at the kitchen clock and my mouth went dry when I saw that it was exactly two o'clock. I left everything on the kitchen table and rushed up to the bedroom. Without taking off my dressing gown I lay down on top of the covers, squeezed my eyes shut and clenched my fists, waiting as the minutes crept by.

Please, no more. Not tonight. The power of three. Let it be over. Give us back our lives. Not…

Even though I had been prepared for it, my body

She

jolted as if I'd suffered an electric shock when the hatch
flew open. Alice gasped and sat up beside me, her eyes
wild and staring. "What was that…" she whispered in a
croaky voice. "Was it…?"

"Yes."

She pressed her body close to mine and hugged me
tightly. Our hearts were together, beating in time,
pounding solace and fear into each other's closed space
at the same time. I clenched my jaw when I heard the
rattle. When the fall and the knocking came, Alice dug
her nails into my chest and sobbed, muttering: "Make it
stop, please make it stop…"

"Ssh…"

She fell silent, and I listened. Something had changed.
The sound of the rope, the creaking, was different.
Louder. It was as if… I heard dry, cracking noises as fibre
after fibre split. My mouth filled with the taste of blood
when I realised what was happening. And then it did
happen. One final, even louder breaking sound, then the
heavy vibration of a body falling to the floor. The rope
had given way.

Neither I nor Alice said anything. We held our breath
and clung to each other as our hearts raced, driving us to
the brink of insanity. We heard a dragging noise from the
corridor, followed by a series of wet crunches, like when
a chiropractor adjusts your joints.

There was silence for a few seconds, then we heard
what we had feared most of all. Footsteps. Approaching
the bedroom door.

What do the dead want of the living?

We would soon find out.

* * *

44

From the documentary
The Village that Disappeared

JANOSZ TOMCYK IS *93 years old, and one of the few who remembers the Jewish village of Krasnywiec, which was emptied of its population and razed to the ground by the Nazis.*

"Their barracks were on the outskirts just here," he says, sucking on his pipe as we sit at a café table in the square in Lvivo. "They kept going in, carrying out their raids until there wasn't a single person left."

"Did no one offer resistance?"

"Oh yes, there was… hm, hm. There was a young girl who set fire to the barracks. They caught her. Hanged her from an oak tree over there, and… hm."

Janosz' expression closes down. He nods to himself, picks up his coffee cup with a hand that is trembling slightly. He peers at me as if to assess my reaction before he continues: "They say that… some people have seen her hanging there. At night, at exactly the time the soldiers hanged her. So… people didn't like going into the forest at night. And why would you do that anyway?"

"You said 'didn't like'—has something changed?"

"It has. A year or so ago a timber company came along and cut down that particular tree. No one had any objections. I think the wood was going to be used for some construction project in Sweden."

Janosz scrapes out his pipe and tips the ash onto the cobbles. He shakes his head and says gloomily: "It's not that easy to escape the past."

LOST AND FOUND

Maria Haskins

SHE WAS STANDING by the window, gazing out at the disappearing frost while sipping the last of the soup from the thermo-jar. The pain in her left foot was always worse just after waking, and she was leaning on the wall to take the weight off until the pills kicked in.

She liked looking at the frost in the mornings. The ground was covered with a thick layer of sprawling ice crystals, and the windows were coated with swirls and intricate patterns, shimmering like glass prisms in the first sunlight. Soon it would all melt away, and trickle down the capsule's metal hull to be absorbed by the sand. Only in the deeper, shaded valleys would the frost remain until afternoon, the sand there hard and frozen, shattering beneath the soles of her boots.

How long now? she wondered, instinctively checking her watch. It was flashing the same useless numbers over and over again. The same numbers the computer gave her as if time had stood still since the crash.

How long?

But trying to remember was pointless. She had lost track of the days and nights sometime after the first two weeks. When she awoke she never knew how long she had been asleep, if it was days or just a couple of hours. Sometimes she would wake at the first light of dawn, but more often she woke up much earlier, laying there in the dark, waiting. In the darkness, sleep and wakefulness blended together, with the wind ever-present. Its high, lamenting, pitiless tone was always there, penetrating even the thick walls of the capsule, piercing every dream and thought.

Maybe one of the others had a watch that still worked.

The thought took her by surprise and made her throw the empty thermo-jar against the wall in sudden frustration.

Stupid, stupid, stupid. Why hadn't she thought of that before?

I could go and get it, she mused, looking out the window at the steep rise, its shadow creeping slowly across the ground as the sun rose higher in the sky. It wasn't far. It would just take a couple of minutes to climb up the rocky bank, shuffle down the slope on the other side, and then she would be there, with them.

She felt the food turn inside her, the vomit burning in her throat.

No. She should have thought of that before she moved them. It was too late now. She couldn't go back—she couldn't face them again.

Two had died in the crash. The third had managed to stay alive the first night, but she hadn't been able to help him. When he too was dead, she had hauled out the bodies one by one, dragging them up the hill and then rolling them down into the hollow on the other side, out of sight. They had been much heavier than she had expected, so difficult to move, their cold skin resembling some kind of syntho-material when she touched them, their eyes still wide open, their mouths ajar as if they were about to speak.

What would you say? she had wondered as she watched them. But she knew it no longer mattered.

When the last one had been placed in the hollow, she had stretched out on the cold ground next to them to get some rest. She stayed there for a long time before recovering enough strength to go back. It had been so quiet, protected from the sand and the wind, and it would have been so easy to stay with them. But night had fallen and the cold had come with it, so in the end she had crawled back up the sandy incline. She had left her gloves behind, and her hands had been so stiff, numb fingers searching for something to hold on to, scratching and scraping.

How long ago now?

She studied the palms of her hands. On the crest of the ridge, she had fallen, slamming her hands hard into rock and sand and gravel. The cuts had healed by now. How long did it take for a wound to heal? A week, two weeks, three? But it must have been longer than that, months probably.

The frost was melting, glistening drops running down the window. She followed one of them with the tip of her finger, saw it join other droplets, becoming larger, heavier, until it finally fell out of sight, into the dry sand.

Falling.

The screech of the emergency signal stabbing her eardrums.

She had always assumed that people would scream in

Lost and Found

situations like that, but nobody had screamed. The only
voice had been the computer's voice, calmly repeating
that the rescue capsule's emergency landing system had
been activated. And then there had been the noise of the
bodies slamming into each other.

The guidance system was defective, she thought,
nodding to herself and wetting her chapped lips with the
tip of her tongue.

She went over what had happened before, during, and
after the crash quite often in her mind: memorizing the
details, recapitulating the sequence of events, making
sure that she remembered everything. Her report had to
be complete and accurate when the rescue team arrived.
She had tried to document it all, had even attempted to
make a voice record of it. It had been like reading a fairy
tale to herself at bedtime, but when she reviewed it the
next morning she couldn't stand listening to it and had
erased the file.

They had to know about the crash by now. The
emergency signal must have reached the beacons. It
wouldn't be long before someone came to get her.

There was so much to do until then. She had put most
of the intact scientific equipment to use, setting up
atmospheric and seismic testing stations in three different
locations. The wireless relays were not working, and the
stations were not situated as far apart as they ought
to be, but all the stats she had gathered so far looked
promising. She was already preparing several terra-
forming proposals as well as a preliminary resource plan,
suggesting which transformation methods would be the
most suitable. In ten years this planet would be ready for
limited colonization and maybe then she could return
here, apply for a settlement permit and get a place of

her own. Ten years of service gave you top priority in the colonies, so they couldn't deny her that.

Her breath was fogging up the window and she wiped off the mist with her sleeve. A few drops on the outside of the glass were all that was left of the frost now, but tomorrow morning it would be back again.

It always came back.

Today she would take readings from the station she had set up by the cliffs. She was always hesitant about going outside and especially to that location because it was so far away from the capsule. But by now the pills she had taken had numbed the pain: her foot hardly hurt at all when she pulled on the thermal suit and put on her boots, tightening the straps of the left boot to give her ankle enough support for the walk.

The inner airlock opened with a sharp hiss, then closed behind her before the outer hatch opened. Dust and grains of sand drifted in, sparkling in the sunlight, and she snapped the UV shield down over her eyes so as not to be blinded.

When she stepped over the threshold, the wind immediately grabbed hold of her, pulling at her hair and clothes as she walked around the capsule to perform the mandatory daily check of its exterior. The wind didn't seem to have changed direction at all since they arrived, and the dunes surrounding the vessel built up higher every day. They almost covered the windows by now. Soon she would have to remove some of the sand, or the capsule would end up completely buried.

Halfway around she suddenly stumbled, causing her left ankle to bend awkwardly underneath her. She banged the hull hard with her fist so that her knuckles ached, sucking on the pain through clenched teeth.

They were back. The tracks were back.

They looked the same as before and trailed across the sand in exactly the same direction. She already knew that trying to follow them was futile: a short distance from the capsule the ground turned stony for a stretch and after that, they didn't reappear.

Crouching down, she studied the tracks. There were more of them this time, crisscrossing each other, coming and going, leaving and returning. Ripples and marks in the sand. Nothing strange about that. Wind patterns. Yes. The wind had made them, and now the wind was erasing them, and in just a few hours they would be obliterated.

She squinted past the capsule, toward the crest of the ridge, but there was nothing to see there, nobody could see her anymore. Turning around, she stood and kicked sand over the tracks, trampling them until the only marks were the ones made by her own boots.

Afterwards, she paused there, a little out of breath, rubbing her still-aching knuckles. The wind was pushing her very hard. It was inside her hood, wailing in her ears, groping her neck with cold fingers. The shadow of the ridge was shrinking already as the sun moved higher. Later in the day, the shadow would fall on the other side, where they were—in the hollow where not even the wind could get to you, where all sounds were so muted and so distant that it almost seemed like silence.

But she couldn't go back there.

Adjusting the UV shield she turned around and began walking away from the capsule, taking long, confident strides. With every step, she put her left foot down hard on the ground to test it. It barely hurt at all. As she walked, she tried not to think of how far she had to go and rattled off snippets of data in a loud voice to occupy her mind: atmospheric oxygen levels, rotation times of other planets they had visited, details of planetary orbits, the periodic table, anything would do. It wasn't like it mattered what she said. The wind ripped the words out of her mouth and scattered them, leaving nothing but sand on her tongue. Still, she kept on talking, putting her head down, leaning into the gusts and striding onwards.

Even though the wind-rippled ground seemed level and unchanging, she was soon unable to see the capsule when she turned around. Out here the wind was all there was. It never left her alone: it screamed in her ears, it whipped the sand against her face, and it blew in under the UV shield, stinging her eyes. She tried to think of something else, something from before, something from back home, but she no longer had any such memories. They had been swept away by the wind, leaving only the high-pitched wail, the sand, and the shadows.

Finally, the cliffs were there in front of her: their sandblasted silhouettes rising like twisted, crumbling towers out of the otherwise featureless landscape. She ran the last hundred metres, limping and panting, the sweat chilling her skin. The station was situated at the mouth of a small ravine, and even from a distance, she could see that the instruments had been knocked over. As she got closer, she saw the tracks looping the scattered equipment.

For a moment she just stood there, trembling in the harsh wind, staring at the destruction. Then she knelt and brushed sand off the instruments, but there was nothing left to salvage. Pieces of smashed plastic and fragments of twisted metal were strewn everywhere, the electronic innards pulled out and shredded. As best she could, she gathered up the pieces and put them in a small pile next to the cliff, then used her hands to smooth over the tracks.

When she had done all she could, she crawled further in between the walls of the ravine, scrambling in on all fours as far as she could until the gorge became so narrow that the rock walls touched her on either side. Between the cliffs, she was protected from the wind, but she could still hear it moan and wail through innumerable holes and crevices. Even though the wind couldn't touch her, the noise of it ripped through her: piercing her, shaking her thoughts and bones and flesh, and she wrapped her arms tightly around her body to hold it together. The wind howled ever louder, its howls sometimes resembling high-pitched cries and voices, frayed and difficult to understand. Now and then she thought she could make out certain words, and after a while, she could even recognize the voices. It was their voices, their words speaking to her out of the cliffs and the sand. They shouldn't be able to talk to her anymore, and yet she could hear them.

Nothing but the wind, she thought, banging her head against the rocks. *That's all it is. There's nothing else. Just the wind. Making ripples in the sand.*

The tracks had been there the very first morning, the very first time she headed out to check on the hull after the crash. She had covered them up immediately, but he had seen her. He had been watching. When she came back inside, he was sitting up in bed, leaning on one elbow, facing the window. She had been so certain that he would sleep longer than that.

"It's just the wind," she explained before he had a chance to say anything.

He just shook his head.

"I saw it," he said without looking at her. "During the night. It was there, outside the window. It was watching me."

Then he lay down, facing the wall.

"We should never have landed here. The probe would have given us info about it. Whatever it is."

She had tried to be understanding. After all, he had suffered from shock, confusion and amnesia after the crash. That made it difficult for him to remember what had really happened during the last few days on board. She had explained it all to him again, that the probe had been sent out and that the readings hadn't shown anything out of the ordinary. Then she asked if he remembered the accident.

"We had no choice," she had told him, holding his hand to comfort him. "The guidance system was broken and we were forced to evacuate to the emergency capsule."

"It's too risky to land without probe info," he said stubbornly as if he hadn't heard a word, and he still refused to look at her.

"It was an emergency landing," she said, speaking slowly and clearly so he would understand. "We had no choice."

But it was as though he couldn't remember that.

"Where are the others?" he asked and she nodded toward the two bodies covered with blankets next to the exit.

"They died. The entry was rough. Don't you remember? Don't you remember that the probe didn't show anything unusual and that the systems malfunctioned and we had to get out of there?"

He had just looked at her then: eyes glazed, a trickle

of dried blood in the corner of his mouth. Still, she had tried to be patient. He was suffering from hallucinations. Nightmares. Just like she was.

"It was watching me," he told her again. "It was standing out there, looking right at me. Even with the insulation, the capsule must give off some heat. Maybe that's what lures them. It must be so cold out there at night."

There had been nothing more to say after that. She had given him his pills and then he went quiet and fell asleep. The next day she moved them. His eyes were still shut when she dragged him across the sand, and finally put him to rest on the other side of the ridge with the others. She had put the memory clip with the ship's log on his chest, placing his hands on top of it. It just seemed like he ought to have something with him. She didn't know for certain whether he had made entries in the log since the crash, but he could have done it while she was asleep, and there seemed to be no way to crack his encryption.

The bodies had looked so lonely laying there on the ground. She had put the first two facedown so that they wouldn't be able to see her, but his eyes were closed, so she had left him on his back. There was nothing to see anyway. Not now. Not anymore.

NOTHING TO SEE, she thought as the cold, rough surface of the cliff scraped her forehead.

The UV shield was cracked. She pulled off her gloves, removed the shield and threw it away, then rubbed her eyes to get rid of the sand, but now the tears came, stinging her nostrils, spreading their salty taste in the back of her mouth.

The wind grabbed hold of her when she stood up to leave, it shoved her in the back, almost toppling her while the cliffs kept howling behind her, calling out tattered words she couldn't escape and didn't want to understand. She tried to get away, didn't want to listen, but the sand was soft and deep and her boots sank into it, it was like treading water. In the end, you always sink no matter how you fight—you're pulled down and under until you can't breathe. The pills were wearing off and the pain in her foot had returned, but she couldn't stay here, she had to get back. So she went on, every step another stab of pain.

When she dared to turn around, the cliffs were gone. The storm was blowing harder now, whipping up swirls and clouds of dust that filled the air and sky, making the landscape look the same in all directions. She could feel the world turning, tumbling and spinning around her until she had no idea where she had come from or where she was going. Standing there, assaulted by the wind, she hesitated, squinting up at the sun until her unprotected eyes burned, vainly trying to remember the position it had been in before.

It seemed to her that there were other shapes surrounding her in the storm, but she couldn't see clearly and they always seemed to stay right at the edges of her field of vision, flitting in and out, uncertain and unseen. They flickered in the wind and the light, then disappeared completely when she turned to face them. Shadows. Sand. Wind.

Maybe it's the search party, she thought. *Sent out to find me.* Maybe they just landed and found the empty capsule. She shouldn't have thrown away the UV shield. It was so difficult to see in the shimmering sand and sunlight.

She screamed, but the sound of her voice being devoured by the wind was so strange that she immediately fell silent again. After a while, the shapes around her disappeared and the air seemed to clear. She was alone and started moving again, more slowly than before, dragging that left foot. The fatigue overcame her then, it entered her mind and her body like a familiar, almost welcome warmth in the chest, spreading slowly into her arms and legs.

It was like it had been when she dragged the others across the ridge. The fatigue had been like an inviting, seductive heaviness—making it difficult to move and even more difficult to think.

Soon, she thought and struggled on, *they'll be here soon. Maybe they're already here.*

WHEN SHE FINALLY reached the capsule, she collapsed inside as the airlock closed, and lay there for a while with her flushed, wind-burned face resting on the floor, listening to the wind howling through the holes and cracks inside her, just as it had howled through the cliffs.

There was nobody there. Nobody had come for her.

She took two pills before sitting down at the work-desk. It was difficult to get the boot off because of the swelling, and the searing reddish-blue bruise had spread halfway up her calf and shin. Carefully, she wrapped her ankle with a cooling bandage and felt the throbbing subside. She pulled up the diagrams and graphs on-screen, all the data she had previously collected from the test sites, and she sat there staring at the screen, trying to make sense of it all. It was so difficult to concentrate, so difficult to see as if the sparkling sand and sunlight were still in her eyes. The report was incomplete, but maybe it would still be enough for a terra-forming licence. It would have looked better with the info from the probe, but it was too late to do anything about that.

I can't do it all by myself, she thought angrily. *They'll understand that. They have to understand that.*

She felt her lacerated forehead and saw blood on her fingers.

The damn probe.

If they had just listened to her, it would have been so much easier, but she had done the best she could under the circumstances. She had done what had to be done.

IT HAD BEEN roughly six months into their trip, barely halfway through their mission.

When she'd accepted the position with the research team, she thought that analyzing and classifying the planets in the sector they had been assigned would challenge her terra-forming knowledge. After only a month on board, she realized that it was going to be very different than she had imagined. The work was monotonous and repetitive and mostly consisted of evaluating long-distance sensor info, not analyzing environments on-site like she wanted to do. The others always found something that ruled out surface expeditions, and soon every new planet became just another source of disappointment.

Scanning the first long-distance data for this planet, she had immediately realized that it was ideal, near perfect for terra-forming, and she had wanted to get down there immediately. It was true that they had lost contact with the first probe, but that was just a technical mishap, and the others ought to have given in when she reported the impressive info from the second probe. Instead, they had requested access to the raw data feed. She had refused because it was unnecessary, but the others remained obsessed with seeing that raw feed. Despite her expertise, despite the well-written reports and the excellent stats she provided, they did not want to listen to her.

SHE ATE EVEN though she wasn't hungry. The whole time she could hear the wind outside—the sand hissing as it drifted over the dunes and rocks. She could feel it on her face, hear its mournful whine through the crevices and crannies of the cliffs. Voices. Their voices. She shook her head when she heard what they were saying. *No*, she said, *no, it wasn't like that*. But that didn't silence them.

She didn't go to bed when darkness fell. It was impossible to see the sunset from inside the capsule, but you could see the sky shift from dark blue to black and then the night sky was split in half by the galaxy's wide spiral arm, its brilliant white starlight casting shadows on the ground. She turned off all the lights until just the screen on the desk remained lit behind her: a cold, pale light fuelled by statistics, data, numbers, plans. More distant than starlight.

It was very cold out there at night. Ice and frozen sand, frost and cold fingers curled as though they were still trying to grab hold of something. Other hands stretched out as if to protect, or fend off. The wind was picking up, she heard the sand scraping against the windows and the hull, and she covered her face with her hands so that it wouldn't get into her eyes.

If it drifts up against the door, she thought. The wind was screaming in her ears now, it could not be shut out. *If it drifts over the top and buries me.*

The screams and the voices rushed at her, the words clearer now, more distinct, but she shook her head because they didn't know, they didn't see, they couldn't know, they couldn't see.

How long now?

She looked at the useless watch that kept flashing the same numbers, the same moment again and again and again.

They would find her. It was just a question of time.

WHEN THEY FINALLY did come, she didn't dare to move at first, hardly dared to breathe so as not to scare them, but they seemed completely unafraid.

I knew they'd come, she thought, leaning closer to see better—just the glass separating her from them now. She raised her hand in greeting, placing it on the window, fingers spread.

After a while, they disappeared and she stood. The thermal suit was hanging in the closet but she didn't need it.

They finally came. I knew they would. I knew they would come for me.

The door closed behind her as the outer hatch opened. She ventured into the darkness, into the cold, where they were waiting for her.

THE CAPSULE WAS almost completely buried when they reached it, and he thought to himself that it resembled a rock or a cliff formation, a part of the planet itself.

"Get going," he said, pulling irritably at his tight silver collar adorned with the black leadership pin. "Looks like we'll have to dig our way in."

The wind pulled at his hood and the sand lashed his face when he turned around, squinting up at the ridge further away.

A noise. Distant.

He tried to catch it again but it was difficult to hear with the hood pulled up over his head.

It took less than ten minutes for the team to dig their way down to the outer hatch. When they were done they stood silent for a moment, leaning on their shovels. In their black outfits with silver click-seams they resembled nothing so much as a gathering of mourners.

The corpse patrol, he thought, brushing the sand off his shoulders. *A well-deserved nickname perhaps, but they could at least have given us suits that look a little more cheerful.*

"Perhaps their comm system has been damaged," he said in a loud voice to make himself heard over the wind. "We can't know for sure. They may still be alive."

When he closed his mouth, grains of sand cracked between his teeth.

The hatch opened and they looked at each other but didn't need to speak: they had all done this before. When they stepped inside they prepared themselves for the smell and sight of death.

"Light," he said and the capsule was illuminated.

Empty.

The tension eased slightly around his shoulders and neck. Most of the interior seemed intact. Only one computer unit appeared to be damaged, its interface panel black and cracked but the screen on the work-desk seemed active. In a corner, they found bloodstained clothing and empty packs of painkillers.

"Somebody's been working here, after the crash," one of his crew said after checking the work-desk.

"Working on what?"

"Looks like observation stats. They must have set up a couple of stations judging by this. But nothing from the probe as far as I can tell, neither the first nor the second one."

"Not surprising considering that we haven't found any traces of them either. Not even a positioning blip."

"Crew of four, right?"

"Two men, two women, the usual. One terra-former, a couple of engineers, a ship's specialist."

"Somebody must have been injured. Almost half the pain pills are gone from the medical supply."

"Okay," he said. "A search party. You three. One k radius to start. Maybe they've collapsed close by. Look for tracks."

"With this wind, it'll be difficult to find any kind of tracks. Anything older than a few hours, maybe even less, will be gone."

"I know. But look anyway."

"If they've spent the night outside, they must be dead by now. It's pure desert and tundra out there."

When the others had left, he haphazardly went through the furnishings, the bedding and toolboxes.

"I don't think they've been here for quite a while," said his second-in-command who was still going through the work-desk entries. "The last info is a few weeks old already. Before that, it seems to have been used almost daily."

"So where are they?" he asked testily. "The life-support systems are intact and as far as I can tell the hull is intact as well. The rest of it is no worse than that. They should've been able to fix it in a couple of days. The food and water supplies have hardly been touched; the solar panels are working. Why aren't they here? Try to find the ship's log. It must be here somewhere."

"Maybe they snapped. Wouldn't be the first time that happened. You and I have been on enough expeditions to know that. The psych problems in these teams are rampant. Even worse than our own."

He was standing by the window, peering out into the sunlight.

Nothing but sand and wind out there, he thought. *Sand and wind*. Finally, he said:

"Out there, when we approached. Did you hear something?"

"Hear something? Like what?"

In the light, he could make out a palm print on the window.

"I don't know," he said. "Kind of a yell, or howl."

"Human?"

"Perhaps."

"I didn't hear anything. Could've been just the wind. This place is not too inviting. Blustery to say the least. That sand gets everywhere and it's as cold as a deep freeze at night."

"No worse than many other places they've terraformed."

"We've found them."

The sudden sound from the comm-link in his ear gave him a start even though he'd been expecting it. He adjusted the volume behind his earlobe: it was always set too loud.

"What shape are they in?" he asked.

"Dead. Have been dead for quite a while. Since the crash is my guess. Frozen solid by now. But there are only three of them here. One of the women is missing."

"Cause of death?"

"Two of them have skull fractures and some serious lacerations. Death was probably caused by a sharp object to the head. Almost identical injuries on both. Could've happened during the emergency landing I guess, but I don't want to speculate. The third has some broken bones and signs of internal injuries. We've found the ship's log but it's useless. Looks like somebody tried to erase it. Not a professional job, but there are only bits and pieces left."

"Erased it? And no sign of the fourth?"

"Nothing so far."

To hell with it, he thought and held up his hand to shield his eyes from the light. *To hell with all of it.*

WHEN THEY LEFT four days later, he was standing by the round observation window in the gathering hall, watching as the planet's illuminated crescent disappeared beneath them. The three bodies were resting in the cargo hold, sealed in shiny metal containers.

"Seems perfect for terra-forming," his second-in-command remarked.

"But without complete stats, they can't begin. And they don't know when the next science team can be sent out here. They're pretty busy elsewhere."

That elicited a derisive snort.

"Busy. Right. If they'd start terra-forming now, it could be ready for colonization within the next decade. Instead, we have to wait for another expedition before the process can begin. Sending out another ship could take several years considering how slowly Search and Science works."

"The regulations are there for a reason."

"But following them is occasionally a waste of time. We both know that. As if we have all the time in the world. As if we can afford to be picky. You know my opinion. These manned expeditions are a waste of resources. A couple of robot teams could make evaluations on a flyby, maybe not all that precise but good enough. We don't have to be so thorough."

He said nothing, just blew on the hot cup of tea he had just poured, watching the steam fog up the window.

"They're running an analysis on the remains of the ship in Tech-lab right now," the other man continued. "But with the crumbs they have to work with, it'll be difficult to determine what really took place."

"What do you think happened to her?"

"Anything could have happened to her. Most likely an accident on the way to one of those useless monitoring stations she set up."

"But no body."

A shrug.

"No body. Maybe she overdosed on pain pills like the ship's specialist. Maybe she committed suicide out there in the sand somewhere. We'd never find her."

"And the probes? Two of them gone and not a trace. And the monitoring stations? Every instrument smashed."

"She must have done it before she killed herself or got herself lost. Psychosis. How many times have we seen that before? A couple of months down there all alone would drive anybody crazy. It was a stupid idea to set up those stations, but I guess it gave her something to do anyway."

The stars were dense here in the inner spiral arms of the galaxy, and they stood silent side by side looking at scraps of white starlight while the ship kept going.

Cold, he thought. *It must have been so very cold.*

"Long shifts for those teams," his second-in-command mused. "Enormous psychological pressure. I don't envy them. Hey. Are you listening?"

He felt the tug at his sleeve and turned, but instead of the other man's face, he saw the ridge and its shadow and the shimmering ice crystals that had shattered beneath the soles of his boots when they had gone down into the hollow to pack up the bodies.

If it wasn't so cold.

He closed his eyes so the sand would not get into his eyes.

"The wind," he said finally. "Almost like voices sometimes even though you can't understand what they're saying."

"What are you talking about?"

But he turned away, staring out the window again.

I wonder what she saw, he thought, placing his palm on the window, fingers sprawled on the glass as if in a greeting, but all he could feel was the cold outside.

SING

Karin Tidbeck

THE COLD DAWN light creeps onto the mountaintops; they emerge like islands in the valley's dark sea, tendrils of steam rising from the thickets clinging to the rock. Right now there's no sound of birdsong or crickets, no hiss of wind in the trees. When Maderakka's great shadow has sunk back below the horizon, twitter and chirp will return in a shocking explosion of sound. For now, we sit in complete silence.

The birds have left. Petr lies with his head in my lap, his chest rising and falling so quickly it's almost a flutter, his pulse rushing under the skin. The bits of eggshell I couldn't get out of his mouth, those that have already made their way into him, spread whiteness into the surrounding flesh. If only I could hear that he was breathing properly. His eyes are rolled back into his head, his arms and legs curled up against his body like a baby's. If he's conscious, he must be in pain. I hope he's not conscious.

* * *

A STRANGELY SHAPED man came in the door and stepped up to the counter. He made a full turn to look at the mess in my workshop: the fabrics, the cutting table, the bits of pattern. Then he looked directly at me. He was definitely not from here—no one had told him not to do that. I almost wanted to correct him: *leave, you're not supposed to make contact like that, you're supposed to pretend you can't see me and tell the air what you want.* But I was curious about what he might do. I was too used to avoiding eye contact, so I concentrated carefully on the rest of him: the squat body with its weirdly broad shoulders, the swelling upper arms and legs. The cropped copper on his head. I'd never seen anything like it.

So this man stepped up to the counter and he spoke directly to me, and it was like being caught under the midday sun.

"You're Aino? The tailor? Can you repair this?"

He spoke slowly and deliberately, his accent crowded with hard sounds. He dropped a heap of something on the counter. I collected myself and made my way over. He flinched as I slid off my chair at the cutting table, catching myself before my knees collapsed backwards. I knew what he saw: a stick insect of a woman clambering unsteadily along the furniture, joints flexing at impossible angles. Still, he didn't look away. I could see his eyes at the outskirts of my vision, golden-yellow points following me as I heaved myself forward to the stool by the counter. The bundle, when I held it up, was an oddly cut jacket. It had no visible seams, the material almost like rough canvas but not quite. It was half-eaten by wear and grime.

"You should have had this mended long ago," I said. "And washed. I can't fix this."

He leaned closer, hand cupped behind an ear. "Again, please?"

"I can't repair it," I said, slower.

He sighed, a long waft of warm air on my forearm. "Can you make a new one?"

"Maybe. But I'll have to measure you." I waved him toward me.

He stepped around the counter. After that first flinch, he didn't react. His smell was dry, like burnt ochre and spices, not unpleasant, and while I measured him he kept talking in a stream of consonants and archaic words, easy enough to understand if I didn't listen too closely. His name was Petr, the name as angular as his accent, and he came from Amitié—a station somewhere out there—but was born on Gliese. (I knew a little about Gliese, and told him so.) He was a biologist and hadn't seen an open sky for eight years. He had landed on Kiruna and ridden with a truck and then walked for three days, and he was proud to have learned our language, although our dialect was very odd. He was here to research lichen.

"Lichen can survive anywhere," he said, "even in a vacuum, at least as spores. I want to compare these to the ones on Gliese, to see if they have the same origin."

"Just you? You're alone?"

"Do you know how many colonies are out there?" He laughed, but then cleared his throat. "Sorry. But it's really like that. There are more colonies than anyone can keep track of. And Kiruna is, well, it's considered an abandoned world, after the mining companies left, so—"

His next word was silent. Saarakka was up, the bright moonlet sudden as always. He mouthed more words. I switched to song, but Petr just stared at me. He inclined his head slightly towards me, eyes narrowing, then shook his head and pinched the bridge of his nose. He reached into the back pocket of his trousers and drew out something like a small and very thin book. He did something with a quick movement—shook it out, somehow—and it unfolded into a large square that he put down on the counter. It had the outlines of letters at the bottom, and his fingers flew over them. *WHAT HAPPENED WITH SOUND?*

I recognised the layout of the keys. I could type. *SAARAKKA*, I wrote. *WHEN SAARAKKA IS UP, WE CAN'T HEAR SPEECH. WE SING INSTEAD.*

WHY HAS NOBODY TOLD ME ABOUT THIS? he replied.

I shrugged.

He typed with annoyed, jerky movements. *HOW LONG DOES IT LAST?*

UNTIL IT SETS, I told him.

He had so many questions—he wanted to know how Saarakka silenced speech, if the other moon did something too. I told him about how Oksakka kills the sound of birds, and how giant Maderakka peeks over the horizon now and then, reminding us that the three of us are just her satellites. How they once named our world after a mining town and we named the other moons after an ancient goddess and her handmaidens, although these names sound strange and harsh to us now. But every answer prompted new questions. I finally pushed the sheet away from me. He held his palms up in resignation, folded it up, and left.

What I had wanted to say, when he started talking about how Kiruna was just one world among many, was that I'm not stupid. I read books and sometimes I could pick up stuff on my old set when the satellite was up and the moons didn't interfere with it so much. I knew that Amitié was a big space station. I knew we lived in a poor backwater place. Still, you think your home is special, even if nobody ever visits.

THE VILLAGE HAS a single street. One can walk along the street for a little while, and then go down to the sluggish red river. I go there to wash myself and rinse out cloth.

I like dusk, when everyone's gone home and I can air-dry on the big, flat stone by the shore, arms and legs finally long and relaxed and folding at what angles they will, my spine and muscles creaking like wood after a long day of keeping everything straight and upright. Sometimes the goats come to visit. They're only interested in whether I have food or ear scratchings for them. To the goats, all people are equal, except for those who have treats. Sometimes the birds come here too, alighting on the rocks to preen their plumes, compound eyes iridescent in the twilight. I try not to notice them, but unless Oksakka is up to muffle the higher-pitched noise, the insistent buzzing twitches of their wings are impossible to ignore. More than two or three and they start warbling among themselves, eerily like human song, and I leave.

Petr met me on the path up from the river. I was carrying a bundle of wet fabric strapped to my back; it was slow going because I'd brought too much and the extra weight made me swing heavy on my crutches.

He held out a hand. "Let me carry that for you, Aino."

"No, thank you." I moved past him.

He kept pace with me. "I'm just trying to be polite."

I sneaked a glance at him, but it did seem that was what he wanted. I unstrapped my bundle. He took it and casually slung it over his shoulder. We walked in silence up the slope, him at a leisurely walk, me concentrating on the uphill effort, crutch-foot-foot-crutch.

"Your ecosystem," he said eventually when the path flattened out. "It's fascinating."

"What about it?"

"I've never seen a system based on parasitism."

"I don't know much about that."

"But you know how it works?"

"Of course," I said. "Animals lay eggs in other animals. Even the plants."

"So is there anything that uses the goats for hosts?"

"Hookflies. They hatch in the goats' noses."

Petr hummed. "Does it harm the goats?"

"No... not usually. Some of them get sick and die. Most of the time they just get... perkier. It's good for them."

"Fascinating," Petr said. "I've never seen an alien species just slip into an ecosystem like that." He paused. "These hookflies. Do they ever go for humans?"

I shook my head.

He was quiet for a while. We were almost at the village when he spoke again.

"So how long have your people been singing?"

"I don't know. A long time."

"But how do you learn? I mean I've tried, but I just can't make the sounds. The pitch, it's higher than anything I've heard a human voice do. It's like birdsong."

"It's passed on." I concentrated on tensing the muscles in my feet for the next step.

"How? Is it a mutation?"

"It's passed on," I repeated. "Here's the workshop. I can handle it from here. Thank you."

He handed me the bundle. I could tell he wanted to ask me more, but I turned away from him and dragged my load inside.

I DON'T LIE. But neither will I answer a question that hasn't been asked. Petr would have called it lying by omission, I suppose. I've wondered if things would have happened differently if I'd just told him what he really wanted to know: not *how* we learn, but how it's *possible* for us to learn. But no. I don't think it would have changed much. He was too recklessly curious.

MY MOTHER TOLD me I'd never take over the business, but she underestimated me and how much I'd learned before she passed. I have some strength in my hands and arms, and I'm good at precision work. It makes me a good tailor. In that way, I can at least get a little respect because I support myself and do it well. So the villagers employ me, even if they won't look at me.

Others of my kind aren't so lucky. A man down the street hasn't left his room for years. His elderly parents take care of him. When they pass, the other villagers won't show as much compassion. I know there are more of us here and there, in the village and the outlying farms. Those of us who do go outside don't communicate with each other. We stay in the background, we who didn't receive the gift unscathed.

I wonder if that will happen to Petr now. So far, there's

no change; he's very still. His temples are freckled. I haven't noticed that before.

PETR WOULDN'T LEAVE me alone. He kept coming in to talk. I didn't know if he did this to everyone. I sometimes thought that maybe he didn't study lichen at all; he just went from house to house and talked people's ears off. He talked about his heavy homeworld, which he'd left to crawl almost weightless in the high spokes of Amitié. He told me I wouldn't have to carry my own weight there, I'd move without crutches, and I was surprised by the want that flared up inside me, but I said nothing of it. He asked me if I hurt, and I said only if my joints folded back or sideways too quickly. He was very fascinated.

When Saarakka was up, he typed at me to sing to him. He parsed the cadences and inflections like a scientist, annoyed when they refused to slip into neat order.

I found myself talking too, telling him of sewing and books I'd read, of the other villagers and what they did. It's remarkable what people will say and do when you're part of the background. Petr listened to me, asked questions. Sometimes I met his eyes. They had little crinkles at the outer edges that deepened when he smiled. I discovered that I had many things to say. I couldn't tell whether the biologist in him wanted to study my appearance, or if he really enjoyed being around me.

HE SAT ON my stool behind the counter, telling me about crawling around in the vents on Amitié to study the lichen unique to the station: "They must have hitchhiked in with a shuttle. The question was from where…"

I interrupted him. "How does one get there? To visit?"

"You want to go?"

"I'd like to see it." *And be weightless*, I didn't say.

"There's a shuttle bypass in a few months to pick me up," he said. "But it'd cost you."

I nodded.

"Do you have money?" he asked.

"I've saved up some."

He mentioned how much it would cost, and my heart sank so deep I couldn't speak for a while. For once, Petr didn't fill the silence.

I moved past him from the cutting table to the mannequin. I put my hand on a piece of fabric on the table and it slipped. I stumbled. He reached out and caught me, and I fell with my face against his throat. His skin was warm, almost hot; he smelled of sweat and dust and an undertone of musk that seeped into my body and made it heavy. It was suddenly hard to breathe.

I pushed myself out of his arms and leaned against the table, unsteadily, because my arms were shaking. No one had touched me like that before. He had slid from the stool, leaning against the counter across from me, his chest rising and falling as if he had been running. Those eyes were so sharp, I couldn't look at them directly.

"I'm in love with you." The words tumbled out of his mouth in a quick mumble.

He stiffened as if surprised by what he had just said. I opened my mouth to say I didn't know what, but words like that deserved something—

He held up a hand. "I didn't mean to."

"But..."

Petr shook his head. "Aino. It's all right."

When I finally figured out what to say, he had left. I

wanted to say I hadn't thought of the possibility, but that I did now. Someone wanted me. It was a very strange sensation, like a little hook tugging at the hollow under my ribs.

PETR CHANGED AFTER that. He kept coming into the workshop, but he started to make friends elsewhere too. I could see it from the shop window: his cheerful brusqueness bowled the others over. He crouched together with the weaver across the street, eagerly studying her work. He engaged in cheerful haggling with Maiju, who would never negotiate the price of her vegetables, but with him, she did. He even tried to sing, unsuccessfully. I recognised the looks the others gave him. And even though they were only humouring him, treating him as they would a harmless idiot, I found myself growing jealous. That was novel too.

He didn't mention it again. Our conversation skirted away from any deeper subjects. The memory of his scent intruded on my thoughts at night. I tried to wash it away in the river.

"AINO, I'M THINKING about staying."

Petr hadn't been in for a week. Now this.

"Why?" I fiddled with a seam on the work shirt I was hemming.

"I like it here. Everything's simple—no high tech, no info flooding, no hurry. I can hear myself think." He smiled faintly. "You know, I've had stomach problems most of my life. When I came here, they went away in a week. It's been like coming home."

78

"I don't see why." I kept my eyes down. "There's nothing special here."

"These are good people. Sure, they're a bit traditional, a bit distant. But I like them. And it turns out they need me here. Jorma, he doesn't mind that I can't sing. He offered me a job at the clinic. Says they need someone with my experience."

"Are you all right with this?" he asked when I didn't reply immediately.

"It's good," I said eventually. "It's good for you that they like you."

"I don't know about 'like'. Some of them treat me as if I'm disabled. I don't care much, though. I can live with that as long as some of you like me." His gaze rested on me like a heavy hand.

"Good for you," I repeated.

He leaned over the counter. "So... maybe you could teach me to sing? For real?"

"No."

"Why? I don't understand why."

"Because I can't teach you. You *are* disabled. Like me."

"Aino"—his voice was low—"did you ever consider that maybe they don't hate you?"

I looked up. "They don't hate me. They're afraid of me. It's different."

"Are you really sure? Maybe if you talked to them..."

"... they would avoid me. It is what it is."

"You can't just sit in here and be bitter."

"I'm not," I said. "It just is what it is. I can choose to be miserable about it, or I can choose not to be."

"Fine." He sighed. "Does it matter to you if I stay or leave?"

"Yes," I whispered to the shirt in my lap.

"Well, which is it? Do you want me to stay?"

He had asked directly, so I had to give him an answer, at least some sort of reply. "You could stay a while. Or I could go with you."

"I told you. I'm not going back to Amitié."

"All right," I said.

"Really?"

"No."

I COULD HAVE kept quiet when the procession went by. Maybe then things would have been different. I think he would have found out, anyway.

We were down by the river. We pretended the last conversation hadn't happened. He had insisted on helping me with washing cloth. I wouldn't let him, so he sat alongside me, making conversation while I dipped the lengths of cloth in the river and slapped them on the big flat stone. Maderakka's huge approaching shadow hovered on the horizon. It would be Petr's first time, and he was fascinated. The birds were beginning to amass in the air above the plateau, sharp trills echoing through the valley.

"How long will it last?"

"Just overnight," I said. "It only rises a little bit before it sets again."

"I wonder what it's like on the other side," he said. "Having that in the sky all the time."

"Very quiet, I suppose."

"Does anyone live there?"

I shrugged. "A few. Not as many as here."

He grunted and said no more. I sank into the rhythm of my work, listening to the rush of water and wet cloth on stone, the clatter and bleat of goats on the shore.

Petr touched my arm, sending a shock up my shoulder. I pretended it was a twitch.

"Aino. What's that?" He pointed up the slope.

The women and men walking by were dressed all in white, led by an old woman with a bundle in her arms. They were heading for the valley's innermost point, where the river emerged from underground and a faint trail switchbacked up the wall.

I turned back to my laundry. "They're going to the plateau."

"I can see that. What are they going to do once they get there?"

The question was too direct to avoid. I had to answer somehow. "We don't talk about that," I said finally.

"Come on," Petr said. "If I'm going to live here, I should be allowed to know."

"I don't know if that's my decision to make," I replied.

He settled on the stone again, but he was tense now and kept casting glances at the procession on their way up the mountainside. He helped me carry the clothes back through the workshop and into the backyard and then left without helping me hang them. I knew where he was going. You could say I let it happen—but I don't think I could have stopped him either. It was a kind of relief. I hung the cloth, listening to the comforting whisper of wet fabric, until Maderakka rose and silence cupped its hands over my ears.

I DON'T REMEMBER being carried to the plateau in my mother's arms. I only know that she did. Looking down at Petr in my lap, I'm glad I don't remember. Of course, everyone *knows* what happens. We're just better off forgetting what it was like.

*   *   *

MADERAKKA SET IN the early hours of the morning, and I woke to the noise of someone hammering on the door. It was Petr, of course, and his nose and lips were puffy. I let him in, and into the back of the workshop to my private room. He sank down on my bed and just sort of crumpled. I put the kettle on and waited.

"I tried to go up there," he said into his hands. "I wanted to see what it was."

"And?"

"Jorma stopped me."

I thought of the gangly doctor trying to hold Petr back, and snorted. "How?"

"He hit me."

"But you're"—I gestured toward him, all of him—"huge."

"So? I don't know how to fight. And he's scary. I almost got to the top before he saw me and stopped me. I got this"—he pointed to his nose—"just for going up there. What the hell is going on up there, Aino? There were those bird things, hundreds of them, just circling overhead."

"Did you see anything else?"

"No."

"You won't give up until you find out, will you?"

He shook his head.

"It's how we do things," I said. "It's how we sing."

"I don't understand."

"You said it's a—what was it?—parasitic ecosystem. Yes?"

He nodded.

"And I said that the hookflies use the goats, and that

it's good for the goats. The hookflies get to lay their eggs, and the goats get something in return."

He nodded again. I waited for him to connect the facts. His face remained blank.

"The birds," I said. "When a baby's born, it's taken up there the next time Maderakka rises."

Petr's shoulders slumped. He looked sick. It gave me some sort of grim satisfaction to go on talking, to get back at him for his idiocy.

I went on: "The birds lay their eggs. Not for long, just for a moment. And they leave something behind. It changes the children's development... in the throat. It means they can learn to sing." I gestured at myself. "Sometimes the child dies. Sometimes this happens. That's why the others avoid me. I didn't pass the test."

"You make yourself hosts," Petr said, faintly. "You do it to your children."

"They don't remember. I don't remember."

He stood up, swaying a little on his feet, and left.

"You wanted to know!" I called after him.

A LATECOMER HAS alighted on the rock next to me. It's preening its iridescent wings in the morning light, pulling its plumes between its mandibles one by one. I look away as it hops up on Petr's chest. It's so wrong to see it happen, too intimate. But I'm afraid to move, I'm afraid to flee. I don't know what will happen if I do.

THE WEATHER WAS so lovely I couldn't stay indoors. I sat under the awning outside my workshop, wrapped up in shawls so as not to offend too much, basting the seams on a skirt. The weaver across the street had set up one of her smaller looms on her porch, working with her back to me. Saarakka was up, and the street filled with song.

I saw Petr coming from a long way away. His square form made the villagers look so unbearably frail, as if they would break if he touched them. How did they even manage to stay upright? How did his weight not break the cobblestones? The others shied away from him, like reeds from a boat. I saw why when he came closer. I greeted him with song without thinking. It made his tortured grimace deepen.

He fell to his knees in front of me and wrapped his arms around me, squeezing me so tight I could feel my shoulders creaking. He was shaking. The soundless weeping hit my neck in silent, wet waves. All around us, the others were very busy not noticing what was going on.

I brought him to the backyard. He calmed down and we sat leaning against the wall, watching Saarakka outrun the sun and sink. When the last sliver had disappeared under the horizon, he hummed to test the atmosphere, and then spoke.

"I couldn't stand being in the village for Saarakka. Everyone else talking and I can't... I've started to understand the song language now, you know? It makes it worse. So I left, I went up to that plateau. There was nothing there. I suppose you knew that already. Just the trees and the little clearing." He fingered the back of his head and winced. "I don't know how, but I fell on the way down, I fell off the path and down the wall. It was close to the bottom, I didn't hurt myself much. Just banged my head a little."

"That was what made you upset?"

I could feel him looking at me. "If I'd really hurt myself, if I'd hurt myself badly, I wouldn't have been able to call for help. I could have just lain there until Saarakka set. Nobody would have heard me. You wouldn't have heard me."

We sat for a while without speaking. The sound of crickets and birds disappeared abruptly. Oksakka had risen behind us.

"I've always heard that if you've been near death, you're supposed to feel alive and grateful for every moment." Petr snorted. "All I can think of is how easy it is to die. That it can happen at any time."

I turned my head to look at him. His eyes glittered yellow in the setting sun.

"You don't believe I spend time with you because of you."

I waited.

Petr shook his head. "You know, on Amitié, they'd think you look strange, but you wouldn't be treated differently. And the gravity's low when closer to the hub. You wouldn't need crutches."

"So take me there."

"I'm not going back. I've told you."

"Gliese, then?"

"You'd be crushed." He held up a massive arm. "Why do you think I look like I do?"

I swallowed my frustration.

"There are wading birds on Earth," he said, "long-legged things. They move like dancers. You remind me of them."

"You don't remind me of anything here," I replied.

He looked surprised when I leaned in and kissed him.

Later, I had to close his hands around me, so afraid was he to hurt me.

I lay next to him thinking about having normal conversations, other people meeting my eyes, talking to me like a person.

I'm THRIFTY. I had saved up a decent sum over the years; there was nothing I could spend money on, after all. If I sold everything I owned, if I sold the business, it would be enough to go to Amitié, at least to visit. If someone wanted to buy my things.

But Petr had in some almost unnoticeable way moved into my home. Suddenly he lived there, and had done so for a while. He cooked, cleaned the corners I didn't bother with because I couldn't reach. He brought in shoots and plants from outside and planted them in little pots. When he showed up with lichen-covered rocks I put my foot down, so he arranged them in patterns in the backyard. Giant Maderakka rose twice; two processions in white passed by on their way to the plateau. He watched them with a mix of longing and disgust.

His attention spoiled me. I forgot that only he talked to me. I spoke directly to a customer and looked her in the eyes. She left the workshop in a hurry and didn't come back.

"I WANT TO leave," I finally said. "I'm selling everything. Let's go to Amitié."

We were in bed, listening to the lack of birds. Oksakka's quick little eye shone in the midnight sky.

"Again? I told you I don't want to go back," Petr replied.

"Just for a little while?"

"I feel at home here now," he said. "The valley, the sky... I love it. I love being light."

"I've lost my customers."

"I've thought about raising goats."

"These people will never accept you completely," I said. "You can't sing. You're like me, you're a cripple to them."

"You're not a cripple, Aino."

"I am to them. On Amitié, I wouldn't be."

He sighed and rolled over on his side. The discussion was apparently over.

I WOKE UP tonight because the bed was empty and the air completely still. Silence whined in my ears. Outside, Maderakka rose like a mountain at the valley's mouth.

I don't know if he'd planned it all along. It doesn't matter. There were no new babies this cycle, no procession. Maybe he just saw his chance and decided to go for it.

It took such a long time to get up the path to the plateau. The upslope fought me, and my crutches slid and skittered over gravel and loose rocks; I almost fell over several times. I couldn't call for him, couldn't sing, and the birds circled overhead in a downward spiral.

Just before the clearing came into view, the path curled around an outcrop and flattened out among trees. All I could see while struggling through the trees was a faint flickering. It wasn't until I came into the clearing that I could see what was going on: that which had been done to me, that I was too young to remember, that which none of us remembers and choose not to witness. They leave the children and wait among the trees with their backs turned. They don't speak of what has happened during the wait. No one has ever said that watching is forbidden, but I felt like I was committing a crime, revealing what was hidden.

Petr stood in the middle of the clearing, a silhouette against the grey sky, surrounded by birds. No, he wasn't standing. He hung suspended by their wings, his toes barely touching the ground, his head tipped back. They were swarming in his face, tangling in his hair.

I CAN'T AVERT my eyes anymore. I am about to see the process up close. The bird that sits on Petr's chest seems to take no notice of me. It pushes its ovipositor in between his lips and shudders. Then it leaves in a flutter of wings, so fast that I almost don't register it. Petr's chest heaves, and he rolls out of my lap, landing on his back. He's awake now, staring into the sky. I don't know if it's terror or ecstasy in his eyes as the tiny spawn fights its way out of his mouth.

In a week, the shuttle makes its bypass. Maybe they'll let me take Petr's place. If I went now, just left him on the ground and packed light, I could make it in time. I don't need a sky overhead. And considering the quality of their clothes, Amitié needs a tailor.

DENMARK

THE FALSE FISHERMAN

Kaspar Colling Nielsen
Translated by Olivia Lasky

HE STARTED FISHING later in life. Since he'd grown up in the city, he didn't know anyone who fished when he was a child; his father didn't fish, nor did his mother, for that matter. None of his uncles or aunts fished, and neither did any of his friends' fathers or mothers, so fishing wasn't really on his radar when he was younger.

HE FIRST STARTED fishing when he was in his mid-forties, so he could afford to buy professional equipment right away. He bought a carbon edge Westin W6—a legendary fishing pole known for extending the length of the fisherman's cast—and one of the best high-speed spinning reels on the market for 5,000 kroner. He bought the most expensive waders he could find since he hated getting wet. He also bought a hat, a kind of oversized sou'wester in cream white, plus all sorts of other odds and ends you need to be a fisherman: a black bucket with a metal handle, a dented metal box for bait, a fold-out case for tackles, lures, spinners, wobblers, flies, leaders, etc., fishing lines, and a pair of pliers. Plus a dagger, of course, that he wore on his belt, a fishing chair, a net, and a smoker.

HE ALSO BOUGHT a pipe that he smoked instead of cigarettes and started taking an interest in the weather. He got a paid weather app that was otherwise used by professional sailors, and when people thought they knew what the weather would be like later in the week or that day, he just nodded and let them live on in their misconception while basking in the fact that he knew better. Sometimes he'd just say: "I suppose we'll just have to wait and see." Or perhaps he would look at their clothing and suggest with a small smile that they were utterly wrong about their choices.

Sometimes he would cycle around with his black plastic bucket hanging from his handlebars, even if he wasn't going out fishing that day.

WHEN HE FISHED, he always fished alone, whether on the coast or in the lakes in Sjælland. He drove out in a used Toyota Hiace that he bought because it had plenty of room for all his gear.

He, of course, had permission to fish in the places where he fished. He started reading about fish: where different fish lived, how deep they swam, what they ate. He studied maps of lakes so he could get a better understanding of the location of the pikes and the perch—or whatever it is they're called.

* * *

He loved fishing. There was nothing he liked better than going out fishing. He would be gone for a whole weekend or a week or two if he could. He dreamt of fishing all over the world, but he mostly just drove up to Lake Esrum or fished from the shores at Amager Beach. Sometimes he didn't fish at all when he went out fishing; he just ate his lunch, which always consisted of thick, uneven slices of whole-grain rye bread cut with a dagger, and without butter, but with a thick slice of cheese or thick slices of cured sausage that he also cut with his dagger. He had a thermos of tea and he might sit on a bench or in his fishing chair and drink a bit of tea or fill his pipe while he thought about whether he wanted to fish that day. He didn't feel like any less of a fisherman if he didn't want to fish. He was just a fisherman who was thinking about whether he wanted to fish.

He hadn't been a fisherman for more than a week before he started noticing the changes both in himself and in the way people regarded him. It seemed like people had more respect for him. They'd talk to him about everything under the sun, but he didn't say anything back—or at least very little—because fishermen don't say all that much. Sometimes he smiled crookedly, tapped his pipe in his hand, and glanced up at the sky as if he were reading the clouds. He would then wish the person a good day, or simply nod and cycle on without saying anything at all. When he was fishing on a fishing trip, children and regular old people would come and look at him. The children wanted to see if there were any fish in his black bucket, which there weren't because he'd never caught a fish, although one time he actually did have a fish on the line.

* * *

THE OTHER FISHERMEN said hello to him and he nodded back, and if they started talking about bait or whatever it's called, or about lures and such things, he'd just start doing something fishermanly until they were done talking. People always stop talking at some point. It's inevitable, just like how a cup becomes empty when you pour out its contents. When they'd finished speaking, when they'd emptied themselves of words, he didn't answer them—he just let silence prevail. They might cough out a few more words to break the silence, or they'd just say thanks and leave, and he could happily note that they seemed a bit uneasy about the situation while he felt as calm as an old oak tree. As a fisherman, you don't have any problem with silence. Silence is the fisherman's friend, while noise and talking are his enemies.

THE OTHER FISHERMEN started studying him inquisitively when they passed by to see what he was fishing for and what kind of bait he was using, since it was clear to everyone hè was a proper fisherman.

Sometimes, he would just stand out in the water in his waders. The other fishermen thought he was silently observing something they hadn't thought about themselves, or perhaps they even thought he could sense fish in the water before he cast out the line.

IN THE EVENINGS, he would Google fishing equipment, but not because he was buying everything new all the time. On the contrary, he was the kind of person who repaired his gear and clothing if it was falling apart. He often spent evenings organising his equipment, and at 10 o'clock, he would go to bed and fall asleep right away and sleep like a rock until the next morning, when he got up before everyone else. Fishermen sleep far better than ordinary people.

HIS NEW IDENTITY as a fisherman also had other unexpected benefits. For example, he could suddenly understand his taxes, and if there were any irregularities, he called the tax administration and discussed it with them. It often involved small amounts, but the smaller the amount, the better the conversation went. They respected him more, and he was right about things for the most part. Perhaps this new ability could be attributed to the composure a fisherman naturally possesses, or perhaps it was the pipe that did it. In any case, he could practically fall into a trance thinking about his advance payments while he cleaned and packed his pipe.

ONE EVENING, HIS wife said: "Why don't you ever bring any fish home? What are you actually doing out there? Are you even fishing?"

After this incident, he would occasionally stop by the fishmonger on the way home and buy a couple of fish since he had, after all, never caught anything himself. He always took off his sou'wester and waders before he went into the shop and put them back on in the car. When he came home, they grilled the fish on the balcony or he smoked them in his smoker. His wife would say there was nothing better than freshly caught fish.

*   *   *

IT WASN'T JUST his life and relationships that changed; his face changed as well. It became tanned in a way, narrower and more wrinkled. He was always sunburned, and his eyes were blue as ice.

He looked like a fisherman even without his fishing clothes now. He was more present with his children. He never got angry or irritated anymore but was always calm and rational. His children would throw unreasonable tantrums because they wanted something or another but he never got caught up in it, he just let them be while he silently watched them, and then he hugged them when it was over. In the evenings, he calmly told his wife about his observations of the children and what he thought they needed. He could tell it confused her and that she didn't like it, but she couldn't say that, because who can criticise their husband for being too loving and attentive to their children? The only problem he had as a fisherman was when he was going to have sex with his wife. It wasn't because he was impotent. On the contrary, it seemed like his penis had even gotten a bit bigger since he'd become a fisherman, but he somehow couldn't muster up the aggressiveness that sex requires or that he sensed his wife expected. When they had sex, she was usually on top and wriggled around until he came. She didn't say anything, but when she turned over on her side to sleep, he could tell she was disappointed. His sperm quality, on the other hand, was top-notch. That was clear even to a layman: there was more of it, and it was thicker, cream-coloured, practically yellow, and it was almost like you could see the enormous fish sperm wriggling around on the sheets when the sperm ran out of her.

* * *

HIS WIFE GOT pregnant with their third child. It wasn't planned. He could immediately sense a sadness in her, even though she tried to seem happy. It turned out to be triplets, and her rectum ruptured during the birth. The doctor said she would never be able to hold in her farts again.

She got postpartum depression and just lay in bed all day while he did everything: looked after all five children, cleaned, shopped. Every weekend, her parents came and watched the children for a few hours so he could go out and fish. It was the only time he had to himself.

HE MANAGED EVERYTHING without getting overwhelmed or upset. It was his level-headedness as a fisherman that got him through that difficult period. His wife's parents also clearly liked him more than their daughter. They even didn't try to hide it but talked quite openly about how unreasonable she was being and how lucky she was to have a husband like him.

AFTER ABOUT SIX months, his wife started getting better. She went on long walks with a friend, and one day she came home and said she wanted a divorce. It came as a bit of a shock for him, or 'shock' might be a bit of an exaggeration, but he was surprised. She felt like she no longer knew him. He regarded her while she was emptying herself of words, and then he said: "Well, then we'll have to look into getting a divorce."

He kept the apartment and the children. They went to court. She wanted custody and was constantly agitated.

He was kind and listened when others said something, and whenever he spoke, it was calmly and carefully, and always in the best interest of the children. It was revealed that he fished in his free time and that she'd had postpartum depression, during which time he'd done everything. She didn't stand a chance. He let her have the children every other weekend and one day in the middle of the week.

HE WENT UP to Lake Esrum the next weekend to go fishing. He wasn't thinking about anything at all while he was driving, and he wasn't thinking about anything when he was standing out in the water in his waders, either, or when he was putting a fly on a hook and casting. The wind was blowing a bit and it started to rain, but he barely noticed. He'd put a bit of cork on the strings of his sou'wester so he could tighten it when it was windy. He reeled in and cast again, and then—he got a goddamn bite! It was a pike, a proper chap weighing more than twelve kilos. It fought for over ten minutes before he landed it in his net. It was the first and only fish he'd ever caught. Several of the other anglers came over and inspected the fish, and it turned out it was a renowned pike that many fishermen had been trying to catch, so from that day on, he was a legend in the area.

HE DROVE HOME with the fish in a plastic bag on the passenger seat. Later he discovered that it had some rather sticky sores with white worms in them on its back and it smelled bad to boot, so he threw it out in a rubbish bin at a gas station.

HEATHER COUNTRY

Jakob Drud

WE TOOK A side road off the remains of highway 15, Hjalmar and I, riding a quad motorcycle built for one. The track was all dirt, occasionally interrupted by hard patches of gravel. Nobody in their right mind would believe that this piece of junk road was the most traveled route into heather country on the West Jutland Isles, or that it supplied New Haithabu with ninety percent of its fuel. But then again, I didn't believe the NeuroClan was sending me out here on urgent business. Sure, a farmer's son had gone missing, but what could possibly be urgent about heather?

The quad's wheels slammed against an unseen boulder and Hjalmar's head bounced against my shoulder.

"I really should have worn a helmet," he said.

Did I sense a wee bit of sarcasm? Yeah, but that was Hjalmar. Head, brain, and tongue. Head: attached to my back and spine. Brain: piggybacking on my bodily functions. Tongue: surrounding my personal hunchback with a halo of words. It'd been three days since the

NeuroClan implanted him, insisting I'd need a biologist for the investigation. To say that we'd gotten used to the arrangement would be like denying that the impact had happened. I couldn't sleep on my back, Hjalmar complained about my farts, and that was just the least of it.

"A little skull-rattling will bring your IQ down a notch," I replied.

"Then who's going to do all the thinking?"

I'd been doing investigations for the past six years. Any case to pay the bills, be it murder investigations, missing dogs, counterintelligence, or cheating spouses. I did it alone, stepping on the toes I wanted to step on without anyone's advice.

"We're here for the money," I said. "Who needs thinking when you owe the Neuros?"

"Well, boo-hoo. I'd give you a nice comforting pat on the shoulder. Oh, except the accountants sold my arms as spare parts along with my inner organs." He shuddered, and though I wasn't supposed to feel him at all, his fear still sent a chill down my spine. "You're not in that kind of debt, Jens."

He had a point, but still. Six years ago, I'd borrowed five hundred thousand Fuel Equivalents for the quad, and so far, I'd paid the Clan back twice. Problem was, the Neuros wanted an investigator on hand, so the accountants just added to my debts. I paid their housing taxes, food import tolls, fuel duties, the ever-popular penalties for not paying my taxes on time, not to mention the tax for complaining to the accountants about taxes. I only truly understood how much they wanted to keep me under control when they invented a private investigator permit stamp.

It was ironic that bureaucracy had survived the impact even when 90 percent of the country's population had died, but the thing was, you didn't want to fight the NeuroClan accountants. Number-crunchers with combat implants and advanced neurological enhancement were an irresistible force.

"We can't bungle an investigation in heather country," Hjalmar said. "It's a fragile ecosystem, and if it breaks down, Haithabu is out of fuel. But if we do it right, you'll be square with the Neuros, and I'll get my spleen back."

"All right, I'll leave the thinking to you. As long as it gets us paid."

The westerly wind began to smell of pig shit as we crossed a pontoon bridge to one of the larger isles. Soon after, we hit a patch of blacktop that hadn't been warped out of shape by the impact, and I wrenched the accelerator, roaring between newly fertilized fields. GMO heather bloomed on both sides of the road, promising a good harvest for the fuel refineries.

We crested a low hill, and I had to pull the brakes hard. Fourteen farmers in blue overalls and coarse-knitted sweaters were marching along the road, determined looks on their faces. None of them were armed, so I kept my shotgun in its holster beneath the handlebar. Their four dogs, all mongrels, ignored the quad, noses low in fertilizer heaven.

"Hey, freak!" one of the farmers shouted.

It took me half a second to figure out that I was the freak. In Haithabu, people were used to stranger creatures than a man with an extra head. But out here, they still believed in the sanctity of God's creation.

"Name's Jens," I said.

"And Hjalmar," Hjalmar said.

"Freaks. You seen my pig?"

The man who'd spoken stood out among his equals, not because he was taller or better dressed, but because he had an anxiety about him that he clearly tried to disguise as anger. Red spots colored his cheeks, and he tried to puff out his chest. It'd have worked better if he hadn't shuffled his feet at the same time.

"Your pig?" I asked. "Just the one?"

"Jow?" The affirmative was drawn out, reluctant, as if saying something positive pained him.

"One pig goes missing and you drag thirteen hardworking farmers off their lands to find it?"

The pig farmer nodded once, stubbornly.

One of his fellows took a hesitant step forward. Obviously, this man wasn't one to annoy his mate, but he must have sensed that everything would move faster if he shared some actual information.

"It's the Gov'ner's pride and joy, see," he said. "She shits like a fountain! It tops everything we've seen. Thirty-two liters a day! Bloody heathers must have gone and took her!"

"And they'll pay for it!" the Gov'ner said.

I got the picture. The ground on these isles was sandy, and heather didn't fertilize itself. Without the heather there'd be no fuel, and so, in this particular corner of the world, shit was king. If the heather farmers had absconded with the Gov'ner's pride and joy, it amounted to robbing the royal treasury.

"There's a reward for finding your pride and joy?" I asked.

"I'll torch their fields if you don't find her. How's that for a reward, Neuro Freak?"

I considered the credibility of the threat and found it

much too real. The Gov'ner and the others paid the Clan for pork export permits, smokery permits for bacon, and probably a health tax too, since bacon was bad for the human intestinal tract. They couldn't directly go up against the Clan and its accountants, since attacking an army of bean counters who had arms the size of boars was pure suicide. But surreptitiously burning down the heather that supplied said bean counters with fuel? Now, there was a move that would hit the Clan right in the spreadsheets.

"We'll find your pig," I said. "But leave the heather alone. Leash your dogs, go home. Be happy with the shit you have and leave the future shit to me."

"Jow," the Gov'ner said. It sounded like a no, but the fourteen men moved aside, slowly. They kept their hands in their pockets and threatened no violence, but the message was clear: Out here, we take care of our own. No one would come to my aid if the quad upended on a wrecked road.

AN HOUR BEFORE dusk, we arrived at the home of Ejnar Hansen and his family east of the former town of Vorupør. The farmhouse was half-timbered, country style: tarred wood, chalked walls, shuttered windows, thatched roof. The ruins of another building lay in the northern part of the yard, reduced to a post-impact builders' merchant, and parked beside it was a surprisingly well-maintained Ford Fiesta with a trailer attached. The only new building in sight was the refinery rising over the yard, a twenty-five-meter steel tank spouting pipes, valves, and ladders.

I parked the quad under a stunted fir that had soaked up the perpetual western winds. Every branch reached east as if it were longing for the polluted Swedish forests around the Forsmark nuclear plant or the wintery landscapes of Siberia—anywhere but this windy coast. I knocked on the farmhouse door, and over the brisk wind I heard someone yell, "Enter!" We barely cleared the low, warped doorframe to enter a chilly hallway the size of a closet, packed with clothes and boots. From there we squeezed into a blazing hot kitchen, where a thin, gray-haired woman of about fifty was tending to a stew on a gas stove. Cabbage and carrots, it smelled like, with enough potatoes on the side to feed an army.

"Ejnar!" the woman yelled. "It's Clan folk!"

Three kids came running from the adjoining living room, the smallest gaping at Hjalmar until their mother shooed them away. Then a man I assumed must be Ejnar entered the kitchen. He had graying red hair and freckles enough to make his face look tanned, but the weather didn't account for all his wrinkles. Some of them were for me. The disgusted double take he did was for Hjalmar.

"They're not staying for dinner, Karla." An outright declaration of war in these parts.

I cleared my throat. "The Clan told me your boy has gone missing. Poul, isn't it?"

"Jow?"

"And seeing as you're the owner of the largest fuel production plant north of Haithabu, the accountants wanted to make sure he hasn't been kidnapped. Don't want your production diverted elsewhere." Particularly not to the oil fund managers, who'd taken over Norway.

"Not my refinery," Ejnar grumbled. "It's a co-op with the other farmers. Much good it does us when the accountants want their taxes."

"But your boy *is* missing?" Hjalmar asked.

Ejnar grimaced and glanced at Karla, who stared back at him. It was a look I knew from my investigations in Haithabu, and it meant *get rid of them*.

"We haven't seen Poul these last three days," Ejnar said.

"It's nothing!" Karla said. "He goes off on these trips sometimes. Comes back when he's ready. No reason to involve the Clan."

Ejnar nodded.

"I drove all day to get here, so I'm already involved," I said. "Where does he go on his walks? Who does he hang out with? Any girls he fancies? Any boys?"

"What he does in his free time is none of your business," Ejnar said.

I could press them, tell them the accountants would drop by to inspect the refinery, but I suspected Ejnar wouldn't say a thing. Besides, playing bogeyman for the Neuros wasn't my style.

"Just one last question," I said. "Have you seen a pig around? Apparently, it shits like a fountain, and there's a reward if you bring it back alive."

Karla slammed her ladle against the rim of the stewpot.

"If I see a pig anywhere on my farm, it goes in the pot. Go look somewhere else, Clan Man, and do it now."

Ejnar put his hands in his pockets, and I got the message. No heather farmer would come to my aid out here. Especially if I was helping the pig farmers. Fragile balances indeed.

"Kidnapped?" I asked Hjalmar when we were back in the yard.

"I don't think I've ever seen the mother of a disappeared child look less worried," Hjalmar said. "She was also cooking for at least another grown-up. I noted an empty space for boots by the entrance, and they'd left stains.

Pig manure is my guess. Someone's not home, but they're not exactly missing. I say we wait here until Poul returns."

That halo of words again, telling me how to do my job.

"What do you have in mind?" I asked. "You cover the back while I take the front?"

I couldn't feel it, but I was sure Hjalmar pulled a face.

"We have to figure out what's what or the Neuros won't reunite you with your spleen," I said. "If the boy's not missing, who tipped off the Neuros? And why don't the parents want us digging?"

We crossed the buckled farmyard to the quad. A man was waiting for us, leaning against the eastbound tree in a way that made him hard to spot from the house. Tall and straight-backed, at least compared to the farm and the tree, he still struck me as crooked. Even in the growing twilight, the pupils in his gray eyes were nasty little pinpoints that kept drifting past my shoulder.

"Their boy's gone missing again," he said. "I'm telling you, he's up to no good."

He was wearing work clothes that must have survived the impact in a cozy, dry warehouse. No tool belt, and though his hands were callused, his face didn't have the farmer's leathery quality from working outside in the sun and wind. His wrinkles had come from myopic squinting, much like you'd find on accountants before they evolved into war machines.

"Impressive deduction," I said. "And you are?"

"Villads Svendsen. I manage the refinery for those ingrates." He nodded to the farm, then started walking to a crease in the landscape that would hide us from view. I followed, already annoyed.

"The boy's not missing," I said.

"What the hell? That boy hasn't been to work the last

two weeks. You think you can just show up and tell me what's going on in my own refinery?"

I interrupted further nonsense by invading his personal space and jabbing a finger into his chest. "You're the one who reported this to the Neuros."

The crease of a manager's well-practiced anger formed between his hard eyes. "They tell you that?"

"It's obvious. You pull me out of view because you're afraid to be seen with the Clan Man. You're pissed at the boy and probably his dad too, working as you do for the ingrates. So please, Svendsen, tell me you didn't drag me out to the boondocks because the son of a farmer is playing hooky."

He actually had the guts to stand his ground. Probably he was so used to bossing the refinery workers around that he didn't understand the limits of his own power. "I called the accountants because the boy's been stealing from storage. A fluorescent cell imager, CRISPR packages, microscopes. He even used his da's old trailer to roll off with a small pyrolysis device."

"And how do you know it's him?"

"Stuff's missing, and so is he."

With logic like this I found myself surprised that any fuel was coming out of this refinery at all.

"Svendsen, tell me you didn't report this because you want the Clan to notice you."

"Who doesn't want to work in Haithabu?" He sighed. "Nothing happens out here. Saturday night fun is a drunken dance in wooden clogs while some farmer squeaks out songs from before the impact. It's that or satanic rituals in the bunkers. But that doesn't change the fact that the boy's a thief. So go find him!"

"Where did he take the equipment?" Hjalmar asked.

His voice made Svendsen flinch.

"How the hell would I know? Just be a good freak and catch him, or I'll tell the Clan you wasted their time and money."

"Like you're wasting our air," I said.

"Joke all you want. The Clan's fuel production is in danger, and I'll tell them you did nothing. Let's see where they put your head after that."

"Up your ass, I'm sure." I turned and strode back to the quad under the eastbound tree. Hjalmar's silent laughter made my back wobble, which told me all I needed to know about Svendsen's expression.

Still, I had no doubt he'd report me to the Clan if I didn't follow the Sacred Orders of the Management. He must already have told them of the stolen equipment like an obedient puppet, so anything else he said would have a sheen of credibility. Especially if it gave the NeuroClan an excuse to keep me working for them. For a desperate second, I wondered if maybe I should just elope with Hjalmar and the quad, leave the NeuroClan, and settle down among the farmers. But I'd be an outsider here, a freak, and the Clan knew it. Even here they had their hooks in me.

"Helmet?" Hjalmar asked hopefully when I got back to the quad.

"No," I said. "It's getting dark, and I need you to look around."

"Afraid those Saturday night Satanists will sneak up on you?"

"We're looking for somewhere to stash a small pyrolysis device and a load of lab equipment," I said. "Somewhere with an intact roof but no inhabitants. The sooner you spot it, the sooner you'll be off the quad."

We took off west, into the wind. Just before the sun climbed below the horizon, we scared up a flock of sheep grazing the moor, which got us yelled at by a bony old man who looked closer to ninety than eighty. Apparently, shepherding was what passed for a pension plan out here. I turned on the headlights as we rolled across sandy terrain where heather fought for right of way with lime grass. The air stung my nose with salt and rotting seaweeds, and moments later we reached the wide, sandy beach. Not a building in sight, nor a place to pitch our tent. Finding somewhere out of the wind was about as likely as me clearing my debt with the Neuros.

It was Hjalmar who caught sight of the bunker a few hundred meters inland. The old block of Nazi concrete from WWII had found a resting place behind a small dune, flipped over on its roof. A weak light seeped over a scavenged wooden door set in the inverted frame, and the steady wind was making a nearby windmill spin happily. It had a roof, all right, but perhaps it wasn't entirely uninhabited.

Close up I caught the now familiar odor of pig shit. It mixed with a sharp stench of offal and gall, a smell I associated with dead bodies and abattoirs after a murder investigation in the ruins of Esbjerg a few years back. Before I found the wisdom to point my flashlight toward the ground, I stepped in something brown and spongy, and closer inspection showed it to be blood mixed with sand.

"Sure you want to look inside?" Hjalmar asked. "Shouldn't we—oh, all right, you're going in, watch out for the frame, careful, mind the head!"

Halo of words.

We made it inside without head trauma. The bunker was surprisingly warm and smelled heavily of pig shit.

A greenish light shone from a circular porthole in a tank in the corner, lighting the single room in eerie colors. A trestle table laden with lab stuff rested against the grimy walls, and I recognized a microscope, a refrigerator, and... well, lab stuff.

"What's all this?" I asked Hjalmar.

"Three guys with clubs sneaking up on us. And a fluorescent cell imager."

I swung around, wishing I'd brought the shotgun from the quad. Firing the weapon inside the bunker would have left us deaf, but I'd have liked to have something to point at the three men blocking the doorway. One of them had a thick, nasty-looking club over his shoulder.

They also had the last evening light behind them, so it took me a moment to realize he was holding a ham.

"You wouldn't by any chance be Poul?" I asked.

The intake of breath was a fine answer.

"Any lights in here?" I asked. "Just here to talk." Or so I hoped. Getting mauled with a ham wasn't on my wishlist for the evening.

After a moment's hesitation, Poul closed the door and flipped a switch. In the light of a single bulb, one of the young men turned out to be a young woman, and the other man a brown-haired boy of no more than fifteen. He filled his clothes out, while Poul and the woman were both thin, bordering on starving. They also had wonderful red hair and freckles. Lots of them.

"Your parents didn't say you have a sister," I told Poul. Which was more than a little clever of them. Allow the detective with all the heads to focus on the missing boy, because that was all he knew about. And Svendsen from the refinery wouldn't have figured it out either. If Poul's sister didn't work for him, he wouldn't notice her at all.

Poul didn't lay down his ham, but the woman gave me a tiny nod. "I'm Gunhild."

"Anders," the boy said, shuffling his feet.

I risked another glance around the lab, such as it was. In the light, the tank in the corner looked like something the NeuroClan could have built. How anyone out here in heather country had gotten hold of this kind of technology was beyond me. I figured Svendsen must have been too embarrassed by the theft to report it.

"What are you trying to do here? The tank?"

Poul took a firmer grip on his ham. "He's Clan."

"Not exactly," I said quickly. "More like an indentured worker. I can call the accountants, but it doesn't look like there's a debt to collect. Is there?"

I expected Gunhild to keep her mouth as tightly shut as the rest of the farmers, but I'd hit her angry bone.

"No debts?" she shouted. "No debts! The Clan lent us fifty million FEs for the refinery, and interests have been piling up. They set the fuel quotas too high, and when we fail to meet them, they fine us. Then we borrowed more money to pay the pigsters for more shit to grow more heather, and still, it's not enough. It's never enough, and that needs to change!"

Her words touched something inside me, some vein of unrest that I had buried deep. Hjalmar released a surprised humming that cued me into the thoughts going through his disembodied head.

I also noticed Anders reddening at the mention of 'pigsters'.

"You're from one of the pig farms?" I asked.

He nodded sullenly.

"Stole the Gov'ner's pride and joy, did you?"

"Don't call him the Gov'ner!" The reddening deepened.

"Finn's just a bloated money-grubber taking advantage of everyone here. It's like Gunhild says. We need a change."

"And change comes in the form of..." I backed up to the tank and let Hjalmar look through the window.

"Organs," he said. "Esophagus, stomach. Kidneys and liver over there. Hmmm, that looks like nerve cords, and... yep, the spiral shape suggests they're pig intestines. Rather large if you ask me. I'd say they have the Gov'ner's pride and joy locked up in here, or at least the parts that matter. Unless you count Poul's club."

"Your very own shit factory," I said to Gunhild. "Does it work?"

"Those guts are really something," she said. "And I have the gene sequence to copy them. With more tanks, I can make more fertilizer, it's just a matter of scale."

Anger was receding, pride taking over, and Hjalmar grabbed the chance.

"Must be hard to keep those intestines alive," he said.

"Not if you know what you're doing," she said proudly. "We feed it heather and a little grain. The intestines digest it and supply nutrients for the fluid in the tank, and the organs draw energy directly from the soup."

I thought back to the mush outside the bunker and wondered how they'd put the intestines in the tank. The source of Svendsen's satanic rituals dawned on me. "That pig must have squealed like the devil himself when you harvested its organs."

They all had the good grace to look embarrassed, especially Anders.

"Hjalmar, does all this work out to a profit?"

"Isn't this a perpetuum mobile?" he asked. "You feed heather into the intestines, it excretes fertilizer, and you use it to grow more heather. There's bound to be a loss in the system. Seems easier to just buy the shit from the pig farmers."

Gunhild ground her teeth, hard enough for the sound to echo in the chamber. "Bollocks to a loss-free system. We just have to be more efficient than the pigsters. They feed their fattening pigs until they weigh a hundred kilograms or more, and a sow weighs nearly three hundred. All we need are the organs, so our metabolic rate is much lower. The pigsters produce grain anyway, so if they'll sell us some, we can produce fertilizer at an incredible rate."

She sounded like a CEO of some old-school corporation. My sympathy for her project was waning fast when Poul took half a step forward, timidly clutching his ham. "We'll finally have enough to eat," he said. "Please. Food is all we ask."

"And you?" Hjalmar asked the pigster boy. "You know the Clan gene-modified your pigs to produce fertilizer. When shit is no longer king, your people will be left with a stinking heap of nothing."

Anders looked at Gunhild as if she was a beacon of righteousness, his face a canvas of resolve and youthful infatuation. "The Clan is ripping us off too," he said. "Finn's just too thick to realize it, but we can do better, producing meat and wheat."

I began to understand why the Clan had seen an urgent need to send an investigator and a biologist to heather country. If Gunhild's plan worked, the pigsters would have to produce fewer pigs or they'd drown in shit. That'd mean fewer bacon taxes for the Clan, plus they'd lose their fertilizer transaction fees. And if Svendsen was right, Gunhild still had a pyrolysis device stashed away somewhere. No doubt she was already experimenting with more efficient ways of fuel-making, and she wouldn't be selling to the accountants. The NeuroClan would want this lab crushed to a fine powder.

"Right," I said. "I have to return the Gov… Finn's pride and joy or he'll burn down your crops. I'll let them know it was an accident, Poul."

It took Poul a while to figure it out. Then it hit him, and, looking at his feet with the regret of the hungry, he handed over the ham.

I WALKED BACK to the quad, ham over my left shoulder, the wind in Hjalmar's eyes.

"What are we going to tell the Neuros?" he asked.

I wondered about that myself. We owed no loyalty to a bunch of farmers. If I traded them in, the Clan would gladly pay Hjalmar and me for upholding the status quo. Maybe Hjalmar could shave off a chunk of his debts. Maybe I'd finally hit zero.

It was just that Gunhild would end up on a spine as a genetic adviser to some unskilled laborer with bad farts who slept on his back, and all for the crime of upsetting a system that squeezed everyone dry. Including me and Hjalmar. I was willing to bet the accountants were cooking up a tax on double brainwave functions to keep me under their thumb.

Maybe I should take the quad, drive north, find a boat to Norway. They said the oil fund managers let people keep their bodies and work off their debts in the salmon industry. But there was another option. Give Gunhild a head start. She probably wouldn't get away with her fertilizer scheme in the long run, but she'd send a waterfall of red numbers through the Clan books first.

Maybe that would be enough for someone to escape their NeuroClan shackles.

"Think you can go a little longer without your spleen?" I asked.

"You want change?" Hjalmar was quiet for a minute. "Why don't we tell them the truth?"

I felt a tingle of panic run down my spine. If Hjalmar told the Clan I'd betrayed them, they'd swap our heads. "And what truth is that?"

"Svendsen was bored out here," he said. "Wanted enough Fuel Equivalents to go to Haithabu and live with the high rollers. He thought, 'Hey, I'm sitting on a warehouse full of refinery equipment. Easy money, just don't fence it to Clan people.' And when one of the local boys figured it out? Svendsen blamed the kid for stealing and squealed to the Clan to keep himself above suspicion."

Halo of words. But I was glad he was around to do the thinking.

"Too bad for him the Clan sent their two finest detectives to investigate," I said.

I mounted the quad, off to Haithabu with a detour to drop off a ham and prevent a brushfire. But before I gunned the engine, I made sure Hjalmar wore his helmet.

THE TRAVELLER GIRL

Lene Kaaberbøl

SHE WAS SITTING in the cherry tree, munching fruit. Her trousers were stumpy, stopping at mid-calf, revealing a pair of rather dirty legs dangling at eye level. They were what had first caught his eye.

"That's our tree!" he shouted, filled with umbrage.

"Oh, really?" she said and spat a cherry pit out right in front of the hooves of Jovin's horse. She was a Traveller girl. That much was obvious beyond any doubt. Those bare feet alone... and the trousers, which no proper Kerner girl would have dared to wear. And the hair. Never had Jovin seen that much hair on any girl. There was no bonnet, no prim braiding, just a cloud of chestnut curls, and nothing, absolutely nothing, had been done to tame the wildness. He could not help but stare.

Strangest of all, though, was the fact that she did not seem to be ashamed. Not of eating other people's cherries, though that was quite bad enough. Nor of being who she was.

"Scram," he said in his toughest voice. "Bugger off. Or you'll get a good hiding." Because that is what his father would have said.

"Oh? From whom?" She did not look particularly worried.

"From me." He straightened, trying to look authoritative. Powerful.

"I see…" The glitter he caught in her grey eyes did not look like fear. More like mirth…

"But to do that you'll have to catch me first!"

She put two fingers into her mouth and sounded an ear-splitting whistle. And from out the depths of the orchard trotted a delicate grey mare, completely devoid of saddle or bridle, or any other visible means of control.

Jovin had heard of the Travellers and their horses. His hand shot out to seize her ankle, but she was too quick for him. With an animal-like litheness, she grasped a cherry branch, swung through the air, and came to a gentle halt seated on the back of the mare.

"Well," she said with a teasing smile, "You were saying—something about a good hiding?" And she and the mare streaked across the ridge, gone in the blink of an eye, and all he caught was the sound of her laughter.

Cursed Traveller scum. Defeat burned and prickled and turned his temper nasty, all the rest of the way to Hansalin. Normally he liked to come here, checking out all the stuff he would own one day. Here was the spot where he would build an extra barn for horses, and here the ground where he would have a quince folly planted, and over there he wanted a tea pavilion so that he could recline, a glass of iced tea in his hand, and gaze across the trout ponds. Next year, when he turned fifteen. Next year, when he and Siri were married.

Of course, he would have to listen to her father for advice in the beginning, at least a little bit. Ebert had after all been running Hansalin for almost an age. But two years ago, Siri's mother passed away, Saint Marten guard her soul, and Siri inherited all of Hansalin. So once Jovin was her Chosen Friend and Protector, he would be the lord of Hansalin. You could see it already in the way he was greeted by the staff, with honour and respect, far beyond what he had been used to in his earlier life.

"Happy Marten's Day," called Ebert from the porch in front of the big house. "So, you've come to look in on Siri?"

"Good Marten's," Jovin returned his greeting. "Yes please, if I may. My mother made cranberry wine yesterday, and she thought Siri might like a bottle." Siri had been ill recently, the way she often was, even in the midst of summer.

"You go on in," said Ebert. "She is in the conservatory, I think." He reached out a wide fist to grab Claro's reins, even as he waved an imperious come-hither at two grooms exiting the ochre-washed stables. "All well at your place?"

"Thank you, yes. And at Hansalin?"

"As well as can be, thank you very much."

An uncomfortable silence arose. Jovin had never known how to converse with Siri's father once the obvious pleasantries had been exhausted. Ebert was a large man, with a full-fleshed face that reminded Jovin of the kind of wide-jawed dog that was usually a good bet at the dogfights in town. The kind that bit down and held on, though all hell broke loose.

"Coming over, I met a Traveller girl at the cherry orchard," Jovin commented, just for something to say.

Ebert's wide jaws jerked. "Travellers?" he said. "Again? I thought we had dealt with them for good, the last time they were here."

"It might not be the same ones."

"It's all the same to me. Thieves and beggars, the lot of them. But we'll see them on their way." He measured Jovin with a cool gaze. "Listen, boy, once you've looked in on Siri, you and I can go find them and tell them what for."

Jovin nodded. "As soon as I've seen Siri."

THE CONSERVATORY WAS so full of green plants that it was like sitting in a forest. Siri minded them herself, he knew, nursing them like they were children.

"My mother made cranberry wine," he said, presenting the small bottle to her.

"Thank you," she said, inclining her head slightly. Her white Marten's Day dress was newly ironed and spotless. She wore the blue bonnet with it, and a shawl to match. The fringes hung perfectly straight and barely swayed as she set the bottle down on the table between them. Siri always moved with such care, as if she was afraid of knocking things over.

He suddenly thought of the Traveller girl. The gleam in her eyes, that shameless direct gaze of hers. Siri hardly ever looked at him. Mostly at the tea cups, her embroidery, or her beloved potted plants.

"Siri?"

"Yes?"

Still, she did not look at him. Through the open door, he could hear the clicking of Aunt Mari's knitting needles—she was nearly always the chaperone when he visited. It rarely bothered him, but today there was something intensely irritating about the gentle racket. Knit, knit, purl, purl, like a nail against a blackboard.

"Siri, why do you never look at me?"

He got the briefest glimpse of her wide, startled blue eyes, then she ducked her head again. "I... do sometimes, I suppose," she said.

"Don't you like me?" Why did he ask her that? He was her Chosen One, they were getting married. Of course she liked him. Or... or did she?

"Yes." A barely audible whisper of affirmation.

"Right. Well, then look at me, please!" He'd said that much too loudly. The sound of clicking needles stopped abruptly in the room next door.

Siri slowly raised her head. The slight glimpse he got of her fair hair was combed back rigidly, so tightly that it might have been painted on. Under her pale skin, the veins at her temple were visible as a bluish tint. "Why should I?" she asked. "Isn't it enough that you can see me? Is that not why you are here? To 'look in on Siri'?"

This was not at all like his usual visits. Normally, they just sat, drinking tea, while he asked her about Hansalin and her family, and she enquired about Caerlin and his family, after which he just left. Now he felt horribly uncomfortable about breaking the usual rules.

Because she sounded strangely un-Siri-like. Almost angry. But what could she have to be angry about?

"Are you mad at me?" he asked.

"No."

"What is it, then? What's wrong?"

"Nothing. Who said anything was wrong? You were the one who asked me to look at you."

And so he had.

They sat in silence for a while. There were a lot of things he wanted to know: what she thought of him, how she felt about the getting married thing, why she had sounded so angry a minute ago. Was she looking forward to the wedding? Or was she nervous? Possibly even scared? There were questions enough he might have asked. But getting started was not easy.

"Do you want a cup of tea?" Siri finally asked.

"Yes please," he murmured, relieved to be back on familiar Marten Day visit ground. And yet... he should have asked. He wanted so badly to know... But Siri just sat there with her head bent impenetrably and answered his polite enquiries about Hansalin without looking at him at all.

"THERE THEY ARE," said Ebert, pointing left, toward a cluster of red and yellow wagons parked in the shadow of the tall poplars.

Jovin had seen Travellers' wagons before. Sometimes they appeared at the town market, and though it was well known that you had to get up early to get the good end of a Traveller bargain, there were still many who wanted to trade with them. They usually had wares unlike any that were normally for sale here—spices from faraway lands, wools and cloth in alien colours, copperware and coloured glass gleaming and sparkling like jewels in the sun. The market in the square for a single day was one thing; but settling down on good Kerner soil with every appearance of wanting to stay for a good while—that was something else.

"Blasted scum," cursed Ebert between his teeth. "Do

they think I've left the good clover grass to grow, just so that their damn Traveller hacks can feast on it?"

Hack was not a word Jovin would have used about many of the horses grazing along Shady Creek. Shiny hides, proud necks, and legs fine and strong like Damascene steel. But apart from the horses, there was no sign of life in the camp.

"I don't think there's anyone home," said Jovin.

"Rubbish," snorted Ebert. "Their horses are here. That means that the Travellers are close by." He rode his own big, heavy gelding in between the wagons before coming to a halt.

"I know you are here," he shouted. No one replied.

"Check in the wagons," Ebert commanded.

Why don't you check? Jovin thought. But he kept the thought to himself. Right now Ebert absolutely looked like a dog that would bite down and hold on. He quelled a ridiculous urge to knock politely. After all, it was just a Traveller's cart, not a proper house. Still, it felt odd to just jerk open the door and enter with no warning.

He had expected the place to be... well, a bit threadbare and dirty. After all, that was the word most Kerners used repeatedly about the Travellers: dirty scoundrels. But the interior of the wagon was almost embarrassingly clean. Clean and tidy and deserted.

"There's no one here," he said to Ebert, jumping down off the stepping board.

"Look in the other wagons too."

But all the wagons had been abandoned.

"They're hiding," Ebert snarled in annoyance. "But I know how to smoke this fox out of its den. Catch one of the horses. You're said to be good at that kind of thing, I hear."

Jovin straightened a bit—he was good with horses, so everyone said.

"Take one of the ones in foal," Ebert demanded.

A lot of the mares had big heavy bellies and were obviously going to drop their foals quite soon. One of these, a fine tall-legged grey, trustingly let him approach.

"Good horsey, fine horsey..." Jovin muttered and settled a rope noose around the slender neck. "Come on then." The mare followed him willingly and trustingly.

"Well done, lad," said Ebert. "Now we go home."

"With the mare?" asked Jovin doubtfully. This was... if it hadn't been a Traveller horse, it would have been theft.

"With the mare. Call it a grazing fee."

Quite a fee, thought Jovin, but swung into his saddle regardless, following Ebert with the mare in tow. They had barely cleared the poplars when a man suddenly appeared on the path in front of them, out of nowhere, it seemed. As if he had grown from the ground.

"That is not your horse," the stranger said in a quiet tone.

"So? This is not your land."

"We're only staying a few weeks," said the man. He was tall and dark-skinned, Jovin noticed, though not as wide across the shoulders as Ebert.

"You're not staying at all," countered Ebert, tensing his dog jaws. "If you are still here by sunup tomorrow, you'll regret it bitterly."

"We only wish peace," said the Traveller quite calmly, considering Ebert's fierceness.

"We will pay you well for the grazing. But it's important to us to stay here until the foals are dropped."

"Not on my land!"

"The Earth belongs to all of us. No one can own it."

Ebert's wide fist shot out and grasped the man's shirt.

"Listen to me, Traveller scum. This land is Hansalin. The dirt you stand on is Hansalin. The air you breathe is Hansalin. Don't try to tell me different, you sorry bastard."

The stranger made a swift move of one shoulder, and suddenly all that was left in Ebert's grasp was his shirt. The Traveller stood several paces away.

"We do not want a fight. How does it hurt you if we stay by Shady Creek for a couple of weeks? Let the mare go. If you are so keen to get your hands on one of our horses, we'll let you have a colt in payment for the grass our herd eats... and the air we breathe meanwhile."

Ebert threw the shirt on the ground with fury.

"Get lost," he snarled. "Sunrise at the latest. Or I'll teach you a lesson about mine and yours that you'll never forget!"

He kicked the gelding forward, making it leap towards the stranger. Or towards the spot where he had been standing because he was no longer there, gone as suddenly as he had appeared. Jovin hesitated.

"What are you waiting for, boy?" shouted Ebert.

"The mare... what about the mare?"

"A suitable fee, I told you. Get a move on!"

At that moment, there was a low whistle somewhere in the bushes. And in that second, the biddable mare stopped being biddable. She froze in place as if turned to stone.

Jovin hauled on the rope. "Come on!" he hissed, "You stupid beast!" But the mare did not move, and all at once, Claro sprang forwards. Jovin held on to the mare's tether a moment too long and simply hung in the air as Claro continued down the path.

"Huffff!" The air escaped from his lungs as he landed on his back in the grass, seeing sun, moon, and stars.

Crunch. A hoof. A horse's leg. Ebert's shadow fell across his face.

"Damn insolent scum," he said. "But they'll get theirs. Get up, boy."

Jovin couldn't. He couldn't even breathe.

"I haven't got the time for this," said Ebert, furious with the Traveller, but also visibly irritated with Jovin. "I've got a lot of men to gather. You find your own way home, boy."

Jovin flapped a limp hand. Ride on, it meant. But he did not think that Ebert would really do that—just ride away and leave him. Bad enough to be left behind like garbage from a picnic. But what stung more was Ebert's parting shot:

"They told me that you could ride, at least."

SLOWLY, JOVIN SAT up and examined his somewhat tender ankle. *They told me that you could ride, at least.* For a moment, he merely sat there, hating Ebert with an intensity so great that it actually surprised him. Claro, of course, was long gone, and it was a very long way home.

Much too long. He let himself slump back in the grass, staring angrily up at the blue summer sky.

"Are you dead?"

The question was hers. The Traveller girl.

At that moment, he almost wished he was. Dead, that was. She had seen everything.

Seen him fall off the horse like a big baby.

"No," he admitted, sitting up again. "Not quite."

"Your horse ran off," she said.

"I know." Behind her stood the delicate grey mare she

had been riding that morning, still completely free of saddle or bridle, and still showing no signs of wanting to run anywhere.

He watched her for a moment or two. Her cheeks were speckled with sun freckles, and her shoulders were wide, almost like a boy's. How was it that he always ended up like this, looking up at her from below?

"You had better get going," he warned her, almost against his will. "Ebert has gone to gather men. If they find you, it will be no garden party."

Her eyes flashed.

"What is it with you people?" she said furiously. "How is it that you always come running with threats and clubs against ordinary decent peace-loving folk?"

He looked at her in confusion.

"We don't," he said, outraged at her suggestion. And then he suddenly realised that this was what it must look like from a Traveller viewpoint. He was just not used to thinking of Travellers as 'ordinary decent peace-loving folk'.

"At least, we don't usually do such things," he finished rather defensively.

"Only when it's us?" she said, "Is that what you mean?"

He made no answer because that was more or less exactly what he had meant. She spun on her heel and started back toward the wagons with the mare trudging behind her like a darn dog on a leash.

"Wait," he called, but she showed no sign of stopping. He had to get to his feet and hobble after her at the best pace his injured ankle would allow.

"You have to understand that you can't just show up and eat other people's grass. I mean, let your horses eat other people's grass."

She finally came to a halt. Turned slowly and deliberately, sizing him up with cool grey eyes that were entirely serious for once.

"Wayfarers have come here for centuries," she said. "Before, no one tried to stop us. We were even welcomed once upon a time. Until one day, when there were suddenly fences and 'no trespassing' and men with clubs claiming they owned the land. As if anyone could. As if anyone could own all this." She gestured towards Shadow Creek, the poplars, the sky—the whole place.

"This is Hansalin land," he said. His land, inside a year or so. Or at least, his responsibility, once he was Siri's Chosen Friend and Protector.

"And then to hell with everyone else?" she said. "Never mind what dreams they may have, and what they want to do."

"What do you mean?"

"Nothing," she replied. "It no longer matters."

"No, tell me—what did you mean?"

She hesitated. Then she looked straight into his eyes.

"There's something here," she said. "In the ground. Or in the water, we don't know. A special power. Horses born here are special. Stronger than others. Faster. Sturdier."

"And that is why you wanted to stay while the mares dropped their foals."

She nodded. "That's why. My father knew it was dangerous. But he was hoping... hoping we could somehow buy the right to stay a while."

"Was that your father we spoke to earlier?"

"Yes."

"So what will you do now?"

"I don't know." She looked down. "Last year... it was bad. My father's brother still can't walk without a limp.

But three foals were born. Three perfect foals... and my father has a dream, you see. A dream of breeding the perfect horse."

"Perhaps I can talk to Ebert," Jovin suggested, wishing he and Siri were already married so he wouldn't have to ask permission from anyone. So he could just say how things would be and who could stay on his land. "Or... if you could perhaps just wait a year..."

"What good would that do?" she asked. "It has just gone from bad to worse, year after year. Why would it suddenly be better next year?"

He did not answer that. He could not bring himself to talk to her of Siri.

"What's your name?" he asked instead.

"Zara. What's yours?"

"Jovin." He extended his hand. After a brief moment, she took it, and they shook. Her palm was warm and tanned and a bit greasy with grass sap and dust. He couldn't help but compare it to Siri's cold, slender fingers. Siri. Zara. Two names that were so alike, and two girls that bore no resemblance.

"Zara, let me try. Ebert appreciates fine horseflesh. Perhaps a deal is still possible." Once Ebert's temper had cooled a couple of degrees, anyway.

"Would you really?" she said. "Would you really do that for us?"

"If I can."

Her face lit up like a bonfire so that all the sun freckles danced for joy.

"Then mother was right after all."

"About what?"

"About there being some good in everyone. Even in Kerner folk."

It was a weird sort of compliment, but he still appreciated it.

"I have to hurry," he said. "I want to get a hold of him before he has gathered too many men." The bigger the group, the harder it would be to get Ebert to back down. The greater his loss of face, he would reckon. Jovin raised his arm in an awkward farewell wave and began to limp down the path towards Hansalin.

It wasn't long before he heard hooves behind him. Zara and the grey mare. "Do you want a lift?" she said. "It looks a bit like slow progress, that."

IT WAS PROBABLY about half an hour. But later, he often dreamt his way back to it, to sitting on the warm back of the mare with his arms around Zara's firm waist, having his cheek tickled by her chestnut curls every time the wind swept them back in his face. Even when she teased him about his lack of bareback experience, it was nice. Irritating, but nice. It would be a long time before he felt that good about anything again.

THE BLOW HIT his jaw and sent him reeling back against the table with enough force that the table turned over.

"You shameless bastard. Is that how you plan on being my daughter's Friend and Protector? Traipsing about with Traveller scum? Wrecking Siri's land because some whore has turned your head? Over my dead body. I tell you; this won't be!"

Jovin's head was ringing, and he could barely see.

But Ebert was in no way done with him. "If the contract had not been signed... if everyone didn't already know that you were her Chosen... you'd be out on your arse in a minute, do you hear? But I have my daughter's honour to think of. Siri's honour, and that of Hansalin. And you will not spit on that, you hear me? You stay here, boy, until we have broken so many heads and backs that this Traveller pack will think twice about returning. And if you ever as much as look at another girl again, so help me God, I will kill you. I mean that. Look at me—do you believe I mean that?" Ebert hauled him up by his shirtfront and kept him upright despite his unsteady legs. Jovin stared into Ebert's face with eyes that wouldn't quite focus. Yes, he believed it. Ebert was capable of killing. And he would do it if Siri and Hansalin were threatened.

"Do you believe me?" hissed Siri's father.

"Yes," muttered Jovin indistinctly.

Ebert let go of him, and he collapsed on all fours onto the tiled floor of the front hallway. "Pathetic. A Traveller girl. How pathetic." And then he left.

A mixture of blood and saliva was seeping from the corner of Jovin's mouth. He could do nothing to stop it. If he took a hand off the hallway floor, he would topple completely. Strange. This morning he had been standing on this same floor thinking he would be lord of Hansalin soon. Even a couple of minutes ago, he had genuinely believed that Ebert might listen to him and change his mind about the Travellers. But someone had seen him sitting behind Zara on the mare. And someone had gone running to Ebert with the tale.

"Jovin? Did he hit you?"

Siri.

Cautiously, he raised his head—cautiously, so it wouldn't fall off. It felt only scantily attached to his neck. She was still wearing her white Marten's Day dress from this morning. It made her look vaguely ghostlike.

"Is he gone?" asked Jovin. "Did he ride off?"

Siri nodded.

"You're bleeding," she said.

"Yes."

"Why did he hit you?"

"Siri... I have to borrow a horse."

Because Ebert's riding off could only mean one thing. He would not wait for first light. Zara and her family were in danger, right now.

"You can't ride. You can't even stand." Her comment was dry as bone, completely without feeling, without pity. "Why did he hit you?"

Jovin did not answer. He braced his hands against the overturned table and made it to his feet. He had to lean against the wall, but at least he was standing.

"Was it about the Travellers?" she asked.

"Yes." He did not want to tell her about Zara. But no doubt someone else would.

Gossip was probably already rife. "Sorry, Siri. I haven't done anything wrong. But I may have done something stupid..."

Now it was her turn to be silent. She just looked at him, her face almost as pale as her dress.

"Siri, please. Won't you lend me a horse?"

She gave him the longest direct gaze she had ever given him. And he had no idea what she was thinking.

"No," she said, and disappeared into the conservatory to be with her plants.

* * *

HE TRIED TO get the grooms to saddle him a horse, but Ebert had obviously given his orders and the grooms had no doubts about whom to fear most. In the end, there was nothing for it but to start walking, buzzing head and painful ankle, as fast as he was able.

It wasn't fast enough. Darkness had fallen before he got there, and even behind the poplars, the flames were visible at quite a distance.

"Oh no," he whispered and stopped in his tracks. The wagons. Ebert and his men had set fire to the wagons... Zara's home. Everything she and her family owned. And perhaps also... An icy fear struck him, and he tilted forwards at a limping run. Frightened horses were galloping back and forth. Men, women and children had formed a bucket line from Shady Creek and were trying to put out the blaze in the one wagon out of seven that might still be saved.

"Zara!" he shouted. "Zara, where are you?"

Nobody paid him any heed. Not even Zara. But there she was, unharmed, reaching up filled buckets from the river. She had a sooty streak across one cheek, and her lip was split and swollen as if she had been punched in the face. She sent him a furious glance before resuming her work.

He did not know what to say to her. 'Sorry' seemed tame and wildly insufficient. 'I tried' was not much better.

"I am so sorry," he finally said.

"Oh really? So am I," she said furiously, slinging the full bucket to the next person with far too much force, causing a squelch. But she could not quite keep up the tough front. Traces of tears were visible on her sooty cheeks.

"I did try," he offered inadequately, despite his earlier forebodings. "He... he just would not listen."

"I see."

"Zara..."

"You had better leave now," she told him. "Go home to your Kerner girl."

"Have they... did they say..."

"Oh yes. Along with all the little details about what they would do to me if I ever touch you with my dirty little Traveller hands again. I got told, all right."

Was that what had happened to her lip?

"Next year..." he began.

But Zara cut him short.

"There won't be a next year," she said forcefully. "This is it. We're not coming back here. Ever."

"But what about... what about the horses and Shady Creek and the foals born here..."

She gave herself a minute break to wipe the sweat away so it wouldn't get in her eyes. "Sometimes you just have to face up to the fact that not every dream can come true," she said. "Go now, Jovin. Before somebody sees you."

'Somebody' clearly wasn't the Travellers, who would have had to close their eyes to avoid seeing him. But Ebert could have placed a man or two in the twilight to spy on him. And Jovin had no wish to cause further hurt to Zara. He left.

IN THE MORNING, the Travellers were gone. Jovin stood looking at the trampled clover field and the six burnt-out wagon hulks. Sometimes you just have to face up to the fact that not every dream can come true.

And he was lucky. He had so much. Siri was a sweet girl. Pretty. Proper. Nice and clean. A bit on the quiet side, perhaps, but that wasn't all bad. Girls weren't meant to be crude and outspoken and strong and stubborn and have wild curly hair which stuck out every which way and bare legs one could not help looking at. Oh, he was fortunate. It would have been completely crazy for him to give up all of that.

IT WAS THREE whole weeks before he ran away.

THE FAROE ISLANDS

THE ABYSS

Rakel Helmsdal

Translated by Marita Thomsen

I AM HANGING from the lowest bar, as I have been for a while now. Knowing there is nothing to see I still stare into the fog.

Cannot recall any beginning, but think I started somewhere in the middle, if there is any such thing as a middle on endless bars. The first years, after it became clear to me that squeezing through them was impossible, I scaled the bars. Thinking that they had to end sometime, and when I reached the edge, I could just climb over and head down the other side, because then I would get down to real life. Exactly how I got to thinking that where I am isn't real life, I don't know. I don't remember ever experiencing anything else.

As I said, I can't recall a beginning, but I do remember how I for years, while I was still just clinging on with my hands and feet daring neither to go up nor down, tried to push through the bars and out the other side, because somehow I knew that I was on the wrong side. But the bars are so close-set that it is impossible to slip through, so I tried bending them, forcing them to open wider. To no avail, it is patently hopeless to shift these thin iron rods even the slightest inch, it was a long while before I finally surrendered and decided to brave the ascent up the bars, up into the fog and the uncertainty.

Initially, it was hard to direct my hands and feet to climb, not just cling onto the bars, but little by little I picked up the pace, and my hands and feet became like eagle claws.

But no edge ever emerged, the haze veiled nothing but never-ending metal ribs.

Despair finally forced me to give up and turn back down. As time went by and I climbed, and climbed and climbed downwards in the mist, a thought began to form, the notion that perhaps there would be something below, once I eventually reached the bottom.

On my long descent, I also started thinking that maybe I wasn't the only one heading either up or down the bars, because one time I thought I, out of the corner of my eye to one side where the fog conceals the bars, saw a black shape clambering down at great speed, like me.

And I *did* get to the bottom, if you can call the end of the bars that. They are set in an infinite wall that vanishes into the blur below me. And so here I am, suspended from the last iron bar where the wall begins. Of course, I have already tried, for an age, to move sideways both this way and that, but have come to realise that it is as hopeless and endless as climbing up.

So this is my situation: here I hang at the end of some thin iron rods at the top of a towering ancient stonewall. Up and to both sides the bars reach into infinity, and below me, there is likely a bottomless abyss. But I cannot see any of this, everything is concealed in the fog. Perhaps

I am surrounded by others, who like me are scrambling up, down, back or forth, or just sag immobile in despair; but this can neither comfort nor frighten me, as I will never get to meet them anyway.

Knowing that climbing is futile all that is left is the *abyss*, and over the years it has become clear to me that there is where the solution lies. The solution to why I am hanging here, what life really is, whether there was anything before the bars, or anything after. Yet it takes unfathomable courage to let go of the bars, and let go I must, because it is not possible to climb down the wall, even if there were cracks for my hands and feet to slot into—they are now so curled up that they would find no purchase, all they can do is hook the bars.

Relinquishing the bars means knowing nothing, having nothing—as long as I keep holding on, I still have the bars and the knowledge that they are infinite. The abyss I know nothing about, I don't even know yet if it *is* an abyss. What will happen when I loosen my grip and let myself fall into the haze, I have no way of imagining. But have I anything to lose? Do the bars mean anything to me except security, *are* they security?

But if I let go, then what happens? Will I fall for time untold, or will it merely be a short drop to shatter against cliffs that so many have met before me?

Without hurry I unhook my feet, only my hands are holding on to the last bar, the rest of my body dangles against the wall, which is cold and damp... I am scared to let go now; my courage is spent... going back up... But I can't, don't have the strength in my arms to pull myself up again, and my hands are growing tired... I can't hold on anymore... I lose my grip... *fall*...

Fall and fall in the fog and everything is just grey and

grey. Nearly lose my breath and consciousness from the speed and terror of the abyss suddenly ending, and me splintering against the razor crags, bodies and bones of others, who also let go.

But as the fall continues terror begins to dissipate, and I gradually come to like falling, just falling, and as fear lifts the fog thins and it is as if I catch glimpses. At first only of shadows in the distance, but little by little those shadows take shape and become buildings and landscapes. It seems like I am falling in a huge, infinitely deep well, and the sides of the well appear as towns, countries and oceans. Mountains and spires stretch towards me, some so close that I can almost grasp them. In freefall I wonder why I know what these are. My recall only stretches to knowing that I have seen such things before. And as memory slowly returns, so do colours and sound.

I float down into memories and shapes, a rainbow swaddles me as strange harmonies float around me, and I wonder why I didn't let go of the bars sooner.

Suddenly a giant eyeball is staring at me. I fall in musical waves towards it, and in passing, I see a human inside. Naked, like me, this person stands with splayed arms and legs reaching for the sides of this immense glass orb, as it turns and turns around itself.

After tumbling past that glare, I notice other eyes staring at me from the well below, and as I approach the next one, I know that the human I saw in the first orb was a person I used to know.

In the next orb there is also a person, someone I have seen and known, and in the third and fourth and... there is my mother... my sister... father... brother... and there is my best friend.

They all look at me with mournful accusing eyes. Fear courses through my veins like a poison, and the colours congeal and the harmonies dissolve.

I fall and I watch these morose reproachful eyes. Inside me, grief unfurls into a big black nothingness.

… No! … there are the eyes, the eyes that I loved, and they hold me in a gaze filled with such sadness that everything inside me recoils and tears well up in mine.

My vision is blurred, but I see full well, as I fall deeper still, that only one solitary eye glares at me now. The dread is suffocating. I drop nearer and the orb appears empty… until I see that it isn't … NO!

Screaming, unhearing, unseeing I tumble into terror. Searing pain is all there is. A tornado of a thousand glass shards tearing through me.

And screaming I hit the bottom. Silent now I take in the emptiness and the stillness.

A long time I lie there. Lie on stony ground surrounded by *nothing*! No nature, wind or weather, no room, no sound, no colour.

I try standing up, but my wizened feet are no use for walking. I am forced to crawl on hands and knees.

Creep across sharp bedrock, wounding my knees and hands. *Nothing* covers me. Then suddenly in the emptiness a looming white door appears. It is just *there*, no connection to any walls or ceiling, and when I approach it, I realise that there is nothing behind it either. The door is ajar and I push it open with my shoulder, it is heavy and cold. I scuttle inside and find myself in a vast hall.

This hall is full of colossal hazy people looming statue-still. Breath trails from their mouths like white mist. Each is holding something: a sword, a little red bird, a severed head with burst eyes, a yellow blossom, a spade, a bowl of poison, a ripe ear of corn... They tower, mighty and stern, and watch me crawl on bloodied knees through the hall towards *Justice*, who presides with her scales on the throne deep in the hall.

And I rise on my twisted feet to ask *why*... but I have forgotten my voice.

ICELAND

THE DREAMGIVER

Johann Thorsson

SOMETIMES, IN THE daylight, I'll find the carcasses of small animals in the brook that runs behind our house. Squirrels and birds, their bodies twisted and bent as if they died in great pain. Always downstream from the house.

IN THE MIDDLE of the dark night I am woken, like so many nights before, by the sounds of our son screaming in his sleep. He's sweating and shaking and his eyes are clenched shut. I try to console him, wake him up but he just turns to his side, arches his back and cries out. He doesn't wake up, never wakes up when I try, just keeps dreaming his terrible dreams through the night. He spends the nights in our bed now, it's just easier for everyone. Our boy can count to ten and pee on his own but he has to sleep in our bed. If he slept by himself, we might miss something. It's been like this for three months now.

The boy eventually settles down and falls back asleep. I get up and sit on the edge of the bed. Yawn and stand up. I stagger sleep-drunk to the bedroom door. The air is thick, full of the breath of three sleeping humans in the late-summer heat. A dreamcatcher hangs by the bedroom door, sagging on a nail. It has a bloated look like it's a balloon and not a twist of strings and feathers.

"Full already?" Greta asks. She is sitting, propped up on one hand with the other feeling the boy's forehead. Stroking fingers through his hair.

"It gets full sooner and sooner, doesn't it?" I reply. "I'll empty it."

I take it down and walk outside. Our house is the only one around, a speck in the countryside, though in the morning, cocks crowing remind me that others live nearby.

There is a small incline in the yard behind our house that leads to a stream. It is here I take the dreamcatcher every night. An almost-full moon lights up the stream, little fingers of gray light reaching down through the trees and touching the water, never reaching the bottom. I walk down, legs still stiff and full of sleep.

At the stream I bend down and shake the dreamcatcher over the water, emptying the subconscious darkness caught in the web. The freed nightmares mix with the water, flowing silently away in the deep dark of the night. I stand up and stretch; for a moment I look at the stars. These are my private moments.

Sometimes, in the daylight, I'll find the carcasses of small animals downstream. Bodies twisted and bent as if they died in great pain. I try not to make the connection.

I go inside, re-hang the dreamcatcher and try to go back to sleep. It hangs looser on the nail now. Light and springy.

* * *

BEFORE THE DREAMCATCHER, the boy would wake up screaming in the night and his nose would bleed. My wife would be raw in the morning, short-tempered during the day and dead-tired in the evening. For some reason, I love my wife more when she is mad at me. Even after she came back, without any shame or remorse on her face or in her heart, I loved her.

We got the dreamcatcher from a store in town that we never found again. That night was the first in a long time that our son slept through. Uninterrupted sleep, free of dark dreams. The dreamcatcher was heavy in the morning, the string holding it up taut on the nail. It was certainly heavier than when I had put it up. It had a sheen to it, almost oily, and smelled faintly of rotting leaves. The nightmares returned and then one night, drunk and inspired, I made a symbolic gesture of emptying the dreamcatcher, calling it useless. But something made me re-hang it and he slept well that night. I then made a habit of emptying it, superstition replacing sense.

ONE NIGHT, AS I bend over the stream in the dark to shake the heavy nightmares out of the dreamcatcher, I am startled by a figure standing on the other side, staring at me. It is tall, hairless and pale, with large eyes that are all black pupils. Its mouth hangs open and the head is slightly tilted. Skin made of glistening white leather. It exhales in a rasp and it speaks as it draws its breath back in.

"You throw my dreams away?"

I am unable to speak. My heart grabs hold of my lungs

and the hairs on my arms stand up as if to escape. The creature looks up at me and then turns its gaze to the dreamcatcher. It exhales and then speaks again as it draws in air. The voice like a violin string played with a saw.

"You throw the dreams away? Are my creations not beautiful?"

The figure keeps its mouth open, and I see it has no teeth. No lips.

"Stay away from me!" My voice is small. Mousy.

I shake the dreamcatcher violently as I back away toward the house. The figure does not follow. In the bedroom, I peek back at the stream through the curtains while my son moans in his sleep behind me. The creature is still standing there, as if rooted to the spot. It looks at the stream, the trees and the moon. Occasionally it turns its gaze toward the house. I hang the dreamcatcher, and my son returns to an undisturbed deep sleep.

"What is it?" my wife asks.

"Nothing," I say as I try to comprehend what I just saw. "I thought I heard an animal."

I do not sleep that night. I call in sick and sleep during the day. The grass has gone gray where I shook the dreamcatcher in a panic during the night.

THE NEXT NIGHT, my son starts tossing in his slumber and I get up to empty the dreamcatcher. Outside, I see the figure again, now on my side of the stream. It stares at me as I approach, mouth open. I notice now that it has unnaturally long fingers, tapered into fine points. I call out to it.

"What do you want?"

The figure speaks in that same drawn-in way. "The dreams are for *you*. Why do you trick them into a net?" My back is a chalkboard, raked with nails.

"We do not want them," I say, the calmness in my voice surprising me. "They disturb my son. Ruin his sleep."

Never has my love for him been so clear. Despite everything.

The figure turns its head toward me, to the house, and back again. It exhales, mouth hanging open, and then speaks as it inhales. "My gifts for you. Unwanted?" The creature takes a step forward. "Unwanted?" It snaps its head in my direction and I flinch and take a step back. "Unwanted?" it asks. "Then name one who would have them. Name a new dreamer."

The crickets grow silent, and so does the world. The soft wind that had caressed the leaves stops. All seemed to wait for my answer.

The creature exhales. Ribs visible, skin sagging. It inhales and speaks. "Dreams are for the boy, for the house," the creature says, and points.

I think about the boy. And then I think about the mother, and all that she has done. I find an anger I didn't know I possessed.

"The boy's father," I say. "Give the dreams to the boy's father!"

The creature, slim and slick, looks away from the house and over to the next farm. It exhales in preparation for speech.

"The father?" it finally asks as it inhales, and blinks.

My stomach fills with ice, but then the creature turns away from me, to the east, and starts walking. It is headed toward the Balknes farm. I always suspected it was him, his eyes brown like my son's.

In one swift motion, I break the dreamcatcher. I make a show of throwing it in the stream.

I sleep sinfully well for the rest of the night, as does my son.

HAMRABORG BABYLON

Alexander Dan Vilhjálmsson

Translated by Quentin Bates

WATCHFUL AND ETERNAL, the Hamraborg loomed over the conurbation, concrete and steel and glass and bones twisted together into a memorial for a city among cities, rising over the low-slung, oppressed settlement, a burg in the middle of the capital village, a metropolis all of its own.

Wind nagged at its brutalist towers, its gentle touches becoming in a moment a bitter blast, but nowhere did a blade of grass flutter or the crown of a tree bend, nowhere was a leaf torn from its branches, the megalith stood unmovable and indifferent like the country's oldest mountains that remember thickly forested lands from ancient eras when the ice age was nothing more than a distant threat. The only movement along its streets were those of plastic bags and battered tin cans; the feathers of a bird's carcass in the middle of the road rippled.

Further along the street, a new movement invaded the concrete wasteland, although these were no ravening barbarians at the city gates, or the roar of tanks and the whine of bombs, but still all the more threatening and pernicious as the solitary invader did the unthinkable, breaking every law of the cityscape, the holiest doctrine of the Hamraborg itself.

In the middle of the street, a woman walked towards the grey-black monolith.

Pedestrian. Ambulant. Car-less. Heretic.

Whether she was aware of how offensive her behaviour was in the eyes of the Hamraborg by approaching the city-fortress in this way, how great was the disrespect she displayed with her ignorance or lack of understanding of the expected deference and ceremony, that her behaviour was worse than that of any louse-infested thrall spitting on the floor in front of the emperor's high seat, is completely unknown.

What was certain was that the Hamraborg followed her progress with deep disdain. The soles of her shoes clapped the tarmac like the blows of hammers, with each arrogant step she unwittingly erected her own gallows.

She was nonplussed as she came to the sheer walls, not knowing where to go, or how to get inside the sanctuary, as there were no steps or doors intended for *pedestrians* anywhere to be found in the outer ramparts of the citadel. She wandered back and forth, but never saw past the corner of the stronghold and clearly had little liking for the thought of spending many days walking around this sprawling fortress.

She summoned up all her resolve, bit the bullet, and broke another sacred rule, like a barbarian hungry for the sweet marrow inside. She continued towards the only visible entrance in the grey castle walls, stooped under and past the horizontal metal bar and went *on foot* into the blackness of the underground car park.

The Hamraborg basked in sunbeams that lit it up in magnificent greyness. Matt windows reflected jagged banks of cloud.

With a rust-toothed grin and a flash of halogen in its eyes, the Hamraborg swallowed the traveller deep into its insides.

THE DAYLIGHT TURNED paler, fading with each step until the darkness enveloped her like hands tightening their grip around a throat. Footsteps echoed inside the vault. The basement smelt of burnt tyres scorched against tarmac, piss many weeks old and a lingering petrol aroma. Something crackled high above, and fluorescent lights flickered into life over her head, going dark again as soon as she was beyond the reach of their sensors. A few more steps and another came to life with a stuttering buzz, and the lights illuminated her way into the Hamraborg's bowels.

No car was anywhere to be seen, or any other sign of activity, other than rubbish heaped in corners and black stains on the concrete that weren't anything like normal skid marks. Whatever had scorched rubber here hadn't been any usual kind of car. She went down a level, keeping all the while to the kerb for fear of a car appearing from the gloom and running her down, but there was neither sound nor movement as she carried on.

She quickly lost count of how many levels she descended into the concrete depths. On one level she saw a flicker of light in the distance and decided to head for it. No lights came on overhead here, and she worried that these were mirages, that the now potent petrol vapour had poisoned her, but the light continued to grow until she could make out a small filling station in the middle of the underground car park.

The concrete walls stretched up into the blackness, fading into a gloom that obfuscated the ceiling from her sight. Next to her were two rusted petrol pumps. Light flooded from a large window, and inside lay empty, dusty shelves scattered like kindling, the floor strewn with ripped crisp bags and crumpled paper cups. The walls inside were coated with glistening wet paint, oil shades melding to swirl together as the pulsating spirals quivered and throbbed, shimmering in front of her under the heavy fumes. The oily graffiti whorled lazily before her eyes. She was relieved that the place was locked up tight.

"Got a thousand krónur?"

Startled, she backed off and looked around in terror for the source of the voice. A stick-thin man stood by one of the pumps, bony and dressed in a beige cassock. His clothes had been tacked together from used car-polishing cloths, adorned with braided rags; with the plastic head of a broom worn proudly as epaulettes. Beneath the cassock was a leather jerkin sewn from car footwell mats, and a tar-black cloth hid his face. An air freshener card in the shape of a green tree hung around his neck, along with a few desiccated human ears.

She backed further away and the man stared. As she stepped back she saw another man lying flat on his back behind one of the pumps. He had a steering wheel around his neck and was dressed much the same. The spout of the petrol pump was in his mouth and he sucked energetically at the steel tube.

"How do I get inside? Into the Hamraborg."

The wretch shrugged. "The car park goes deep. Very

deep. Unless you're driving." His laughter was like a tractor starting up.

"How do I get in?"

"That'll cost you a thousand."

Their voices echoed back and forth in the void. The wraiths of voice continued the conversation even when no more was said. She fumbled in a pocket and pulled out a creased thousand krónur note. The man with the pump in his mouth moaned. The thin man took the note, neither agitated nor threatening and made nothing of her being like cornered prey opposite him. He smoothed the note and started fiddling to get the self-service pump to accept it.

"Where do I go?"

The machine whined as it drew the thousand note inside. The petrol pump hummed into life. The man on the floor pulled again and again at the trigger in the hope that the fuel would start to flow.

The wretch pointed into the darkness, without taking his eyes from his companion, trembling with anticipation. "The lift's that way."

She peered but saw nothing, although something flickered in front of her eyes, it could have been an imagining or just a tiny streak of distant light.

She hurried away from the petrol station in the direction of the half-imagined light. Behind her she heard the pump at work and the man whispering to his companion in a voice full of gentle anticipation:

"Pump and smile. Pump... and... smile."

A DESERT OF darkness separated her from the lift. For forty days and forty nights, she walked until the steel doors stood facing her. She pressed a button and stepped into the maddening fluorescent light of the lift cage.

There were just two buttons on offer.

K1

K2

She pressed K2 and the lift dropped like a stone.

A GENTLE MURMUR, a soft *ping*. She came to on the floor as the lift came to a halt. She had passed out as the lift dropped and gravity betrayed her. The doors opened and the cage was filled with the din of the street, so loud after the silence of the underground car park that her ears hurt. On unsteady feet she hauled herself upright and peered past the piercing neon light, the sour stench of pollution making her cough.

The feverish craze of Hamraborg welcomed her.

Packed streets meandered like skeins of twine, their grip ever tightening like a noose, the throng bustled through an oppressive gloom kept at bay by exhausted neon signs, which called out to her wherever she looked, imploring her to treat herself to a beer, electrical goods, a fuck, a puff of a hookah, antique furniture, a flogging, a falafel or a visit to church.

Every step swept litter along and she found herself wading through ankle-deep garbage. The sour smell was overpowering, as soot and oil and burning plastic and sweat and sex and competing perfumes sought domination, fried meat and rotten, vomit, booze, charcoal and gas and opium and ammonia and desperation.

People stared at her, either backing off or pressing themselves close, as she tried to stare through the throng and failed, unable to do it, the duress was too much and the Hamraborg too overwhelming, sweaty and slick up against her cheek, whispering filth in her ear, tempting and dangerous and disreputable from top to toe.

A chink in the blanket of garbage showed a glimmer of light underfoot, and she saw another identical street underneath, all the way down, until she was foolish enough to look up and see in the ceiling above was yet another street, and that the ramshackle houses built of pilfered cement and rusting corrugated iron stretched upwards as well as down, leaving her caught in the heart of a maze with neither end nor beginning and from which she would never find a way out. Even if she wanted to, she would never find her way back now that the lift was out of her sight.

"Darling! You're so lonely, come on, come over here!" A woman in a suit, wearing a mask with the face of a young woman, white as bone and with rouged cheeks, gestured at her stall, where all kinds of strange and alien sexual organs writhed with life, glistening with slime under green-red lights. "This one'll put colour in your cheeks, sweetheart," she continued, running a finger the length of a plait of three swollen organs, purple with pink veins and trembling soft fins along the shaft, and as she touched the penises, they shivered in delight, emitting a thick fluid that squirted into the air. "First refill's free!"

She hurried away from the smorgasbord of flesh and tried not to think of those sexual organs as being genuinely alive, meat and veins and bodily fluids, as people yelled angrily at her as she pushed her way past them. Panic was setting in. People stared. *A rural stench on this one*, someone said, and she hurried into the nearest bar.

The fug of fried food hung in the air, every surface glistening with grease. In the narrow bar, there was just space for a row of stools, tight to the counter, behind which stood the owner, barbecuing whole sewer rats over glowing charcoal, a clutter of poison-green bottles covering the shelves behind him. She took a seat and the other two customers surreptitiously looked her up and down.

The owner picked up a rat from the barbecue and slapped it on a large loaf, the bread so yellow and soft that it could have been made of sponge, before dousing the rat in mustard, remoulade, ketchup and both fried and raw onion. Finally, he took a pinch of tangled material, adroitly stretched it out and placed the hot rat on it. She realised that it was human hair, all kinds of hair, in all sorts of colours, of all kinds of people.

"What d'you want?" the owner snarled and wiped his hands on his belly. His high forehead was tattooed with 2 0 0 in bright green letters outlined in white and his broad arms were patterned with shaky crisscrossed scars. "I don't serve them from Reykjavík."

"I'm from up country," she replied and slapped a wad of notes on the counter. He raised an eyebrow.

"That explains the stink," said an older woman, hoarse with smoking, two cigarettes in her mouth as she lit up a third. The bowl in front of her was empty but for two rats' tails that lapped over the edge like worms in a bath. Mouth full of rat and remoulade, the other customer kept quiet.

"Looking to rent a video," she said with determination, eyes fixed firmly on the barman. He turned over one of the rats as its skin burst and the fat inside it cracked in the heat. He licked his fingers without taking his eyes off her.

"That'll cost you more than just money," he said, scooping up her notes and stuffing them into his trousers. "I'm not sure you'll find the way, even if I were to give you directions. The streets in Kópavogur always turn out to confuse strangers."

SHE WAS LOST. The neon lights were fewer and the gloom of the inner Hamraborg took their place, black night illuminated by staccato flashes in the concrete desert. Flickering beams from shacks where not every window had yet been boarded over. It seeped from above wherever she went, and her jacket was damp with the foul-smelling scum.

A body lay on flattened cardboard boxes and under a greyish, tattered skin, in front of locked shutters and the lopsided door. The iron hatch was marked with an icon of a broad smile, far too broad and with way too many teeth, while one tooth, gold in colour, had jumped out of the mouth, the cartoonish figure smiled brightly and invited customers with toothache to step inside. She nerved herself to address the tramp, as she felt it was preferable to get no more lost than she was already.

"Excuse me. I'm looking for the market."

The man started and shied away as he looked at her, fumbling under the foul-smelling pelt for a weapon. He waved a rusty meat hook at her with trembling hands. This boy was just a teenager. He had sliced an ugly wound in his forehead which was still healing; 2 o O.

The lad stared at her, lowered the hook, his eyes opened wide and he instinctively sniffed the air.

"You smell of the sun."

"Do you know where the market is?"

"The countryside. The countryside and the sun."

"Sorry to disturb you."

She was about to walk away when he scrambled to his feet and she yelped, certain that he was about to attack her, but he raised his hands in peace and asked her to be calm.

"I know where the market is. But there's a price."

"I have no money."

He slipped a pair of children's scissors from a pocket.

"One lock of hair. Please."

She thought it over but knew she had no choice. She snatched the scissors from him, snipped off a mouse-grey lock of hair and handed it to the boy. He held the hair close to his face, drawing the scent of it deep, held his breath, not letting go until his lungs could stand it no longer, then stowed the skein in a pocket, with elaborate care, thought for a moment, and pulled a single hair from the tangle and put it in his mouth.

"Come on. Let's rent a video."

V H S ANNOUNCED DOZENS of flashing neon signs, icons of scantily dressed ladies moved in lascivious three-phase routines, aces of spades smouldered, jacks of diamonds laughed and currency symbols from around the world flickered in every colour of the rainbow. The name of the place was spelt out above the door in warm incandescent lights, some bulbs dead or heading that way, in the beautiful script of a past age of glamour and elegance that had never made its way inside the walls of the Hamraborg.

The Market.

The clatter of a hundred slot machines flooded the inside, the noise maddening and the aisles without end, on the floor a zillion little balls that the machines now and again spewed out. The haze of smoke was thick, an antique in itself, a cultivated atmosphere that it had taken decades to nurture.

She coughed, but the hunched slaves to the game didn't look up from the blinking promises of their machines.

The casino gave way to shelves that reached high up the walls, stacked with video tapes. The further she went into this video collection, the din receded until she could hear the tinny sound of corny nineties love songs. She picked out a video at random and made for the counter.

The man behind it was watching a small tube TV on which a man was swallowing goldfish whole while a narrator did a voice-over. He wore a soft waistcoat, pale white with black slashes. Sealskin.

She placed the videotape on the counter. After a long while the man looked at her and sniffed.

"No Reykjavík types here."

"Can I get a tape rented?"

"No. Fuck off." He turned up the volume on his TV. "And talk proper Icelandic."

"I need a haircut." He ignored her. "An *artistic* haircut."

Greed gleamed in his eyes.

"You're a pilgrim."

"I don't know what you call it. I'm on my way down."

"I understand." He switched off the TV, hauled himself to his feet and opened the door to the store room at the back.

She followed.

*   *   *

A DISPLAY OF sweets, snacks and candyfloss lined the
route to the black-walled video storeroom, and behind
that lay a dark staircase that echoed. He led her through
one door after another until she entered a small hall, well
ventilated, and she took a thankful breath.

Then the lights came on and she smothered a cry.

Before her stood a short woman in a bright pink dress,
all unicorns and rainbows and kittens and hearts, her
face hidden behind a sugar-sweet, big-eyed anime mask
so synthetically cute as to be unnerving. In the hall were
screens showing acts she had no wish to see, of which the
least bad was a pale, skinny man who sat at a banqueting
table enthusiastically eating soil.

"The sun," the woman said. "The sun has arrived."

"She's come for a haircut," said the sealskin-clad video
guy. The woman took out a pair of blunt scissors.

"Half," she said, suddenly uncertain. "I want to keep
half."

"You're on the way down," the woman said.

"Yes."

The anime mask looked at her expectantly.

"What an exciting performance."

SHORN, AND WITH half of her hair in a bag, she followed
the anime woman towards the church. It looked to her like
a warehouse, unmarked and unlit, its windows broken and
nobody to be seen, no sound but dripping water and the
squeaking of rats. Two bruisers lounged outside, bald and
shirtless, wearing sealskin waistcoats, outsized sunglasses
and their foreheads tattooed with 2 0 0. The anime woman

conferred with the pair then convinced them to let the woman in by herself. The lock snapped shut behind her.

She padded down the steps in the darkness and banged her head against a door, someone opened it for her and she stepped into this holiest sanctum, the Hamraborg's best-kept secret.

Music carried from run-down loudspeakers, cheery but distorted, every table half-full, every glass half-empty, but the beer frothed and the hard stuff hit the spot, and so worship was conducted every evening that never came to an end.

A raised stage stood at one end of the bar, a vast icon of a faceless woman filling the wall behind it, a halo encircling her head and a skull held in her hand. There was a throne of beer bottles on the stage and on it sat an enormous toad, as fat as lard, wart-covered and mould-green, with wrinkles beyond count, bulging yellow eyes, its mouth fixed in an eternal frown. A royal cloak of red fur was fastened at the toad's throat, barely covering its shoulders.

The man at the toad's side gestured for her to approach and she obeyed. He was hairless and wore sunglasses, his only garments an albino white sealskin waistcoat and drooping tattered jeans, or no, she caught a glitter of very thick platform-soled trainers that had been white back in the days of yore. His skin was pale and damp with sweat and hung on his bones as if all the air had been sucked out of him. His bare chest was covered with the mark of the Hamraborg, although it wasn't easy to make it out on the slack skin. The Hamraborg had been sketched in abstract, jagged white outlines, against a background as green as poison, and beneath it was a symbol, white and strange and hard to decipher. At first, she thought it was a person prostrating and then realised that it was most likely supposed to be a seal pup.

She was the only person present without a tattooed forehead, while he was the only one marked 2 0 3. Around his neck hung a collar with a chain fastened to the toad's nipples.

She addressed the man and not the toad, as the anime woman had instructed.

"Lord Hunger, I bring gifts." She held up the bag of hair. "In my pilgrimage to the grave of the saint."

The man's face betrayed no emotion, his jaw still hanging open as he turned to the toad.

"Who are your people?" the vast man-frog rumbled in a deep tone that came all the way from his gut.

"I'm from the Northeast."

First gradually, and gathering weight, like the beginnings of a terrible landslide, then unstoppable and murderous, the toad began to laugh. Lord Hunger followed suit, and the other guests obediently joined in.

She tried to defend herself.

"My roots are in Thingeyjar…"

"Nobody asked where your grandparents grew up!" Lord Hunger snapped. "Where is a good place to live?" he yelled out over the hall, suddenly energised with strength and life and cranked-up arrogance.

"KÓPAVOGUR IS A GOOD PLACE TO LIVE!" the throng yelled back and went wild, knocking back drinks, rows of shots were filled on the bar and dispatched in a flash. The toad joined in with their shout and the depths of its bass voice with its overwhelming weight almost had her collapsing to the floor

"I grew up in the Hlíðar district in Reykjavík," she confessed as the tide of jubilation receded.

"In the countryside," Lord Hunger corrected.

"I grew up in the countryside."

Hunger looked up at the toad. It winked lazily. He reached for her bag and snatched it from her, immediately ripping it open to take a deep lungful of the sun-sweet aroma of hair. He handed the bag to a muscular woman with 2 0 0 on her forehead, wearing diamond-studded sunglasses and a snow-white sealskin cloak that reached to her ankles. She smelled the hair, tasted it, and nodded.

"Eau du soleil," she said, satisfied, and Lord Hunger's gold teeth shone.

"Take the pilgrim to be tattooed. And for the saint's sake, dress her properly and get rid of those countryside rags."

THE SPIRAL STAIRCASE was built of blocks of stone, the steps worn into smooth depressions by the footsteps of the ages as uncountable pilgrims had crept down into the dark and the past buried beneath the Hamraborg.

There was a pervasive smell of earth, damp and ancient and overpowering. The tattoo stung, a searing spider's web stretching across and up her forehead, down her cheek and along her neck, spreading across her shoulders. The black, vascular network covered her and marked her out as a pilgrim, a chosen individual on a sacred journey, excluded from the community and the city and from the sun itself.

The steps finally came to an end and passages that haphazardly meandered took over, illuminated by dim, yellowish torchlight.

She stepped over the threshold and into the catacombs.

Its walls were lined with thigh bones and skulls, bones upon yellowed bones stacked in their thousands and millions, down here in the guts of the Hamraborg where she kept her children, laid them to their final rest, the citadel gave them life and raised them in its grinding misery, and finally, its citizens ended up in the belly of their mother to attain new life though an age of ages, and in a new role as building blocks served as hardcore to form the foundations of its endless streets.

She had no idea where she was headed, but that didn't matter. Either she would find her way, or she would become part of the fabric of the catacombs. The cold gnawed and she drew the sealskin cloak tight around her, and as it had no arms, she was still cold and the new and ragged clothes she wore held no warmth.

The bones showed her the way.

THE GRAVE OF Saint Catalina was in devotion to selflessness and longing for death. The crypt was lined with bones, the floor a packed circular pattern of ribs that fought one another for dominance, the concave walls lined with spiral after spiral of limbs, a maelstrom that consumed the pale torchlight. At the centre, bones were arranged in the image of a skull, built on a vast scale, its form shaped by hundreds of skulls, empty-eyed and yellow-brown; the teeth were huge, whole bones that she couldn't recognise, maybe from whales, and in the great eye sockets of the icon glimmered gems, whole chunks, carved into the shapes of skulls that glittered with an inner light of their own.

Before the awful skull sculpture stood a worn statue of a faceless woman, her head lowered, clad in a tattered shawl. Arms at her sides, palms faced forward in surrender or acceptance, she couldn't be sure which. Ragged flowers lay at her feet, and they certainly weren't anything that had ever lived, not down here in the Hamraborg's deepest dungeon, but instead had been cleverly twisted into the form of flowers from strips of newspaper.

A man knelt before the statue.

He was aware of her presence but made no acknowledgement, she feared that he was dead, frozen through the ages in worship, thanks to the blessing of rigor mortis. After some time she heard his lungs creak with every drawn-out breath. His black clothing obscured his form. Grave clothes. His clasped hands were sewn together with thick leather thongs.

She knelt before the figure and lowered her head in mock reverence. Before the statue was a glass case, containing a red cushion, and on the cushion rested a tiny yellowed bone. This was all that remained of the saint. She couldn't tell from where in the body the bone had come.

"I have come to claim my brother," she said and her voice echoed around the shrine.

"His bones have already been required to make new pillars of foundation," the man replied, without taking his eyes off the saint.

"I don't give a shit about the Hamraborg."

The blasphemy didn't echo, smothered in the deathly hush.

To her surprise, there was no angry reaction from the man. Instead, he murmured in sympathy.

"Then go and find him. But the Hamraborg will never let go of you."

She had no reply to make to such a prophesy. She stood up, shook the dust of bones off herself and searched the catacombs.

* * *

AN ETERNITY LATER an empty-eyed skull stared at her from the stylish bone mosaic of the wall, its jaw part of a wing pattern that was supposed to form a terrible bird. That familiar look, accusing and tragic, tore at her heartstrings. But she let no feelings show as she tore her brother from the wall, ripping a wound in the Hamraborg's side as the feel of the bone made her nauseous, and that was when she broke, that was when she wept with sorrow or regret or relief.

She tried to find more of his remains, but it was impossible to identify ribs or limbs or digits, all were rendered equal in their transformation into building material. She kissed the forehead of the skull and wrapped it in cloth.

THE CAVE RESONATED as the stalactites sweated and the still water was disturbed, the rings expanding wider and wider until they faded into nothing and the far side of the lake was a void. Out there was nothing but darkness. A slowly pulsating red brilliance radiated from the depths, but she couldn't make out the source of the light.

Under the Hamraborg, under the basement and the labyrinthine streets and the catacombs, lay the last refuge of Kópavogur's original inhabitants. Refugees who had fled the cruel season of slaughter that had practically wiped them out in the settlement years.

They lay on the rock like spirits, their black, deep eyes all on her. Their pale white pelts shimmered like moonlight.

Nothing but the sound of her breath and of falling drops broke the silence.

The cold was so great that she didn't feel it as she stepped into the clear water and plunged into the light.

NORWAY

AS YOU WISH

Tor Åge Bringsværd

Translated by Olivia Lasky

THE STEADY HUMMING from the excavators outside. The smell of eggs and bacon. "How do you want me?" The words are quiet and careful, almost like a whisper. She's standing over by the window, grey morning light filtering through the half-open blinds. "How do you want me?" She puts her hands on her hips and gyrates slowly from side to side, her long, dark hair cascading down her bare shoulders.

"Let me wake up a bit first." It's Friday. You have the day shift. There's no reason to get up yet. Not for a while.

"How do you want me?"

"Stop nagging!" You try to rub the sleep out of your eyes. "Why don't you get me a cup of coffee instead?"

She fills a mug from the tap on the wall and hands it to you along with the breakfast tray. "Older?" Her forehead and nose wrinkle up. "Or younger?" Her face smoothes itself out again.

"I said *stop nagging*!" You slosh coffee on the bed and swear.

"But I have to know," she says—the one you call Liv. The one you've called Liv for almost two months. "I have to know how you want me…"

You look at her and shake your head. You don't know if you should be annoyed.

"I have to know!" The voice is hoarse. Her hands open and close.

Suddenly you smile. "You're good enough just the way you are," you say.

"Are you sure?"

"I don't want you any other way." You watch how she relaxes, how her body takes on its soft catlike grace again. "Come here," you say, making room next to you on the bed. "Come here for a bit."

YOUR NAME IS Brageson. You work in Mine Blue-14 and share a ditch with a Japanese man named Kato. "How long have you been here?" Kato asks.

"Seven weeks."

"And you're already having problems with her?"

"Yes."

"You have to show her who's boss," Kato laughs. "And she's sturdy, you know." He nudges you in the ribs and grimaces. "Don't be afraid of pushing the limits with her. She can handle more than you think."

You try to laugh, too, and shrug, shaking your head.

"It's just a transition," the short, stocky Japanese man says.

Kato has a ten-year contract.

He has a partner he calls Tanika.

* * *

THE DITCH IS a cramped hell. Full of toxic gas. Dark and damp. It'll be better once you're allowed to set up your own control panel and can rig a ditch by yourself. You and Kato work well together, it's just that the ditches aren't meant for two. You know Kato is getting paid quite a bit extra to train you. Apparently, it's even worse in other places, like the Red Mines, for example. That's the kind of thing people must talk about here to make the time pass. You and Kato operate fourteen work robots, but most things just run themselves. "The routines are put in place so we don't fall asleep," Kato says. Actually, it would be pretty boring to be all alone, but that's how the system was built. It's enough to have one man in each ditch, not to mention cheaper for the company.

BUT THE WAGES are good. It's the money that's the real draw, not the wanderlust. If you're willing to give up between two to ten years of your life, then Nova Thule's a place where you can work on your finances and get back on your feet again, or lay the grounds for a better, richer life than you might've gotten to live otherwise.

That's how the advertisements make it seem, at least.

EIGHT HOURS LATER, you're back under the dome—the big, shimmering-gold bubble of human light and warmth. You can finally breathe without a mask here. You can walk around without a protective suit. You can think about something other than crackling traces of colour on flat screens.

* * *

175

SHE'S STANDING IN the doorway, waiting. Laughing. She throws herself around your neck and helps you out of your work clothes, pulls off your boots, asks if you want something to drink before dinner. You're not really in the mood to say anything at all; you just let her take care of things. You can hear her singing in the kitchen.

YOU'RE TOO TIRED to go out but there's hardly anything to do anyway. In the canteen, you can play cards and pool, or watch old movies. Or just drink. But you don't have any friends, you don't know anyone here, and you can't bear the same old drunken drivel. Listening to sad stories, tales of troubled childhoods, fantasies about castles in the sky and how everything's going to get better... sometime in the future... when life finally begins... just up ahead, around the next turn. You can't be bothered. You've seen too many canteens. It isn't appealing anymore. Better to just stay at home.

YOU'RE SITTING BY the window, looking out at green fields surrounding a small grove of trees—a Norwegian spring landscape. Blue skies, twittering birds. Once you even spotted a few hares. You know that if you wait long enough, you'll see deer and foxes, but you've never had enough patience to wait. You yawn and press a button. The window goes dark. Liv comes in at the same moment. "Did you turn it off?" You don't respond. You know she likes this window most; it's always on when you get home. For a moment, she stares at you in silence. Then she smiles. Tenderly. Affectionately. "But you make the decisions here," she says, tilting her head. "Yes," you answer gruffly. You don't meet her eyes. "I make the decisions." You press another button and the window shows a turbulent ocean, water as far as the eye can see. The waves crash against the glass. Spindrift. Is it the Atlantic or the Pacific? You can never remember what's written on the disk. You turn up the volume and shut your eyes, letting the sea roar. Nova Thule. A patch of fog drifting around a strange, distant star. Never a sunny day. Never a clear sky. You think: *What am I doing here?*

"IT DOESN'T MAKE any difference if you talk to them," Kato says while you're sitting in the ditch. Two of the robots have gotten stuck, and now you're chatting about your partners as you wait for a green tinkerer to come. "Because they don't understand anything you say anyway. All they know is what they've been taught." You see that his mouth is moving, but his voice is in your ears. You're both wearing helmets and protective suits. It makes you look like divers in old newsreels. Or maybe slow-moving beetles. "I mean, you don't actually believe they got like that by themselves?" His laughter makes a crackling noise. "Oh no, my good man. By the time they make it onto our laps, they've already been kneaded and moulded like you wouldn't believe. And spaded on both ends!"

A green tinkerer waddles into the ditch, steaming from its long air-stilts, its rotating warning light casting shadows in all directions.

YOU DREAM YOU'RE back on Earth. You're married with three kids. You fight. The kids can hear it. Every day. Morning and night. Slinging insults at each other over every tiny thing. And the kids are listening. Nothing is as it should be. Never satisfied. Always something to nitpick. Something to jab at. A wound to keep open. Something to twist the knife in. Out of bad habit. The children are watching. The children are listening. Hiding their thoughts in dark corners. But it's too late to stop. It's too late to hit the brakes. It's moving too fast. You don't even have time to think. You don't have time to pay attention. Everything has just become the way it is. You call each other ugly things. Without meaning it. Without really wanting to. But you can't stay quiet. Your mouth just moves automatically. Your tongue runs on a closed loop. You don't even notice that the children are getting smaller every day. Smaller and smaller. Then they aren't children. They're dwarves. Bearded. Grey-haired. Their small, wrinkled, apple-faces staring at you, cackling toothlessly. But you don't see anything. You have enough to think about between the two of you. Then the dwarves barely reach your ankles, they disappear beneath the table—and in the end, they can be swept under the rug like crumbs and dust.

You wake up, dripping with sweat, a bad taste in your mouth.

"Is something wrong?" A soft hand gently strokes your forehead. She's crouching down next to the chair. "Is there something I can do differently?"

You shake your head.

"Are you sure?"

You don't want to make the same mistake twice.

*   *   *

YESTERDAY YOU WERE called in to see the psychologist—a short, fat man who was constantly licking his lips and scratching one side of his nose. "You must learn to reject her. She must know her place."

"I don't like hurting her."

"Using that kind of phrase—about an idunn—is utterly absurd. And you know that." Concerned lip-licking.

"I know."

(No one at home told you about idunns. Not a word was said about them when you enrolled. But they're absolutely everywhere here on Nova Thule. Everyone uses them.)

"You're letting her get too close to you."

"I can't help it."

"So, it's best that we take her back."

"No! I need her!"

More lip-licking. "You need to find balance. Face the facts. We're giving you a deadline." More nose scratching. "If you aren't able to normalise the relationship in a week, we're coming to take her."

SHE'S NOT A machine. She's not an android or a biomat. She's not the result of artificial mutations or genetic experiments. She's an idunn.

THE QUESTION IS really whether they can be called independent life at all. All newcomers had to watch a movie about it. The movie talks about how the mining company utilises idunns as an integrated part of the well-being offering. How practical it is, how hygienic, how morally sound. In the past—in corresponding

179

male-dominated societies on Earth—it was normal to introduce a certain number of prostitutes for common use. On Nova Thule, they used local resources. There is guaranteed to be no risk of venereal disease of any kind. Infection can't possibly be transmitted between a human and an idunn. Offspring is physically impossible. And perhaps most importantly: they don't actually have anything to do with women at all. The scheme was therefore even approved by the UN Council for Gender Equality and the joint committee for national women's fronts. Idunns also can't be characterised as animals. Or plants. The closest thing you can compare them to are crystals—and there currently isn't any interest group for the protection of crystals, the film commentator laughed. In other words, they can be used for any purpose you could ever want. Crystalline beings. Creatures without human intelligence or animal instincts but with a highly developed sense for imitation. A kind of extension of the same ability that parrots and monkeys of the past are said to have had—two species that have naturally long since disappeared. And to make it perfectly clear: the film emphasises that it is solely due to the sexual preferences of the majority that most idunns are 'female'. Men who want a partner of the same gender will of course be helped just the same way as everyone else.

"HOW DO YOU want me? Is it good like this? Are you satisfied? Do you like it when I do it this way?"

"THE STRANGEST BIT is that you can get them to look like anyone at all," Kato says. "I change her face and body every Saturday. I have a whole catalogue with pictures of girls. Girls I know and don't know. From any time in history, even. Then it's practically like a whorehouse if you think about it! But I guess a lot of the fun is gone when you look at it like that…"

YOU KNOW: SOME make them look like their mothers or sisters. For a while. You know: some of them treat them like daughters. For a while.

"WE'RE WORRIED ABOUT you, Brageson." The psychologist has called you in today as well. "Let me put it bluntly. We don't know if you fit in here with us. Do you understand what I mean?"

BUT DO ANY of us really fit in anywhere? Who can be sure of where he belongs? You think of someone who left you, someone who'd had enough, someone who took the children with them. Because… one day you just no longer fit together. So who can know anything? Know something *for sure*? You only remember: you wanted to change each other, like most people try. But this is what went wrong between you and her. You wanted to change each other…

"DOES EVERYONE WANT an idunn?"

"No, not everyone." (The psychologist licks his lips.) "And at least not right away." (Licking again.) "But *you* did?"

"Yes."

"You needed it." (Scratches his nose.)

THE OCEAN ROARS towards you. The waves are sky-high. It feels like the whole room is rocking. She turns around and smiles—warm and inviting. "Is it better now? Is that how you want it?" You walk wordlessly to the panel by the sofa and change the disk, chasing the sea away, letting the soft spring landscape fill the window. She looks at you, confused, but before she manages to say anything you've wrapped your arms around her. You kiss her like you haven't seen each other in weeks.

THE IDUNN YOU get delivered to you upon arrival should typically last as long as you remain in the service of the company. At the end of your service, you are obliged to return it in the same condition as you received it. Loss of the aforementioned idunn or damage to one's own or others' entails liability for damages in the form of salary deductions in accordance with the attached checklist.

— Excerpt from the *By-laws for Mining Crews on Nova Thule.*

"HOW DO YOU want me?" She blows herself up. "Should I put on weight?" Now she shrivels up again. "Or maybe lose a few pounds?" She twirls around, her hair lifting like a cloud around her head. It changes colours as you watch—all the shades, like a rainbow. All lengths and hairstyles. You laugh and clap your hands. She laughs back. She likes when you laugh. She likes pleasing you.

"How do you want me?" she shouts. But you just laugh, hiccupping now. Until your eyes are full of water. She just keeps dancing like a whirling dervish. Her nose changes. Her cheeks. Her breasts. "I have to know." Her voice goes up several octaves. "I have to know! I have to know!" Until she suddenly understands that you're crying.

YOU'VE PICKED UP snippets of conversations in the canteen. Sometimes you've asked questions yourself, but mostly you've just listened. They say they were found by chance during a test drilling, somewhere the ice had melted. No one knows for sure, but it definitely wasn't here at the Blue Mines—because then you would've known. Maybe at the Red Mines, or the Yellow? Some say they were chiselled out of the mountains in great big chunks. Others say they were found in the form of a viscous slime—a huge pond you could just scoop them up from. An underground sea. But aren't they crystals? Yes, in a way—but also not just that. Or perhaps in another way. Who knows? They are said to be dehydrated before being injected with sugar. Sugar? Yes. And human hormones, too... There's often some drunk who starts raving about smuggling them out. A tanker. A tanker full of idunns. Just imagine the price they would fetch on Earth. Some others say that the mining company must have thought of this a long time ago. Because there's big money here. But first, everything has to be tested. Up here. So, in a way, you're guinea pigs. All of you. And you toast to that.

* * *

"BUT I DON'T understand why you never want to trade," Kato says. He and Tanika have stopped by. Tonight she's fat and blonde. "Isn't that half the fun?"

But you shake your head. Liv is mine, you think. You put your arm around her, feeling her leaning into you.

"You can't take her with you anyway." Kato shuts his eyes and takes a couple of deep drags from the hookah.

You pick up a little, green-striped disk from the table in front of you. "Do you want me to put on the new window that you brought?" You stretch your hand towards the panel in the wall without waiting for an answer.

The window turns on, opening onto a busy city street.

Kato straightens up, taking in the traffic, the hubbub of people. "Can you turn it up a little bit?"

You turn up the volume.

Tokyo thunders past you.

Kato takes another deep drag from the hookah and strokes one hand over his face. "Good God," he says quietly. "I've been here for five years. I'm only halfway..."

Liv and Tanika look at each other. They smile.

KATO IS SMOKING too much. His eyes are getting shinier and shinier. Late in the evening, he asks Tanika to change her hair colour. He stomps on the floor and claps his hands until her hair is red as blood. He wants her to wear it in an updo, with barrettes and long hairpins. Liv helps her. "They're easy to train," he says. "You can get them to do whatever you want." You look at Liv, at how soft and supple she is, how quickly her fingers are working. Neither of the two idunns says anything. After a while, you notice you're feeling dazed and dizzy. You've smoked too much as well. "You're not listening!" Kato shouts.

He grabs your collar. "I'm telling you about everything I've taught her... belly dancing, chess, sitar-playing, all kinds of tricks, but you don't even give a damn!" He has his nose right up in your face. "I'd rather have her just as she is," you mumble. Kato breathes angrily. "I don't think you've even read the goddamn manual a single time!"

SHE CAME WITH an instruction manual.

An idunn is prepared to please, it says. *She wants to be used, to delight, to be of service.*

It further states that you can quite easily teach your idunn almost anything at all. Authorised teaching programs from a variety of subject areas can be borrowed from the library free of charge.

And finally—to top it all off: after quite a short time, you'll have a partner you can actually live with!

"YOU HAVEN'T MADE a single change to her. Nothing at all. We've checked." The psychologist leans back in his chair, putting both hands behind his head. "Interesting, but also concerning. A little confusing, perhaps? Is there something you want to tell us?"

No.

(How are you supposed to get him to grasp the tenderness you feel for her? He'd just call it unnatural and tell you it's abnormal to connect so strongly with something like her. Maybe even dangerous?)

* * *

"You can't be satisfied with me all the time"—her voice is loud and piercing—"you say everything is fine. Constantly. But that's impossible. There must be something you want to change." Her eyes dart around the room like birds that have suddenly been caged. "Something. Not much. But a little bit… something that you want… me to do… differently?"

But you shake your head. You look down at the floor and just keep shaking your head.

"But I can be *anything*!" she shouts. "Anything you want! Don't you understand? I can be *anything*!"

You clench your fists. "I don't want you any different," you say quietly.

"But I can't stand it! I can't always be the same! No one can always be the same! It's not fair!" She paces back and forth like she's in a cell, slamming her head against the walls. "It's not fair!"

She doesn't understand you.

No one understands you.

No one has ever understood you.

The sound of excavators outside hurts your ears.

You find the window that makes the most noise.

The sea.

You stare at the colossal waves.

You feel the bitter thoughts running out of your head.

You notice that she's carefully putting a blanket over you. You pretend not to notice.

You see her going out.

You pretend not to notice.

* * *

You HAVE THE night shift. When you go to work, she still hasn't come back. You've started to worry.

Kato doesn't have any sympathy for you, though. What did you expect? "You only think about yourself," he says. "Actually, you're really just fucking selfish! Do you actually think it's in *her* best interest for you to act the way you do?"

You don't know if you should laugh or cry.

"And imagine if she actually disappears," he says. "You know you're financially responsible for her, right? Have you reported it? Is anyone looking for her?"

You tell him to mind his own business.

THERE'S A LIGHT in your window when you get back to the dormitories. You sprint through the entrance, fidget in the elevator, wrench the door open, call her name. But it isn't Liv. It's the psychologist and a representative from the Company. What do they want? What are they doing here? They ask you to sit down and tell you that you really should listen carefully. They say this is a lot more serious than you realise. But you don't listen, you're just full of questions: Where is she? Where is Liv? Did they find her? Do they know anything? They say you need to calm down. They're not going to talk to you until you pull yourself together. They say that they have her. Not here. But they have her. She'll be able to come back to you again. But you have to promise to be careful with her. Because who knows what can happen when an idunn runs wild? It's never happened before. But it most likely isn't a pretty picture. You don't understand what they're talking about. They say that if you don't promise to accept an idunn for what it is, they'll have to take it away from you. They're talking about Liv. But they're suddenly calling her 'it'. You don't like that. You snarl internally. But you know they're being serious. Best to pretend. Best to obey. Best to submit. The representative from the Company clears his throat: "There have been complaints about your work as well," he says. "You're not as attentive as you should be. According to the plan, you should be getting your own ditch on Monday, but we doubt whether you can manage it. You think too much about... *it*." He clears his throat again. "It's almost become an obsession for you." You assure him that you're ready for your own ditch. But he doesn't look all that convinced. "Brageson," the psychologist says. "We've been keeping our eye on you this whole time, and this is your very last chance. You'll be assigned your own ditch. As planned. And we'll make sure you get your idunn back. But just on a trial basis. One mistake from you and..." He scratches his nose and shrugs.

They tell you to sign a few papers.

Where is she?

They promise it will be sent back to you at some point today.

YOU'VE HAD AN exhausting night. You kick off your boots and take a sleeping shot. You want to be well-rested and in top form when she gets back home. You turn on the window she likes the most—the peaceful spring landscape—and lie down on the sofa. You listen to the birdsong. Is that a fox you just spotted? You sit up. Is that finally the fox? You almost regret having taken the sleeping shot. Then you suddenly plunge into a deep darkness. You're falling. You extend your hands straight out from your body, feeling the slippery walls of the well racing past. Powerless. You can't do a single thing. Falling. Doesn't matter. Nothing matters. You're as good as dead. Suddenly the fall stops. The bottom is soft. It doesn't hurt. You landed on top of a huge stuffed animal. A teddy bear. It's your old teddy bear! You recognise it by the ears and the wisps of fur on its stomach that you coloured with a marker. It throws itself around your neck. You embrace each other. Crying. You've always loved each other. Circumstances separated you. But now you've finally found your way back to each other. But you still know that you must kill it. You don't understand why. You just know you must do it. It really should have happened a long time ago. Many years ago. It just never happened. But you can't run anymore. You must kill your old teddy bear. Why else would you have a knife in your belt? It doesn't look at you. It closes both eyes. It growls and presses itself against you. Is it trembling? No. You're the one who's trembling. Your hand shakes. But you lift the knife. Forgive me! you shout. Forgive me! And you press the knife into its stomach. The little teddy bear buckles. Without a word. It withers in your lap. You understand: It's no longer alive. It can never sleep in your bed again. You pull out the knife. Old sawdust sprinkles off the blade. But you're the one who's bleeding. You're the one who's hurt. You hold on to your stomach with both hands. Blood pumps out of your navel in long, heavy spurts.

Then you wake up.

She's standing right next to you, leaning forward.

You stretch your arms out and pull her down to you.

And kiss her.

* * *

BUT THIS ISN'T where you live? At home, the ceiling is grey. Here, it's brown and slanted, and you're not lying on the sofa, you're lying on a hard bunk made of transparent plastic. You're not alone, either. You turn your head. What is he doing here? There's a figure sitting on a chair by the window—a *real* window—scratching his nose. He has an old-fashioned notepad in his lap that he's scribbling notes onto. You want to say something. You want to get up. But he shushes you. He indicates that you should stay calm. Look over there, his finger says, pointing at the door. It opens. In comes—but it isn't possible!—in comes... you topple off the bunk... you look from one Liv to the other... they're completely identical. "How do you want me?" they both say. First one. Then the other. What is going on? "It's your fault!" you shout at the little nose-scratching twat. You take a threatening step towards him. But Liv—one of them—gets in the way. "How do you want me?" she says. The psychologist licks his lips. His narrow eyes glisten. "Brageson," he says. "Let me assure you: I had nothing to do with this. Not directly..." He points at the door again. "Look—there's another one of them." A third Liv comes in. "How do you want me?" she shouts at the top of her lungs. The two others shout as well. All three of them start screaming. Again, and again and again. They come towards you. You back away. They take each other by the hands. They make a circle around you. You see the psychologist leaning over his notepad. He's scribbling like a madman. You're more afraid than you realise. But is there anything to be afraid of? You try to laugh. And then she's laughing at you. All three of them. With white teeth. "Which of you is Liv?" you say. "Which of you is the real one?" But they just keep laughing. Loudly, heartily. "I'm tired of playing around!" you yell. "Answer me!" But the psychologist answers for them. His voice trembles with childlike anticipation. "They're all real— all three of them!" he shouts. "That's what's so special! It explained it to me. It can be as many as it wants! Just watch!" A fourth Liv shows up behind you. She wraps her arms around your waist. She puts her mouth against your ear and whispers: "How do you want me?" And she's strong. You feel how she tightens her grip. You gasp for breath. "Let go of me!" But she doesn't let go. Another Liv falls to her knees and throws her arms around your legs. Now you can't move. "Help me!" You try to meet his eye. But he looks away. "Brageson," he says. "Try to understand. This is a unique opportunity for me. And I've given them my word!" A third Liv puts her hand in front of your mouth. Her fingers smell sweet. They taste sweet. Your lips moisten. You swallow a sticky liquid. You see that her hand is flowing into a quivering lump. The four figures move closer and closer around you. Their bodies merge. Their facial features disintegrate. Nothing looks like Liv anymore. Your vision goes blurry.

YOU DON'T KNOW how long you've been out. You thought you were going to die. The fear is still sticking to your mind like barbed wire. But you're alive. You can look around. You're still in the same room. You're lying on the floor. In a big puddle of white, viscous slime. You want to get up. But you can't. Why won't your legs carry you? Where have your hands gone? Then it hits you. And you understand. You're not floundering in a puddle of slime. It's *you*. You are the slime!

He's still sitting there, taking notes in the chair in the

corner. He's pulled his legs up beneath him. His face is red and excited.

Liv is also here. Somewhere. Around you. On all sides. Liv... and all the others she's been.

How many can this slime contain?

How many others has she been? How many more is there room for?

You/she/you are covering the whole floor. Filling the room from wall to wall.

You're not afraid anymore. You're not cold anymore. You're warm. Strangely calm and relaxed. You're like an undulating sea. Or a quiet cove... with tiny little ripples. You speak to each other. Greet each other. Stroke each other. Meet and part. Undulating. Swaying. Meeting and parting. Like a melody that keeps coming back.

You are an idunn.

You see him getting up from his chair. Now he's wading around in you. Staring down at you. Licking his lips. Scratching at his nose. You so badly want to say something, but you can't quite find the words or your voice.

He's the one who speaks first. "Brageson," he says, crouching down. He scoops you up with both hands and lets you filter out through his fingers. "Brageson... I know you're in there."

You gather all of your whispering voices. You make a whirlpool of slime. You form a huge, white mouth. And you hear your old voice. The one you once owned. The one that isn't yours any longer. Not just yours. You hear how it murmurs and sings.

Now he kicks you. Angrily. Spraying slime every which way. "Answer!" he shouts. "Brageson... I know you can hear me!"

You fight with the sounds.
You form them into words.
Slowly... they drip... from the huge mouth.
"How do you want me?" you say. "How... do... you...
want... me?"

THE CORMORANT
Tone Almhjell

THE PEOPLE OF Grip say I'm half seagull.

That girl living out on the rock, they say, she's always got her face to the wind, her mind to the sea. But they are wrong. I'm not a seagull. I'm not white against the storm, far above the waves. I'm not fearless and loud in their midst. Instead, I'm black and slick with water. I dive into the swell and out of sight.

I'm a cormorant, and if I spread my wings, death follows.

My mother knows this. Why else would she be watching in her mirror, looking for signs of him?

It's always a question of which story she chooses to tell about my father. Whether it's the short one where he left her or the legend where he flew away. Whether she is mending nets with numb fingers or gutting fish with dirty knives.

I don't know which is closer to the truth. But sometimes I feel it rushing through my veins: The black cuttle of wakeful depth, the thinning mist above morning banks, the cold secrets beneath the surface of the sea. I am like him, but only half so. The rest of me is like her. Stuck on this island, soles cut by barnacles, toes in the winter sand.

Griptown is a gleaming necklace along the beach on the other side of the strait. I can only see it if the wind is kind when the waves don't rise like heaving walls, shutting us off from the world. When my mother and the sea are both calm, we bring our fish across the strait to sell it, rowing hard to beat the currents. I know the salt-pocked cobblestones, the chill-swept streets, the stubborn lanterns against the settling dark. I know what the Griptowners say about us, too, but still, I'm hungry for their voices. I'm hungry for the lights because the lights mean people. Meals shared. Talking. Laughing. Dancing, maybe, in the fisherman's inn? I might like to dance, if I didn't worry the music would lift me and cast me adrift. I might like to dance with the boy.

He's there, somewhere in the glow of one of those lamps. Maybe he leans against the wall in the Draug, quiet with his sketchbook and pen, watching them. He turns their faces into ink and their talking into stories. They don't understand, but he's like me. His eyes change color like the sea, and I list them like a prayer. Green and promising like spring melt. Gray and waiting. Dark and not for anyone to fathom.

I've felt them on me, walking along the stalls of the fish market. He watches everyone, like everyone watches me. But one time I passed him drawing on a crate by the docks, and I caught a glimpse of long, dark hair on a page as he quickly closed his book. The drawing must have smeared between the pages. His work ruined; his precious paper spent. The ink spread in his eyes as he realized his mistake. I'm not sure why that made me happy. Maybe I like his eyes like that, black and other. Maybe I just like ruin. After all, I am made for it.

That's what my mother says, on the fish-gutting days.

It is a fish-gutting day.

My mother squats on the stone quay, rocked back on her heels, net pooled around her like a nest. Her knife is fast and blind. The fish still struggle in their crate, twitching for air like living silver. But she cuts them quick, slices throats, slashes bellies, scoops out guts, tosses them into the barrel. Already it's almost full of slowing tails and jelling eyes.

"He was generous today," I say, *He* being the almighty sea for most people around these parts. But then he always is. My mother and I live alone out here. We have no other arms to pull up the catch than our own, no other nets than the ones we've had for as long as I can remember. Our boat is too frail to take out to the edge of the kelp woods where the big shoals roam, so we set our nets just beyond the little quay. Yet they never come up empty.

She darts her blade through a pale, soft belly, grunts. "What is owed must be paid." Her back is hunched inside her spattered shirt as she adds, "Such is the pact."

I wait for her to lapse into her story of the boy who washed ashore in a storm, won her heart, and flew away. But she doesn't. Instead, she cuts and tosses, cuts and tosses, until the crate is empty and all the silver is dead. I draw a bucket of seawater and slosh it over the stone. Scales and blood rinse over the edge of the quay, but the smell lingers.

'Pact' is not a word for fish-gutting days. 'Pact' is for when the winter dark leans in from all sides and the ocean holds not a glimmer of hope. 'What is owed must be paid,' she'll say, 'but not yet.' I used to ask what she meant, when I was younger. She never answered. She just stared into her mirror. Sometimes at me, eyes distorted by the buckled glass. Sometimes past me, out through the glazed panes.

I don't ask anymore.

"I'll take the barrel to the smoke shed," I say instead. This is our usual way: I clean up the mess and carry the fish, she mixes the herbs for the smoke.

Mother's smoked fish is the best in all of Grip. Traders come all the way from Maisincourt to buy it. She keeps the recipe a secret, even from me. When the southern ships come in, she goes to the fair to buy some of the spices. The rest of the ingredients she gathers in the mountains: For a whole day she leaves me in Griptown while she trudges around the heath, searching for frostberries and fox cub femurs, goldmoss and footprints in old summer snow.

This is the story she tells in the Draug, to those who fear her but love her fish. But I don't think it's just the herbs that make the fish taste like that. It's the driftwood, too.

The pieces wash up by the hundreds on the beach after every storm, salt-cured and hung with strange weeds. We shouldn't use them for fear of inviting the dead to the fire. But there is no other wood on our island.

It's all we ever burn.

SHE NEVER LETS me into the smoke hut, and this day is no different. The door is closed behind her, but I wait on the path outside in case she needs me. In case the smoke finally decides to take her, like it ought to. I imagine her walking around in the darkness of the hut, hanging the fish, tending the flames, while the smoke obeys her, swirling around her fingertips but never daring to pass her lips.

This day is different.

Before the first gray tendrils curl out of the chimney, the door opens and my mother bends under the lintel. The room behind her is cold and empty save for the rows of fish shimmering under the ceiling. No roiling smoke serpents. No fox bones smoldering.

"What's the matter?" I ask, searching her face. It's smooth and still as always. The people of Grip say my mother keeps like her fish, untouched by years. But I see what's beneath the smoothness. She's worried.

"The wood won't catch," she says.

"It's not dry enough?" I ask, even though it can't be so. This wood has been left out on days of blustery sun.

"Yes, that's it. Not dry enough. Must have been tainted with something." She turns away from the wind, and her hair whips across her cheek, covering it. "Go to the beach. See if you can find more."

"But—" I begin, but I close my mouth. We both know there's been no storm, that the beach will be empty.

"I'll wait," my mother says. She bends under the lintel, closes the door once more to wait in the fish-smelling dark. I walk away to do her bidding.

OUR ISLAND IS shrinking.

When I was little, it held entire kingdoms, connected by tuft-buckled paths. Tall cliffs rimmed by seaweed.

Heathers and bogs. Cauldrons where the sea churned in, licking the stone hollow. But for every winter, the paths seem to shorten. The cliffs sink under my feet until they are weary rocks, no good for keeping anyone sheltered. My mother tells me this is also my doing. 'You grow too fast,' she says, and not in the gentle way I've heard spoken, mother to daughter, in Griptown.

I take the north path. It winds up from the shallow bowl where our house crouches, scales the cliff, skirts the edge like a scar, brings me over the tallest point of the island. The ocean unfolds, choppy and muddled, until gray clouds swallow it beyond the kelp woods. The beach is a dark lip at the foot of the drop. It is not tangled with driftwood. It is not empty.

The sky and sea are dull, but specks of light lie scattered in the sand, as if yesterday's reflected sun has washed up on shore. I make my way down to the beach and pick up one of the shining objects. This might be driftwood after all, maybe ebony. Except it has been carved to look like a feather. It is knife-narrow with silky fronds divided along the shaft, black, but so fine the edges show gray, so polished they gleam. Or could it be a real feather, encased in some mysterious glass? Or even magic?

I put it to my tongue. The salt cuts me.

I set my basket down and walk around the beach, gathering up the treasure. There are three feathers, none alike, and when I run my finger along them, my skin prickles. I feel restless with wonder. I need to know what they are and how they came to be. Did someone carve them for love, only to set them adrift? Were they an offering to a nameless god? Or maybe a flock of wooden birds waged war above the kelp woods, shedding feathers as they fought and died?

I fold the feathers in my apron and run back up the hill. My mother must be told.

Outside the smoke hut, I stop, overtaken by misgivings. It is a fish-gutting day, and I left my basket on the beach. What if the dark mood takes her? What if she decides to punish me and burn the feathers? I try to think what I will say, how I should present the gift of the ocean and make her wonder, too. But before I have shuffled my words, the door opens, and my mother is there. She takes in my face, which is probably flushed from running, lowers her gaze to my apron. She frowns. I show her.

No words are needed after all. As soon as she sees the feathers, her eyes glaze over. She darts forward and tugs the edges of my apron out of my hands. The feathers spill onto the path as the tears spill down her cheeks. I feel dizzy. I have seen her cold and angry, wild and angry, sad and still, small and brooding. But never crying.

"We could burn them," I say, my voice pulling up into a question.

She shakes her head and I know better than to ask. The meaning of the feathers is hidden from me. But not from my mother.

Her steps are like stabs when she walks past me and heads for the house. A snap sounds under her boot. "Fetch your coat and gloves. We are going to town."

On the path behind her, one of the feathers lies broken in half.

MOTHER SITS AT the bow with her back turned to me.

I don't know why. The strait is wide, so we always take turns at the oars, to let our shoulders and arms rest. The one who is resting always sits at the stern, so we can switch places in the boat without jostling one another.

When I was too little to row, we would only make the trip twice a year, for the late summer fair and at the end of the cod season. For days after, my mother would grimace and rub her neck, and we would stay in the inn for two nights before going back. I remember the first time she let me help, how important I felt, how grim she looked.

I put on the gloves, which are soft leather and cost a fortune. But we need them for this trip. I dig the oars into the water. The island fades slowly, white-flecked rock blending with the bleak tufts, while the briny smell of shore clears up into salt and wind. To begin with, rowing feels pleasant. I like how the blades carve into the heavy water, how the sea pushes back to match the strength of my pull. It feels like speaking with a friend, a friend I am forbidden to meet.

I cannot swim. Water is a border I have only crossed twice and never truly. Yes, I've dropped my hand over the gunwale when my mother rows, letting the wake slip over my skin. I've stood where the tide floods the beach, and with each wave sunk a little further into the black sand. I've bathed in the brackish pools, too, cut my knees because I tried to float. But swim I cannot. My mother won't let me.

My first memory is her holding me too tightly, digging her fingers so deep into my sandy hair it hurt. I must have gone into the water, though I don't remember that part. Then, when I was seven, I wanted to fish for crabs and fell off the quay. The ladder was right there, so I climbed up and dried my clothes in the sun before I went back to the house. I thought she hadn't seen. I thought she had been mending nets by the boathouse all afternoon. But she knew.

Afterward, she must have felt bad, or at least felt the need to explain, because she told me this is how it is for all island children. You learn to fear the sea, or you die. Which might be true. I've never met any other island children.

My shoulders grow sour and my arms sloppy. Each time the blade cuts the surface wrong, the oar twists in my hand. Even with the gloves, my palms chafe. We have long since passed the shallows where we always make the first switch. I look over my shoulder, but Mother hasn't stirred. She sits half-twisted, facing the mainland as I face the sea. She is holding the mirror up, watching me in the glass, her eyes sharp as if daring me to complain.

I do complain, but not until we have passed the second switch mark and my arms ache so I can't swallow the lump in my throat. We are still only halfway across the strait.

"Mother," I say, and it comes out whiny. "I think my hands are blistering. Can you—"

"No. You need to learn."

The words are hard, but her voice isn't. It's more pitiful, like mine.

"Why?"

I don't mean why I need to be able to row to the mainland alone. I understand that. Mother could get sick, or have an accident, and then what would I do? What I mean is why now, when it's not necessary? Why are we going into town with no fish to sell? And why is she sitting with her back turned, looking at me through the mirror?

I've thought about breaking that mirror.

She bought it in Griptown when I was little. I remember the peddler, with his big mustache and gold tattoos, his carmine coat, and jingling boots. Not a peddler, a shadow witch, some people said, and drew the ward mark across their chest.

My mother held me back when I wanted to see what the fuss was about. But in the evening, alone and locked inside our room in the loft of the fisherman's inn, I pressed my eye to a crack in the floor and saw my mother in the booth below, sitting with the carmine man. I saw her put her hand on his sleeve, saw her whisper in his ear and press a coin into his palm. She got nothing in return that I could see, not then. But the next summer, when we rowed home across the strait, the mirror was there in her bag, and the pouch of coin we usually bring home from the fair was not.

And the carmine man had been there, though I never saw them together.

I've never looked in the mirror. It's not very good. The surface is scratched, the glass buckled and yellow. It bends lines and pulls at shapes, twisting things ugly. When my mother looks at me over her shoulder, her forehead stretches, her nose bloats. I don't understand how she can bear staring at herself in that thing, all through every dark mood and every storm. But that's not why I don't look. I'm too afraid.

"You need to learn," she repeats. "In case you need to row back again."

She makes me row the entire way.

THERE IS WEATHER brewing, I can tell.

Everyone can see a storm hit, right before it does. But I live on a bare rock in the sea. I can read more than clouds and whitecaps. Sometimes it's a silvering in the seam between water and air, sometimes a flock of too-scattered birds, or a hum at the back of my head. This time it's a small, gray rent in the sky near the horizon as if the above is pouring into the below through a hole. And we are out here, two souls in nothing more than an empty shell, easily tipped over.

I point it out to Mother, and in the mirror, I see the whites of her eyes grow full. But she says nothing, not until the sky is too dark to show the rent anymore and the sea flattens out under the hull. It's the breakwaters. They reach out to enclose us like arms, sheltering us at the last moment. The lights of Griptown flicker across Mother's back.

"Tie the boat," she says as we thud into the pier. "We leave in the morning."

WE DON'T LEAVE in the morning.

It's not possible. The storm still bears down on Grip, rattling the timbers of the Draug, making the windowpanes in our small room bulge. There is still daylight outside, a murky kind that loses against the rain. The harbor is crowded with ships seeking shelter from the weather, but I can't see their masts. I can't even see the buildings across the street. There are no people out.

Except Mother. She slipped out the door at first light and told me to stay in the room. I have done as she said, though there is no food and the smell of soup that wafts up from the taproom downstairs hurts worse than the blisters in my palms. If Mother intends to make me row back when the storm lifts, I have a secret plan to refuse. We know that I can do it now. There is nothing more to prove.

Her bag sits on the bed. I haven't touched it, but now it occurs to me that maybe she has brought food. I open the lid. There is no food. But she has brought her lace blouse and beaded shawl, her small stack of letters. The money pouch is there, fat and full, and the mirror, wrapped in its oilcloth sheath. She wouldn't even let me pack an extra shirt for the trip home. There wasn't time, she said. Yet she has brought all the treasure she kept in the casket under her bed. Is she planning to leave me? Is that why I need to be able to cross the strait? So I can go home alone?

But she couldn't have gone anywhere, not in this. Hail pelts the panes now, builds at the sill like piles of milk teeth swimming in water. I can't see the ocean, but the ocean has come to me. I'm glad. I don't like being away from the water. Even climbing too far up the mountainside makes me restless and dizzy. My mother says it's because I'm an island child. But I'm not a child anymore.

I stretch out on the floor. It is old and creaky, full of gaps where the wood has turned. Voices stream up from the taproom. Men mostly, who were out drinking and got caught in the weather. There is no dancing, only gloomy conversations about the violence of the storm, how late and sudden it is, and how the ships in the harbor will be late sailing east for the herring.

For a brief while, the world outside is trapped in here with me, and I want to savor it. I press my face to the planks. They smell like smoke and salt, worn soft by many boots. Dirty, but I don't care. I like how the floor punishes my body, how it erases my breasts, how it doesn't care who I am or that I am a woman now. Through a crack, I peer into the room below.

I see the innkeeper, busy at the bar. When I was little, he was one of my favorite people. My mother used to pay him a coin to let me stay in the taproom while she went gathering. I loved it. I was supposed to stay in a booth, but I trailed him everywhere, to the kitchen, out back to throw out the slop or feed the chicken.

One day, my mother was late getting back, and I was getting weepy. So the innkeeper gave me a piece of candy. I sighed and dangled my legs from the barstool, all melty with happiness that this man, who laughed so much more than my mother, treated me so nicely.

"I wish you were my father," I told him. I remember the glint that came into his eyes, but I didn't understand what it meant then.

"Where *is* your father?" he asked. "Maybe I can give him the rest of this." He shook the candy, which rattled in its paper bag. "The two of you could share it."

"Oh, no," I said. "My father isn't here. Anyway, I don't think he has teeth."

The innkeeper spit into a glass and began polishing it with a rag. "No teeth! He must be a very old man."

I shook my head. "Not old! Or a man, anymore." I leaned forward and whispered across the bar. "He's a secret. And magical. And he can *fly*."

The innkeeper laughed but didn't look at me, and it was from this not-looking I knew I had made a mistake. My whispers weren't quiet enough. I glanced around and found a roomful of eyes on me. To my horror, my mother's were among them. She had come down from the mountain just in time to witness my betrayal. Dark of face, she yanked me off the stool and dragged me upstairs. The next time we came to town, I stayed in our room.

I thought it was unfair then, but not anymore. There are some things you can't talk about in town. People want to learn your secrets, but they're scared of them, too. And when the innkeeper spits in the glasses, it's not just to clean them.

It's a warding.

Being trapped in a storm is thirsty work. The innkeeper pours and hands out beers, greedy fingers reach out to grab them, gold and foam puddle on the bar. One of the drinkers wears a knitted sweater that has frayed at the sleeve, and his hand is speckled with black smudges. He is only there long enough to pay and take his drink, but it's enough. My belly somersaults. I crawl over to the other cracks in the floor, searching. Then, in the booth where my mother once sat with the carmine man, I find him.

The boy is here, right below me, drawing. He must have arrived last night after we took our supper upstairs, but before the storm got bad. Which means that this entire day, there has been nothing between us but air, a few dirty planks, and my mother's words.

For a while, I'm content watching.

The boy sits alone. He leaves his beer untouched, speaks to no one, but he glances around now and again. The way he leans over the table, I can't make out what he's drawing, but I see the edge of his sketchbook and the tip of his straggly, old feather pen. He makes it dance with elegant strokes and careful sweeps. I long to touch the hair that curls at his ears. But it's not until he leans back in frustration that I realize what I must do.

My mother has brought her treasure. But so have I.

*   *   *

The din of the room falters as I enter. I don't let their narrowed eyes stop me. If I stop, I might lose heart and turn around. So I make myself a wave that is carried across a beach, all the way to his table.

The boy is the last to look up. Unlike my mother's, his expressions are easy to read. They move from surprise to confusion, to uncertainty. But before all that I see a spark of startled joy, which is what I had imagined during my breathless rush down the stairs. The spark catches in my chest. I have never walked up to him before. I have never spoken to him before. I am thudding with courage as I hold my hand out.

"Here," I say, which is not what I had imagined, but it will have to do. My gift speaks for itself, better than I ever could. I see his thoughts shift again, like fresh water pouring into a current. He lifts his brows, a question.

"I saw your pen was broken," is my answer.

If he wonders how I could have seen the pen splinter, it doesn't show. He takes the wooden feather from my hand, holds it up against the lantern. The light tints the edges orange, reflects in his eyes. Orange and alive. I add it to my list, for the next time I'm standing alone on the island, watching the distant lights of town. The thudding in my chest becomes violent.

"You could sharpen the tip," I say as if this is a necessary thing to point out.

He nods as if I've told him something useful. "Did you make this?"

It was a gift, I think, but I don't say it. "I found it. I think it's ebony."

"Then you should keep it. It's too fine for me." He tries to hand the feather back, but I ignore it and sit down opposite him.

"You should finish the drawing."

We both look at the open sketch book between us. The pages are wet with ink, a looming wall of black, a giant wave topped with froth and wind. At the heart of it, soon to be swallowed by the wave, there is a space of white, shaped by the darkness into the form of a soaring seagull.

I wonder if the boy, too, recognizes that this means something, that his breaking the pen means something, that me seeing the drawing from above carries significance. It is why I came downstairs, the source of my courage. The seagull is supposed to be me.

He smiles.

"They like to play in the wind," he says.

"Not this wind," I say, and a gust slams hard against the window. I smile, too.

Yes, he must see it, that the storm is playing along, making us the creatures riding the updraft. I consider telling him that he is wrong, that seagull isn't the bird for me. Against a wall of black, I would be invisible. But how could I tell him? Cormorants aren't welcome birds. They are harbingers of death, come to let you say goodbye. And I don't want to stand alone in the sand anymore.

"No, not even seagulls go out in this," he says, "only madmen would do that."

I feel my smile stale. The weather is brutal, not safe for man or beast, mad or sane would make no difference. But still my mother is out there. Where is she? What is she doing? I don't want to think about her, but now she is as good as sitting next to me in the booth, pale and reproachful. What would she say if she knew I had brought one of the feathers? That I have carried it across the strait inside my blouse, feeling its sharpness against my skin, feeding it my warmth? I can't help glancing over my shoulder at the door.

The boy looks at the door, too, then at the feather. His eyes turn black. "Is this hers?"

I frown. "No," I say. "I told you. I found it."

But he leans back, and I lean back, too. I want the orange light to return, but I can tell my mother has put it out. For the first time since he looked up, he turns and considers the room. The Griptowners have returned to their steaming bowls, and the rasp of beer voices fills the inn once more. But I have grown up with their hidden stares. They are watching us now.

"Have you ever thought of leaving the island?" He speaks quickly, quietly.

I say nothing. I have thought about leaving the island since I was old enough to remember. I have longed to live here, in town, with people, shops selling fresh cakes, and cats that curl their tails around my legs. With grass that is soft to lie down on. With him.

But leaving the island means leaving my mother. He knows that, because he says, "It is one thing to live out there by choice. Another to be held captive."

I shake my head. I'm not held captive. Am I? I think of my mother rowing back to the island, her face smooth and still. Of her gutting fish. Of her digging her fingers into my sandy hair, of her whispering over and over, 'Not yet, not yet, not yet.'

"I don't care what the others think," he says, softly now. "They can spit all they want. You're not like her. You should leave." He reaches out and places his hand over mine.

Another memory floats up in my mind, where I scream

at her. 'Why do we have to stay here? Why can't we live in town like other people?' I can't remember her reply, only her sadness as she gathered me in and let me rest my head in her lap. As if there was nothing to be done. As if this was not her choice. But if it's not her choice, then whose is it?

I look into his eyes and though they are green now, green and promising, he is right. I'm not like her, and I'm not like him, or any of them. His hand still covers mine, but I feel him float away from me, like a piece of driftwood that was never mine to keep. I don't have time to explain, because before I can pull my hand back, there is a loud bang, and my mother stands in the doorway.

Her fists are scratched, her coat torn. The storm cracks a bolt of lightning behind her, and I hear someone mutter the prayer of warding. But it's her expression that scares me. She looks utterly lost. When she sees me, she stumbles toward me, seemingly without noticing that I am leaning across a table with the boy, that he is holding my hand.

That there is a black feather between us.

She clutches the fabric of my shirt. The wind has ripped her hair into rags that bleed water down her shoulders. She doesn't speak, but there is so much anguish in her face that she might as well be screaming. I let go of the boy's hand and rise quickly.

"Mother, you need to dry off," I say, and she allows me to steer her across the floor.

I don't look back, but around the tables we pass, people are spitting in their mugs. I feel his eyes on my back. I left the feather on the table, like a beautiful piece of wreckage. It's his gift now.

In our room, things are worse. She sags to her knees. I

help her out of her coat, but she is soaked through. Her skirt is a cold bog that tries to suck her in.

I squat down before her, help her unbutton her shirt. "Where were you?"

Her head hangs down. "They won't sail. None of them. I begged them to take us, but they won't leave. Not for any heap of money." She throws her arms around me and weeps.

WE EAT OUR supper upstairs. The soup is thick and creamy, salty with fish and sweet with carrots. There is fresh bread that steams against the candlelight when we break it. Mother has hung her wet clothes to dry by the black stove. Her tears are already dried, her calmness in place. She doesn't ask about the boy, and she doesn't speak of the feather. This is her way of proposing a truce, but I can't abide by it. I have too many questions.

"Mother," I say. She must have been waiting because her spoon settles into her bowl. "What is the pact?"

"It's not a pact. That would require both parties to agree, and I never agreed to anything. I was just told." She gives a small shake of her head. "It's more of a postponement, granted out of pity. Or love. Or what passes for such where he comes from."

It's been years since she answered my questions like this, all reasonable and calm. I try to keep my voice calm, too. "You mean my father."

She reaches out and cradles my cheeks. "We only ever borrow, my child. Only for a brief while and then it is gone. The only difference is that I have known all along that the day would come."

"For what?"

She lets me go. Her hands settle in her lap, white and still against the black of her skirt. She looks so tired. "For me to give it back."

I don't understand. If the fish we caught is the pact, and the driftwood is the pact, how can we give it back? It's all gone. Eaten, sold, burned. Apart from the contents of her bag, we have nothing of value.

"Mother, give what back?"

She turns away from me, toward the window. "Everything."

Her eyes close, and I think that we are done. But then she smiles. "I always knew running would be no good. But there is one thing left to try."

She won't say more. Not why we need to leave, not what she is going to try. Not what it is that we have borrowed and must give back. Whatever she says, it can't be everything. No one owes someone everything.

I don't ask again.

When I climb into bed, she sits next to me and strokes my hair, as she used to when I was little. The storm still howls outside, but I don't mind. I feel safe and drowsy. She watches me as I fall asleep. Not once this evening has she brought out the mirror.

At the edge of a dream, I hear her say, "I will buy a choice."

When I wake, the room is silent. The storm has given in. In its place, snow falls silently, white against the gray clouds. My mother is gone.

I suffer a moment of panic until I realize her coat is still draped over the chair by the stove, and her bag sits next to her bed. I open it. The money pouch is there and the letters. But her beaded shawl and lace blouse are not, nor is the mirror.

I dress quickly and run downstairs. My mother is not there. The taproom is nearly empty. The boy is gone, and so are the men who were trapped here with him, released home to their wives and beds. I don't see the feather anywhere.

The innkeeper is behind the bar, cleaning up last night's mess. His eyes slipped off me when I entered the room, but when I walk up to the counter, he says, "There are no eggs yet, but I can make you oatmeal."

"Where is my mother?"

There it is, that same glint I saw when he gave me candy and asked about my father. I can read it now, though. Disgust swirled with greed. "She went out right before the storm died down," he says. "But she wasn't dressed for it, so she won't have gone far. She's not out back?"

That must be it. I hurry outside. Maybe she's feeling poorly? Though it beats me why she would dress in her finest for that.

Out back there is no one. The yard is an unrumpled blanket of white. I rush to the front of the inn, look up and down the street. Griptown is sleeping in after the storm. Smoke rises from the bakery chimney, but no one is out yet. The street is as pristine as the rooftops.

The snow has erased any sign my mother may have left behind. But I know her, know what she does after a big storm, and the innkeeper is right. She won't have gone far.

I run down to the docks. There is no wind, but the sea is still in turmoil. Old waves roil under the skirts of the dock, jostling the ships that lie at anchor like chained giants. The pier is a finger of white that sticks out in the pewter gray. I walk out on it. Our boat is still there. My mother is not.

I allow myself hope. There are many places she could have gone. Up into the mountains, maybe, to search for winter moss. Or she might have persuaded the bakery to let her in early, to buy us fresh buns. Or she could have gone to see the captains again, to try and book a passage now that the weather has let up. But then I see a glimmer of glass at my feet.

I bend down and brush snow off the mirror. It distorts my fingers into claws. My mother must have stood here, shivering in her thin blouse. I can almost hear the beads on her shawl click and rattle as she lifts her arm to look in the mirror. And then what?

I look over the edge of the pier. The water is shrouded by snowflakes that disappear as soon as they touch the surface, white flecks going under. Even so, I think I would have seen the beads of her shawl down there. I do not. But the mirror is a shard in my hope. She would never have cast it aside like this. She called it her window to truth.

I pick it up and hold it at an angle. I'm afraid to look in it.

But my mother is gone, and this is the only clue she left behind. If I am to find her, I need to know what she saw in there. I'm not certain that the carmine man was a shadow witch. He could have sold her nothing more than a framed piece of old glass, one that holds no danger. And if not? Glass can be broken. I tell myself whatever I see can be ignored, if not forgotten. I tell myself that truth is not always set.

I look in the mirror.

* * *

I AM NOT sure what I expected. That I would see a monster? That the carmine man would catch my soul and bind me?

There is no binding that I can sense. I see myself. The glass warps my eyes, making them big and terrified. The scratches tear my skin. The brassy color adds a strange silver tint to my irises. But it is me. Only me.

I didn't think my expressions were so easy to read. Fear, replaced by relief and shame. But between those, a glint of disappointment.

The mirror captures the edge of Griptown, obscured by the thickening snow. The string of lights which I have longed for isn't lit. The houses feel remote and dead, as distant as they have always been. I can't see the farm where the boy lives. I don't care.

I turn around and look over my shoulder at the sea.

It is the same, restless and unmovable. Yet something has changed.

By the right breakwater, there is an iron pole that marks a rock under the surface. Now a creature has settled on the tip of the pole. Through the snow, I try to will the shape into my mother, legs pulled up, arms reaching, but of course, it's not her. It's a cormorant, resting after the storm. A harbinger of death, come to let me say goodbye.

I call out my mother's name. The snowflakes cut my voice into pieces that are too small to carry. The bird takes flight and turns seaward, disappearing into the snow.

There is a rumble under the pier, and I look over the side as a wave breaks over our boat, drenching the snow that has been gathering there. There is a feather in the bottom. It dances around, clacking against the frame, wood against wood. I stare at it. I can't tell if it's the one I gave the boy or a different one.

I climb into the boat. The feather is unsharpened and not his, I think. My mother must have brought the third feather from the island, then left it here. Did she leave it as a sign? Does she mean for me to follow? Is that why she tested my rowing? My mother's riddles are as inscrutable as ever. I should have asked more. Not been so afraid of her dark mood. Not been so afraid of the answers.

But this I can guess: She must be out there somewhere.

I set the feather beside me on the thwart, untie the knot and push out. The waves try to beat me back, but I sink the oars into the water and bend its force to my will. *Help me*, I think. *Help me find her.*

As I row, I work through the sequence of events since the fish-gutting. The wood that didn't burn. The feathers on the beach. The storm that chased us ashore. The storm that died down when my mother disappeared. 'I will buy a choice,' she said. But what sort of choice?

Her fingers in my hair, her words like heartbeats. 'Not yet, not yet, not yet.'

It's snowing harder. The town fades away, then the great beast of ships. I pass the empty pole, a bleared cross in the thickening snow. I keep rowing. The sea grows quiet. The swells are still powerful, but they have nothing against which to break. I hear only the oars cutting the water, the drops raining down from the blades, the groans of the rowlocks, my breath. And with every pull of the oars, a question.

Where did she go? Why did she leave? Is this the pact? That she must abandon me?

The mirror lies facing up in my lap. I imagine I catch a glimpse of something dark in there, but when I look around, there is nothing but the next wave and the previous, the falling snow and the close sky.

I row until my palms bleed. They're so cold I don't feel the pain. I don't know how far I have come or where I am going. Maybe my soul is caught after all, in an empty pocket of gray winter.

I look in the mirror. I am too pale and too red in the wrong places. Snow crusts on my lashes and in my brows. My tears leave warm streaks that turn bitter.

With the other hand, I pick up the feather. I can't feel the details in the wood, or the smoothness of the grain. I think of my mother's face when I brought them.

'Not yet, not yet, not yet.'

Not yet what? I see her struggling out on the pier, dressed in her prettiest clothes, armed with the mirror and nothing else. To try one last thing. To buy a choice.

Perhaps the mirror finally shows me the truth, because suddenly the riddle unravels in my head. The choice is not for her. It's for me. The pact is not that she must leave, but that I must. The thing that she must try was to offer herself in my place.

The thought sluices through me, cold and terrifying: Then she is gone. Truly gone. No more fish-gutting days, no more mending of nets. No more secret spice blends or fingers that bury themselves in my hair. No one who tells me what to do. No one who loves me, only me, without pause or reason. Even if it's only for a while. Even if she knows she must give me up.

I am alone.

I hear a rush of wind behind me, followed by the sound of soft dripping against wood, and I am not alone anymore. Someone is there, behind my back. My chest thuds. I am too afraid to turn around. My hands shake as I lift the mirror over my shoulder and let it look for me.

A cormorant perches on the bow, black and slick with water.

Its neck is elegant and curved, its beak a startling yellow. The drops patter, the boat creaks, the snow whispers. I whisper, too.

"Did you take her?"

It cocks its head and watches my mirror-face with beady eyes. Is there something familiar in the tilt of that neck? In the eloquent silence? Or do I just feel kinship with this bird because we are both bound by words to loneliness? That girl living out on the rock, she's always got her face to the wind, her mind to the sea.

"Are you my father?"

The cormorant unfolds its wings slowly, holding them out to dry. They shimmer, long and smooth like silk. They are more beautiful than any drawing or piece of polished ebony, but they are not perfect. There are three gaps in the plumage.

There are answers in these gaps, I see that. I brought my mother three black feathers from the beach, and she rushed me away from the island, away from the sea. Why, is a question of what I choose to believe. Whether the feathers are driftwood or a message. Whether I am lost or called home. Whether I can turn and go back to Grip or if my mother bought me nothing but loss.

I put the mirror down and turn to face the cormorant.

"Have you come to take me?"

The cormorant looks at the feather in my hand. I hold it out. The yellow beak darts forward, takes it. Then the bird gathers its wings, dives into the deep and is gone.

For a moment I stay in this position, arm stretched out, palm open, left behind.

Unmoored and unbound.

I stand up. I have never learned to swim. But I feel it rising in me: the black cuttle of unseen depths, the thinning mists above the banks. Swim I cannot, but I am half like him. I am certain that if I will it so, I could fly.

I climb up on the thwart. The snow has let up. The ocean unfolds around me, dark like silver, gray like pearls. I see the horizon, but no island and no shore. In this kingdom, there is only sea.

Now I feel it, the wave rising, rocking the boat, tilting the world.

I spread my wings and choose.

Dedication: For my sweet, kind mother, a goodbye.

THE DAY JONAS SHADOWED HIS DAD

Thore Hansen
Translated by Olivia Lasky

HIS NAME WAS Jonas and he'd become what you would call 'grown up', but that happened not that long ago and he didn't think it was anything to get all worked up over. He felt like most of the adults he knew were distant, somehow. He had the same feeling about his father as well.

When his father came home from work, he'd almost always fall asleep in front of the TV after dinner. He'd sleep there until it was time to go to bed, so nothing ever really happened at home.

That was fine with Jonas. It had been like that since he was a child so he didn't know any other life, even though he'd noticed that some fathers were more cheerful than others.

He didn't remember his mother; she died just a few weeks after he was born. A yellowed photograph on his father's nightstand showed a smiling woman. He could see that she'd been incredibly beautiful.

Now, it was just the two of them in the old house that

his father's grandparents built a long time ago, back when the city was smaller and everyone knew each other.

His father left the house to go to work every morning at precisely a quarter past eight. Jonas didn't have a clue what kind of work his father did. He received only vague answers when he asked, so he stopped asking.

His father almost always dressed the same way: a worn-out jacket that used to be brown, shoes that were almost just as worse for wear, and a little leather satchel he'd inherited from his father. His father kept his lunchbox in the satchel. It was the same lunchbox he'd had when he went to school. There was a faded colour print of *The Lone Ranger and Tonto* on the lid. Probably his father's favourite book as a child. Written by Fran Striker, if Jonas wasn't mistaken. Inside the lunchbox, he had two slices of bread with goat cheese and one with liver paté and pickles. He had the same meal every day. When it rained, he wore a hat. The hat had also seen better days.

Some evenings, his father came home with grass stains on his knees and leaves in his hair. *You don't get those in an office,* Jonas thought. But he didn't ask. His father clearly didn't want to talk about it. Jonas felt that he had the most subdued and secretive father in the world.

IT WAS A grey Tuesday in autumn when Jonas decided he would find out what his father actually did. He followed him when he left the house in the morning, but at a distance, so his father wouldn't notice.

Jonas kept close to the walls, ready to hide if his father turned around. He didn't. He walked calmly towards the centre of town, greeting acquaintances now and then, but he didn't speak to them. He just tipped his worn-out hat and nodded politely. Jonas saw that some of the people his father greeted stared at him after he'd passed by. Some of them exchanged whispers, but Jonas didn't hear what they said; he just understood that they considered his father odd. Clearly, he wasn't alone in having some questions about his father.

Suddenly, his father stepped off the sidewalk, ducking into a narrow alley with tall houses on either side. There wasn't a single person to be seen, just bleak facades with windows without any flowers or curtains. It looked like the buildings had been abandoned long ago.

The street wasn't long. It opened onto a plain where a couple of cows stared at him with wide eyes and chomping jaws. The forest behind the plain was tall and dense, and Jonas watched as his father moved in between the trees. He was walking with the same determined steps as before, but Jonas thought it seemed like he was swinging his satchel a touch more cheerfully now.

This was getting stranger and stranger. Jonas knew the forest was immense and that it had very few structures, and definitely no offices. What did his father have to do there?

His father disappeared between the trees. The treetops cast long shadows. It had been raining most of the night, so his father's footprints were clearly visible on the damp forest floor.

It was almost completely hidden between the thick bushes and tree trunks, but Jonas spotted a small house. It didn't have any windows, and the unpainted walls practically blended in with the surroundings. The roof was almost completely covered in birds. They sat in silence, their heads tilted. The door was ajar and Jonas saw his father's footprints out in front. He hesitated, then pushed the door open. Inside, a steep staircase led straight down into the ground. It was like a black hole. Jonas still saw nothing of his father but could hear his footsteps on the stairs beneath him. They grew weaker and weaker until stopping entirely and all Jonas could hear was the sound of his own steps.

Jonas considered shouting for him for a moment but didn't. Somewhere down in the dark, his father had a secret—Jonas was quite sure of that. No one had an office deep down in the ground in the middle of the forest. Why hadn't he told him about it? Did his father have a secret he didn't want to tell anyone else? Not even his own son?

The steep staircase ended in a narrow tunnel carved into the bedrock, weakly lit by small torches. The smooth stone glittered with shades of brown and red. There were a few places where he saw winding yellow stripes and strange figures. Jonas thought they resembled some kind of written language. Perhaps stories and thoughts no one could even remember anymore...

He spotted something far away toward what he thought was the end of the tunnel—a light that looked like sparkling sunshine.

Strange, Jonas thought. Only a few minutes ago, he'd been surrounded by a cloudy autumn day. Now he smelled the scent of deciduous trees—a scent that didn't belong in the autumn landscape he'd just come from.

Shortly after, he heard birdsong and cries he didn't recognise. Animals, he suspected.

Then he was out of the tunnel.

Jonas looked around in confusion. He couldn't believe his own eyes. He was surrounded by tall grass and iridescent green ferns that reached all the way up to his chest. In the distance, he caught the sight of a tall, dark forest. The sky was cloudless above the treetops, and he felt the sun's rays stinging his face. The air was warmer than it should be at this time of year.

He kept looking around, not entirely understanding what had happened. Everything seemed like it belonged in a dream, far away from his reality.

"Dad!" he shouted… but he didn't get any answer. The birdsong stopped for a moment before the treetops were again filled with twittering and flapping wings.

To his surprise, he discovered his father's clothes, folded over a tree branch. His shoes were placed neatly at the base of the tree along with the worn-out satchel. Jonas felt concern rising in his chest. What had happened to his father? All kinds of thoughts started to pop up, but none seemed plausible.

He kept shouting for his father, again and again, but the only sounds he heard were the birds and a light breeze rustling through the trees.

There! Tracks from bare feet, in the damp earth between the ferns. The footprints continued into the forest, between the tall trees with thick crowns.

They must be my father's, Jonas thought. He trudged ahead through the lush green with his head bowed, eyes fixed on the footprints, passing ancient trees, walking where probably few people had ever set foot. The foliage rustled around him, and now and then he caught sight of animal eyes, but he felt strangely safe.

The tracks disappeared occasionally, but he always found them again. He was almost certain that it was his father he was trailing. The steps were short, just like his father's.

Jonas didn't know how long he had been tracking them.

He stopped and shouted for his father now and then, but still, there was no response besides the sounds of the forest. Once, there was something that growled from somewhere nearby—a terrible growl he assumed must have come from a big animal. Terrified, he was searching for a tree he could climb up when he suddenly heard:

"There you are!"

It was his father's voice. He was standing beneath a colossal fern, smiling and dressed in nothing more than his short blue boxers. He was holding a spear in one hand. Jonas stared at him, his mouth agape, unable to utter a single word. He couldn't grasp that this was the quiet, serious man you could set your watch by and who never did anything surprising. The man who fell asleep in front of the television every night, even when there was something exciting on.

This father seemed like he belonged in the forest. He looked different from the serious man who went to an office every day.

His father kept smiling at him.

"But Dad," Jonas said. "What is happening? What is this? We're deep underground... and you're walking around in nothing but your underwear."

"It's a bit difficult to explain," his father replied, "so it'll take some time, but I'm going to give it a shot. Whatever I don't know or can't quite explain, we'll figure out together. Deal?"

Jonas nodded. He was still confused, his mind was racing and refusing to settle down.

They continued walking deeper into the forest—a forest without paths and where the enormous treetops blocked out most of the sunlight, creating shadows in shades of brown and green. His father said he didn't recognise this place, and yet he never seemed to be in doubt of which direction to go.

He walked in front with the short spear over his neck and his forearms resting on the shaft. From time to time, he turned around to make sure Jonas was still behind him. He was still smiling broadly and looked like a father Jonas had never known.

At dusk, they set up camp by a small pond.

"We can sleep here," his father said. "We won't make it back home to our own beds. That probably won't happen for a while. I hope you don't have anything against sleeping beneath an open sky?"

"That's fine," Jonas replied. "I assumed we'd be doing that."

He moved a few pinecones before lying on his back in the tall grass. The birds had quieted down, but in the dark, he could hear other sounds he guessed were coming from padding paws.

A half-moon reflected in the glassy, blue-green surface of the pond, creating something that looked almost like writing.

His father fell asleep almost immediately. He snored quietly like he always did, but Jonas stayed awake for a long time. He stared up at the starry sky that he could just make out beyond the dark treetops. The stars glittered more than he was used to in his own world. He could hear that the night's hunt had begun in the trees, and a fish occasionally breached the surface of the pond. Then, he finally drifted off to sleep—a restless sleep. Time and again, he forced his body into a better position on the hard ground.

* * *

THEY WALKED THROUGH the forest without trails for days.

"Where are we actually going?" Jonas asked when they stopped again for the night. "Isn't it about time you told me what we're doing here?"

"I'm not sure of the direction," his father murmured. "I just know that somewhere in here, there's another kind of world. A world where dreams can become reality. Doesn't that sound nice?"

"It sounds strange, at the very least. Where did you hear this?"

"I heard about this world many years ago. A sailor told me, someone I met when I was out at sea, long before I met your mother. He'd been searching for this wondrous place his whole life, but never found it, but he claimed he'd gotten close."

"And you believed him? Aren't sailors known for telling tall tales?"

"Some of them lie just like everyone else, but not all of them. He was an old man when he told me this story. He died only a few days after we spoke, but he claimed he'd gotten close."

"And you believe his story?"

"Time will tell if it's true. Anyhow, it doesn't hurt if we believe him for a while and look around a bit, does it? At the very least, we've ended up here, in an underground world. That's pretty weird, isn't it? I searched for years before I located the way down here, and I did that with help from many others besides this sailor. There have been others who have written about a hidden world. Stories that were written hundreds of years ago. When I finally found the way, I didn't dare tell anyone. They would've thought I was out of my mind if I said there was a world beneath our own. There are some things you should think about long and hard before telling anyone. Imagination can open doors, but we don't all share the same dreams and fantasies, so there are many doors that are closed to us."

"Are you sure you're going the right way now?"

"No," his father sighed. "It's quite possible I'm wrong. But either way, we've ended up somewhere not many people know about. We haven't seen a single person since we've been here. That's pretty exciting, isn't it?"

"Of course it is," Jonas said, moving closer to the fire.

The half-moon hung above him. An animal screeched somewhere in the dark before the screech was abruptly cut off.

THEY DIDN'T KNOW how long they had been walking through the endless forest, but his father thought it must have been over a week. Neither of them even considered turning and going back to the world they'd come from.

Then, one evening at sundown, they spotted a shadow moving just over the treetops. The wings resembled a bat's, only much, much bigger. Every time the massive wings moved, it sounded like the crack of a whip. They both realised what they were looking at, but it had been over 150 million years since this animal lived. Blood-red eyes stared down at them and they heard a scream neither of them had ever heard before.

"It's a flying reptile," Jonas whispered.

"Pterodactylus in Latin," his father said enthusiastically. "I've seen countless illustrations of them, but I never thought such a beast would fly right over my head. Now I'm positive we're heading towards something unusual. Exactly what I've been dreaming about for most of my life."

They only caught the one glimpse of the enormous animal, but the sight was enough to keep them awake for most of the night. They sat side by side, gazing at the sky, but saw only distant stars and a moon that had gotten a bit narrower.

The next day had more surprises in store. They suddenly happened upon a thin path covered in white sand. There were no signs of footprints, wheels, or hooves, just the occasional plant that had sprouted out of the fine sand. The path stretched almost perfectly straight from east to west. They stood there for a moment, perplexed, doubtful about which direction they should choose.

"Where do we go?" his father asked.

"No idea," Jonas replied. "Should we flip a coin? You've always said that most things are based on luck and circumstance. Should we say that heads is west?"

He pulled out a five-crown coin and flipped it. The coin showed tails, so they went east. They moved more carefully now. Both had the sense that anything could happen at any moment.

And it did. The path took an abrupt turn. They were now surrounded by tropical trees and breathed in the scent of thousands of flowers, many foreign to them.

Suddenly, something started moving in the treetops. It was a figure dressed in a leopard-skin loincloth. The man swung elegantly from tree to tree, a flock of colossal apes behind him.

"Is that…"

"It is." His father smiled. "That is, without a doubt, Tarzan, but I thought he would be bigger and stronger."

A moment later, Tarzan and the apes disappeared into the distant treetops.

The path sloped down toward a city that consisted of

buildings from many eras and styles. Some buildings were unfamiliar, with towers you couldn't see the end of. In every direction, they spotted figures that belonged in the imagination; immortal creatures that had captivated humans for hundreds of years. They recognised several from books and illustrations, but most were completely unknown.

The path widened out into a broad avenue with many side streets. It seemed like the street they were following was getting longer and longer with every step they took. All the while, they were met with smiles and cheerful greetings. Seven dwarves danced around them, asking if they'd seen Snow White. On one side street, they caught a glimpse of a man on a white horse. He wore a masked helmet and was dressed in a tight blue suit.

They stopped outside an inn, looked at each other quizzically, then hesitantly went inside. Eyes from all kinds of creatures studied them for a moment before continuing with whatever they'd been doing. They found an empty table with a narrow window overlooking the street. Outside, a gigantic sea serpent was creeping south, probably looking for the ocean. On a dark side street some distance away, a vampire awoke after having slept through the day.

Without asking, an enormous troll placed two foaming mugs of beer in front of them. The troll mumbled something they didn't understand before it went back to its place by the beer barrels.

"I think I could stay here for a while," Jonas grinned.

"Me too," his father said and raised his glass in greeting to the giant troll.

A LION ROARS IN LONGYEARBYEN

Margrét Helgadóttir

ELECTRICITY WAS RATIONED at night in Longyearbyen, yet a few lights blinked stubbornly over the empty streets. Automated trash collectors alternated from side to side. One of them paused, as if sensing the tall man's presence, then buzzed on, sucking up glittering confetti from the frozen ground.

The man lit a cigarette and tilted his head back, trying to discern the tops of the towering skyscrapers, but the buildings were engulfed in darkness. The city's residents were still in their beds, many sleeping off hangovers after the Third Light Parade. But even if they had been awake and peering out their windows, they still might not have seen him. Between his height and the huge rifle strapped to his back, you'd think he'd be fairly noticeable, but he was so calm, so unnaturally quiet, that he blended in with the shadows. Only the tiny swirl of smoke from his cigarette gave him away.

He'd been one of just a handful of passengers on the flight from Wainwright. Nearly empty planes were rarely permitted to take off nowadays, but on the last night before the holiday madness started, not even the airport staff in Danmarkshavn had bothered with questions when the plane landed to recharge.

With the massive Christmas Parade only a week away, he knew people would soon be flocking to Longyearbyen to see the spectacle, despite the recent steep rise in flight costs.

The city's light festival lasted all of December, with smaller parades every week. It was as if the inhabitants wanted to block out the winter darkness and use every opportunity to bring lights and noise and fun to the streets. But the grand finale—the Christmas Parade—was exceptional. Svalbard archipelago, a haven long known for its religious and cultural mix, welcomed new citizens from all over the world, and the Christmas Parade had thus evolved over the years into a synthesis of traditions from everywhere; no one would be surprised to see a man dressed up as an odd combination of Scandinavian barn gnome and scary goatlike Krampus standing with a Catholic priest or an imam on one of the floats.

The tall man gazed at the trash collectors wheezing past and sneered at the innocent cheerfulness of it all. The pulsating Arctic metropolis was—in his view—merely a puttering, provincial town.

He observed lights coming on high above, one by one, in the ocean of windows. The city was awakening. He tossed his cigarette on the frozen ground and twisted it under his boot a little.

The townspeople, he mused, had no idea how lucky they were that he was not here for them.

* * *

ON THE OTHER side of Longyearbyen, in a building at the mouth of the Advent Valley, Trym yelled at his alarm clock to make it stop. Unfortunately, it hadn't yet learned to recognize his groggy morning voice. Not even hurling a pillow was effective. Grumbling, he dragged himself out of bed, turned off the piercing noise, and then glanced out the window, a habit he'd formed over the past week.

In the summer season, he could see the tall mountains surrounding the valley. But on this December morning, he saw only lights from nearby windows and the little gathering of people waiting outside his building.

Narrowing his eyes, he studied them. They didn't hide their presence. On the contrary, several relaxed in camping chairs, chatting, lanterns at their feet. Now and then they'd glance up at his window, and one of them even waved to him.

"Vultures!" he muttered and yanked the curtains shut.

Seething, he pressed the small bird-shaped tattoo concealing the chip in his inner arm, activating Thelma. Instantly, the big screen stretched bright and colorful across his kitchen cabinets.

"Thelma," he commanded, "one triple espresso!"

The coffee machine whirred into action, and the rich scent of freshly ground beans filled the air. Trym plopped down onto a kitchen chair.

"Open the inbox!"

If you went by the flood of messages he currently received, not even counting the advertising junk, Trym had become a celebrity. Most were inquiries from journalists or letters from people he'd never met but who still felt like expressing their views. "Delete, next, delete, next, delete, next," he muttered.

Skimming through the news, he noticed that the Third Light Parade was the main topic, with lots of pictures and interviews with enthusiastic onlookers. Trym frowned. He'd never grasped the point of the whole December spectacle. The food was OK, but all those parades and costumes, not to mention the crowds—he just hated it.

Then, below all the merry news, the headlines he'd been looking for:

Still No Sign of Levi

Police Widen Search to All Basements

Governor Promises Levi Will Be Found Before Christmas

Fans Fear Levi Is Dead

The articles were accompanied by various pictures of Levi and, to Trym's shock, pictures of himself. Swearing, he told Thelma to switch to phone mode. Thelma's soft voice flowed into his ears: "Your voice mailbox is full. Your first message is from…"

Impatient, he listened to only a word or two of each notification before commanding, "Delete!" Only four messages caught his attention—one from his boss: "It's chaos here, Trym. Stay away until this is sorted." One from his co-worker Kaya Kunene, the zoo's public relations and communications manager (and—more importantly—his ex): "Good news! The film company has moved up the documentary's production. The crew is here working with me already, and they've hired a really esteemed director to attach to the project! We'll be famous! Call me!" One from his mother: "Why haven't you returned my calls? I'm your mother. It's Christmas, and you haven't even told me if you'll make the family brunch!" And one, received just minutes earlier, from an Ernst Douglas: "I know what you did. We need to talk."

He told Thelma to send noncommittal short replies to the first three and sat mulling over the last one. The man's voice was so cold, so sure. Unnerved, Trym listened to the message a couple of times but still had no clue: Who was Ernst Douglas?

He jumped when the doorbell rang. Then, with a loud beep, words popped up on the kitchen cabinets, a text message from Ernst Douglas: *Let me in. I'm at your door.*

In the corridor stood a tall stranger, slightly hunched, with the low-set brim of his hat hiding most of his face. Trym's eyes widened as he saw the rifle sticking up behind the man's neck, the muzzle covered in worn leather. The man stared back at him, a steely glint in his eyes. When he spoke, his voice was hoarse:

"Where's the lion?"

THEY SAY IMPORTANT things happen by coincidence. If the city hadn't been so distracted by the Second Light Parade, Longyearbyen Zoo would have been packed with the usual crowd. If the zoo hadn't been left on its own but for a couple of security guards with hangovers, someone would have noticed the vacant cages sooner. But as it was, no one had noticed the penguins were missing until a shop attendant stumbled across one in the freezer room at Nordlys Supermarket. Since the zookeepers were occupied with catching the squeaking birds, it went unnoticed that the lion Levi was missing until its keeper arrived with the cat's usual nighttime snack—raw factory lamb. By the time the alarm finally sounded and the zoo's manager called the governor, the animal had gained a head start of several hours.

You might find it strange that a missing creature could

create such a fuss in such a big city. But then you haven't comprehended the significance of either the zoo or the lion. The zoo animals, despite all having been created in laboratories—though not in the factories, mind you— were great entertainment. The zoo itself was an important social gathering spot on weekends. It had shops and cafeterias, even a roller coaster. The animals were the main attraction, of course, weird as they were with their fur and claws and many limbs. But the animals also tugged at the humans' souls, reminding them about the lost world, about things they knew only from pictures in ancient books.

And then there was Levi.

The zoo owned two male lions. That there were two was, in itself, sensational. The zoo's manager had never heard of any other zoo that possessed more than one.

And of the two, the older lion was one of a kind.

No one knew for certain where this lion had come from, except that it'd stayed for a short time in the Copenhagen Zoo and St. Petersburg Zoo. The mystery surrounding the big cat had resulted in countless myths about its origin. Though critics claimed that the tales were fabricated by Longyearbyen Zoo, many believed the lion was the real thing—born in the wild, some even asserted. Levi had a dedicated website and fan club, managed by Kaya, and people traveled to Longyearbyen solely to see it. The lion meant big business and money.

But for the people who visited every weekend, Levi's existence meant that the world had not completely fallen apart, that there was life where they'd thought there was only death.

Levi meant hope.

* * *

SVALBARD HAD BECOME a popular center in the Arctic Ocean after the Great Ice vanished. Then, as the world became increasingly uninhabitable, people sought out the Arctic for more than holidays and business. Fleeing the deadly sunlight in the south and the wars that had broken out in the wake of the fatal climate change, the swarms of refugees had steadily grown over the past century. This posed a challenge for Longyearbyen, which in its very earliest days had housed only a few thousand hardy people. Now, centuries later, it wrestled with the limits of how fast a city could expand. Temporary barracks housed the new arrivals outside the city while the governing council debated what to do with them.

In December, it was difficult to tell when a day started and ended, but Kaya figured it was midday. Although Arctic winters were still dark, they were not as they'd been in ancient times, when snow had covered everything. The ground still froze hard once the sun left for the winter months, but much of the surface ice thawed in the daytime. In Refugee Town, though, ice glazed the narrow alleys all day. And now it glittered in the white beam of the police spotlight.

Kaya stood huddled outside the barricade tape, watching the officers work. The cold breeze ruffled her curls. Her toes felt numb inside her boots. She wiggled them, trying to get the blood flowing, and glanced at the small group of refugees waiting in silence behind her. *Frightened*, she thought. As newcomers, they hadn't yet acquired the affection the locals had for the lion. To Kaya, they seemed as fragile as the windowless buildings surrounding them. The governor had proclaimed that the temporary shacks were built of sturdy material, but Kaya suspected that any powerful gust of wind could easily blow them over.

Unaffected by the police officers' scowls, she leaned over the tape to scrutinize the package on the ground. She couldn't see its contents clearly from where she stood, but she knew it was factory meat. Despite the frost, there was no mistaking the smell. She wrinkled her nose.

"Officer, is it factory lamb?" she called to the uniformed man standing a few meters away.

Not really wanting to answer but hesitating because she had such a lovely smile, he muttered, "We don't know yet. Got to take it to the lab."

"It looks like it's wrapped. That indicates someone put it there, right?"

"Could be."

"What do you think? Was it meant for the lion?"

He shrugged and made a gesture that could be interpreted as either yes or no.

"Do you think it's poisoned?"

An officer, his face wrinkled, stalked up, his broad shoulders stiff.

"We'll send out a press release later, Miss Kunene," he said gruffly, then turned his back to her. His colleague quickly followed suit.

Amused, Kaya studied their backs briefly, then sighed, realizing she wouldn't gain anything further of interest in the refugee settlement. Before having to settle for the zoo gig, she had wanted to become a real journalist, an investigative one even, or a leading spokeswoman for an important cause, and she found it energizing to question the authorities. She made her way out and over to her parked sail rover. It stood out with its pink sail, but its somewhat decadent look portrayed exactly the image Kaya wanted. Fondly, she patted the vehicle and climbed onto the sturdy seat.

She didn't put up the sail right away, just sat gazing at the bustling scene. Since cars were so expensive, Longyearbyen's streets were full of rovers whooshing past its many bicycles. The city had so many rovers that competition to train as a sailmaker's apprentice was fierce. Tram systems crisscrossed the archipelago, with major stations at the university, airport, and Platåberget space station. Yet many inhabitants preferred the sail rovers, even though they couldn't rely on a constant wind flowing between the skyscrapers. Still, at this time of year, the days were more often windy than not.

Kaya thought hard. It could be that someone wished to poison the lion, of course, but she had another hunch: The meat in Refugee Town had been put there by an abettor, someone who wanted to feed Levi, someone who had probably placed similar packages all over the city. Someone who cared about Levi …

Trym.

Frowning, she activated her Thelma. The screen flashed over her hand. Trym had replied to her call with a short text: *Fabulous news! I'll call you later.* She mulled it over. Kaya knew Trym well enough to be alarmed by his contrived cheerfulness. They had worked together for several years, and their workplace alliance had escalated into a short-lived romance, followed by an unfortunate de-escalation back to a flirtatious workplace alliance. That was the way with Trym, a frustrating pattern of two steps forward, one step back, that even his mother complained about. The more Kaya cared for him and confided in him, the more he seemed torn between reciprocating and placing distance between them. Distance had been winning out in recent weeks, and forced cheerfulness was Trym's preferred means of staying detached. She knew that something wasn't right.

She couldn't have come this far without trusting her gut.

Never ashamed, Kaya didn't hide her ambitions. She simply knew she was destined to be something greater than a lion's publicist. The prospect of a major documentary film about Levi offered an unexpected opportunity after what had seemed like an unfortunate detour in her career. It had taken some persistence to persuade the film company, but Kaya had succeeded— just before Levi's flight became global news. Kaya couldn't deny she relished the limelight the film would now provide, and she had tried hard to convince Trym that this attention could prove advantageous to him and his cause as well. But being in the spotlight was definitely not Trym's thing—even if the zoo manager had enthusiastically endorsed the idea—and the present holiday cooling in their relationship coincided with the greenlighting of the film project.

And the lion?

No one needed to know the truth, but *indifference* came close to describing her feelings for the animal. If she were honest and not being paid to flack for the feline, she would call it ugly, hairy, stinky, and very, very scary.

Maybe she was just jealous of old Levi?

Trym appeared to prefer the lion over the company of humans. He cared for Levi for Levi's sake. For Kaya, the lion's significance lay in advancing other things: her career and her connection to Trym, which she was eager to preserve and deepen. But too often, the lion they had in common seemed to deepen the chasm between them.

Trym wasn't the only one obsessed with the lion. Levi had hordes of dedicated fans. They volunteered for the many search groups. The children drew pictures of the lion and hung their art on the zoo walls. Priests gave intercessions for the big cat's survival. More and more fans gathered outside the zoo, waving homemade posters proclaiming what Levi meant to them and how much they wished the lion would come home.

Even the other lion seemed upset at Levi's absence. The zoo manager had told Kaya the younger cat had started to pad restlessly back and forth in the lions' enclosure, panting and growling.

Fascinated, she observed the mass hysteria surrounding Levi's disappearance. You'd be a fool not to capitalize on it.

Kaya Kunene was not a fool.

As someone with unrestricted access to the zoo, and one of the last people to see Levi in captivity, the police had questioned her, of course. She didn't mind; she'd used the opportunity to look around the police station and chat with the officers. It was a coincidence, she had told them—a stroke of luck, you might say. She'd been in the zoo that night talking with Trym about the documentary film, trailing after him when he'd gone to feed Levi, so she was with him when he found the lion's cage empty.

Trym.

Her mind kept coming back to him. Creasing her forehead, she examined his message again. He'd seemed upset and sad at the police station, but she'd spotted an amused gleam in his eyes too, as if he were secretly pleased by it all.

The media folks surrounded his apartment building and followed him everywhere. But Kaya believed they watched him closely only in the daytime. Anyhow, day or night, she suspected he could easily escape his stalkers. Like Kaya, he was a local and knew his way around the city.

Did he know where the lion was? Would he try to capture it? She inhaled sharply.

"Thelma, call up the cameraman!" In seconds, his voice spoke into her ear. Not bothering with niceties, she said, "I have an idea."

While talking rapidly, she raised the pink sail and steered out onto the busy street.

IN LONGYEARBYEN, A lion roared in the darkness, the sound so powerful it shook many humans out of their sleep and out of their beds, frightened by the wild presence in their streets.

The lion roared, raging against the foreign night smells, so different from those of the zoo. Then it whimpered and became quiet.

THE NIGHT, A peaceful balm, was Ernst Douglas' favorite time to be in a city. The quiet hours, when even the most stubborn nightclubbers have headed home and before the city has woken up. He found Longyearbyen nights particularly pleasing, since most of the lights were turned off so early.

The battered sign outside the old airport hung at an odd angle on its tilted pole, but the image on the rusty surface was still visible: a red triangle with a polar bear in the middle. Shaking his head a little, Ernst marveled at the thought of the giant white bears waddling freely about, a deadly threat to any unfortunate humans crossing their paths. He'd seen photographs, of course. Breathtaking fierce beasts that feared nothing.

Oh, how I wish I were there.

Often, Ernst felt sure destiny was playing games with him—there had been a mistake; he was meant to live in another time, back when the world was filled with wild animals. These days, a hunter had to be content with tracking down the rare stray animal, usually an escapee from the laboratories. There was more money in manhunts, assignments received through the dark web.

He contemplated his conversation with Trym. The police reports had said nothing Ernst hadn't already guessed. Nevertheless, the meeting with Trym had been revealing. It always paid to be a little bit aggressive with people. Not that the younger man had admitted anything to do with the escape of either the lion or the penguins, but Ernst had a gut feeling the zookeeper had played a significant role in both incidents.

Ernst Douglas always hunted on instinct.

So now he was keeping watch over the zookeeper. Not hanging around outside his apartment like those media lunatics, of course, but tracking Trym, certain the young man would lead him to the lion one way or another.

He felt he understood Trym now.

Whenever he was out on surveillance or a hunt, Ernst took pride in getting to know the individuals he stalked. The so-called superiority of humans made him laugh. In his eyes, most humans were like animals: easy to read, their movements so very easy to predict.

But even so, he always felt a deep respect for the object of his pursuit. To really get close to someone or something—to get under their skin, to understand their fears and pleasures, their desires and wants—you had to accept that it went both ways; you had to become involved in the relationship, use the necessary time to build a close connection.

The hunt was a commitment.

A hunt was also the truest form of relationship Ernst knew: the forming of the bond between hunter and hunted. The kill was, in the end, merely a necessary trifle. Ernst was not one of those hunters who needed to decorate their walls with the heads of their dead prey. What Ernst hungered for was the prey's growing acknowledgment that he, the hunter, was the one who would end its existence. This was what Ernst craved, this final acceptance. Ernst didn't view himself as a religious man, but he saw this acceptance almost as a sacrament.

Hunting a predator was the supreme challenge: It forced the predator to admit that it too was hunted. *A true survival of the fittest*, he thought.

And the lion…

The lion would be his ultimate test. Not an animal fabricated and genetically modified by humans but a beast of pure instinct. Of course, confinement in various zoos for so long might have muted the lion's wild nature. Ernst realized that. But he hoped—oh, he longed—for its free spirit to still be there, hidden beneath that thick fur: a true predator.

He'd sensed its presence all the time he'd been in Longyearbyen, its pungent smell carried in the wind.

And that roar the other night. Goose bumps rose on his arms just thinking about it.

Grinning, he saluted the bear on the sign, then strode to the runway, his boots crunching on the ice. The runway, unused for centuries, was barely visible under the mosses and stubby arctic grasses growing there undisturbed.

Perhaps it was nostalgia for the old days, maybe cultural heritage preservation issues, but this spot was curiously one of the few in the city that had been left to its own devices. With the housing crisis the city was enduring, he guessed it was only a matter of time before massive building machines interrupted the peace of this place.

He pushed the rusty gate wide open, its metal hinges squealing, and set his package down behind a dumpster, tearing open a corner to bare the contents.

Ernst had calculated that it would be hard for Levi to find food, habituated as it was to humans feeding it on a regular schedule. It could seek out restaurants and grocery stores. However, few places threw away food these days. Ernst suspected that Trym had planned to feed Levi somehow, but that would be difficult with the media watching him.

The lion would be hungry. Awfully hungry.

Ernst had been leaving these packages around Longyearbyen for several nights, in places where he knew the lion would be able to find them—not downtown, but at the fringes of the city. Refugee Town had been a blunder. The lion would want to stay away from people.

The factory meat from Ernst would curb the worst of its hunger. And because the meat packages would smell like Ernst, the animal would associate the food with him and hopefully track him down outside Longyearbyen.

There, it would meet its end.

LEVI LIFTED ITS broad nose up in the air, sniffing. Following exciting scents that were both familiar and not, the lion headed out of the city. It didn't move quickly; its limbs were stiff with age and the chill of the night, yet it trod smoothly, silently, its heels never touching the ground, the large footpads cushioning the sound of its footfalls.

PERFECT. SATISFIED, ERNST surveyed the entrance of the cave and the view outside. He'd placed the last package of factory lamb below the opening. When the lion found the package, Ernst would have good aim from just inside the cave. The valley was deserted except for the space shuttle launch site in the middle. The station was only a black silhouette, but the towers were clearly visible against the night sky. He guessed the station was abandoned, since no tram tracks led to it. Not many could afford to travel to the space colonies anymore, and the few who did would leave not from here, he reasoned, but from the newer station at Platåberget. Anyhow, most people would be at the Christmas Parade tonight, so he'd have the place to himself. *Perfect.*

"Sure took you long enough."

Ernst swung around, raising his flashlight high to illuminate the inner cave. "Who's there?"

Astonished, he stared at Trym, who was walking toward him. Ernst burst into laughter.

"Wow," he said after a while, catching his breath, still chuckling. "Not many have surprised me. But you…" He reached over his shoulder to loosen the rifle from his back. Shaking his head, he narrowed his eyes. "How did you know I'd be here?"

"It wasn't that difficult when I got why you were in Svalbard."

"You understood?"

"Oh, yes! You're a hunter. Of course Levi would be a temptation. It wasn't a smart move to seek me out first thing, though. I'd never heard of you before and would have proceeded in blissful ignorance, but your visit made me curious. I did some research to find out who you are. You're not a very popular guy, are you?"

Ernst listened, his mouth set in a hard line. He held the rifle loosely by its strap.

"I followed you, of course," Trym continued.

"You followed me?"

"Yes. Not that difficult, actually. I'm also aware you've been trying to keep an eye on me. You probably didn't think I'd notice, but that hat of yours is easy to spot. Did you think I would lead you to him in case you didn't succeed with the meat? I gave Levi food the first week, you know, made sure he had warm places to rest during the day. But when you arrived and started feeding him too, I had to change my plan." Trym shrugged. "It was easy to guess you planned to kill him somewhere deserted, someplace where you could lie in wait. I guessed a cave, since we don't have many mines anymore. This cave is close to the city, so I took a chance and waited for you here. And it fits nicely with my original plan for Levi."

"Why didn't I see your sail rover?"

"There's another entrance that only locals know about. I hiked here often as a kid."

Ernst was silent. He noted that Trym, unlike everyone else, referred to the lion as *he*. He pondered this, along with everything Trym had just told him. He was pleased to have been surprised. *There's a lesson here somewhere*, he thought, his lips curling up at the corners. With his other arm, he felt around in his pocket and pulled out a cartridge. He'd underestimated Trym for sure.

A shuffling sound made him go utterly still. Wordlessly, he watched the lion emerge from the depths of the cave and pad around Trym. It stopped in front of the younger man, keeping its golden eyes fixed calmly on Ernst. Bulging muscles trembled under its thick fur. Its tail whipped from side to side. Levi appeared to be protecting Trym.

It's enormous! Despite all his preparations, all his expectations, Ernst felt awe. Its head alone was almost three times the size of a human's.

He sensed greatness in this animal, something old and majestic. Underneath that matted mane, something powerful and wild lurked. He could easily picture it lying in the shade of heavy baobab branches on the African savanna, just like in the images he'd seen in ancient books.

He smiled broadly. "Thanks, Trym. I've not had this much fun in a long time. But now I must ask you to leave. You see, there's a bond between the lion and me. I needed to hunt it; I need to kill it." He sounded almost apologetic.

The lion cocked its ears and growled as if understanding what he'd said. The hair on Ernst's arms bristled. He raised his rifle and aimed it at the animal. The lion was a little too close for his liking, but Ernst always followed his instincts—and they told him this was the way it must be.

Trym stepped in front of the lion.

"Get out of the way. I don't want to hurt you," Ernst snarled.

"No!"

"All right." Ernst pointed the muzzle at Trym. "If you insist."

Levi roared, the deep sound reverberating through the cave. Its dagger-like fangs glinted in the dim light.

Distracted, Ernst fumbled with the trigger. With the lion's roar still ringing in his ears, he never heard the thud of paws hitting the stone floor, approaching rapidly.

ALONG LONGYEARBYEN'S MAIN avenue, the Christmas Parade moved downward toward the docks. The floats inched past the crowds cheering from the sidelines and from the thousands of windows. Out on the fjord, brightly lit ships of all sizes glided by. Even the colossal wind turbines far outside in the Advent Fjord were festooned with lights.

Longyearbyen Zoo's float displayed a gigantic lion covered with blinking lights, a Santa hat, and a banner displaying the words *Come Home, Levi!* The zoo manager stood at the front, waving to the crowds, which went wild with chants of "Levi! Levi!"

TRYM HOISTED ERNST up by his armpits and sat him with his back against the mountain wall, then picked up the rifle and sat down on the other side of the cave opening, facing the hunter. He anchored his flashlight in a rocky crevice behind him, the light beaming toward the ceiling, bathing them in a faint white glow.

Ernst held his hands over his stomach. Trym squinted, unable to see much in the meager light, but the bloodstain on Ernst's torn shirt appeared to be growing. The lion had not bitten the hunter but had swiped his powerful paw across his chest and stomach, and Trym guessed the extremely sharp, strong claws had dug deep into the man's flesh.

Levi sniffed at the wounds. Then it huffed, came over

to Trym, and laid its large body down next to him with a thump and a heavy sigh. Trym reached up and scratched behind Levi's rounded ears. The animal leaned toward him, rumbling deeply, and bumped its head against Trym, almost knocking him over.

Trym's gaze flicked back to the hunter.

"You weren't supposed to be here," he said, spitting the words out in anger. "This…" he tapped the rifle. "This is not right. It's not fair."

Disgusted, he pushed the weapon away, the metal grinding against the rock floor. Levi looked at him, eyes glimmering yellow, then lowered its head to rest on its forepaws.

Outside, northern lights swept the sky. Trym admired the display for a moment before eyeing the hunter again.

"I have planned this for too long for you to destroy it. You see, Levi is old. No one has ever heard of such an elderly animal before."

Ernst's eyes were closed, his face twisted in pain, but Trym knew he was listening.

"Levi is unique," he continued. "I feel closer to him than to anyone else. We have a bond you could never understand."

Ernst opened his eyes and squinted at Trym. "You're wrong." Grimacing, he shut his eyes again and grunted: "I understand better than you think."

Trym nodded.

"You thought he followed you. But he was following my scent. He trusts me. I've been his keeper since he came to Longyearbyen. I know him."

Shivering, Trym leaned closer to Levi, seeking the lion's warmth. It didn't open its eyes, but Trym felt it press tighter to his side. *I should make a fire*, he thought.

There were firestones in his backpack. But he didn't want to leave the lion alone with the hunter.

"He's dying. The past few months, he's been stiffer and stiffer, though I massage him every day. I've known for a while that he'll die soon. He'll die tonight. My gut tells me so."

His eyes glistened with tears as he gazed at the northern lights dancing green across the sky.

"I decided to free him when the boss told me they'd started searching for a female. They hoped for cubs," Trym said. "They weren't sure it would work with a lab female but wanted to try while Levi is still alive. His offspring would bring lots of money. They all wanted to use him. Money, fame, careers. It's disgusting!"

The hunter sat motionless, head bowed.

"Now he will die in peace," Trym said. "No cameras filming, no people fussing and gawking all the time, commercializing his misery." He thought of Kaya with regret, wiped his tears away, and smiled wistfully. "Now he will die as a free animal."

Far away, behind the mountains, the Christmas Parade fireworks burst into myriad colorful stars and other shapes.

"Did you know that the people of the North used to celebrate the turn of the sun, the return of the light and the warmer seasons?" Trym said. "Christmas should be a new version of that, a pure celebration, but instead ..."

His voice trailed off, as he realized there was no longer anyone there to answer.

"THEY HAVE TO be here," Kaya whispered. She pulled a red cap down over her curls, flicked on her flashlight, and began to walk up the slope, treading carefully. She'd been trying to locate Trym's whereabouts for several days before thinking of the cave, where he'd taken her for a hike on one of their first dates.

The cameraman unpacked his equipment from his sail rover, yawned, and followed Kaya. They had started out quite early. He'd stayed up too late after the Christmas Parade, but Kaya had been so sure on the phone, so convincing—"We must reach them before they leave!"—so he'd said yes. He regretted it now. Even if Levi was quite possibly born in the wild, probably the last real lion the world would ever see, the thought of encountering a large lion in a cave was terrifying, to say the least.

The camera was heavy, the frosty ground slippery. The land was nothing except sand and rocks with a few tufts of grass here and there. At the top, he spotted Kaya standing motionless. Then he saw it, too. Out of habit, he lifted the camera onto his shoulder, but Kaya pushed it down.

She shook her head, staring at him intently, her eyes filled with tears. "You can't film this."

He gave her a long look, then slowly set the camera down.

The gap in the mountainside was right in front of them. Three figures were visible in the dimness of the opening, as if on a stage. On one side, Trym sat with his back against the wall, sleeping. The lion lay halfway over him, its great head covering his lap and legs.

The golden eyes staring toward them were empty, just like the eyes of the unknown man who lay so still on the other side of the opening, one arm outstretched toward Trym and the lion, as if he'd been trying to reach them.

Trym stirred, blinked, and watched them for a while,

unseeing. Then, as if becoming aware of their presence, he shoved at the lion, trying to get up. The cameraman quickly walked over to help him. Finally, Trym was able to stand. He gazed at the big cat, then crouched down and stroked its face.

The cameraman leaned over the hunter, shaking him a little.

"It's no use," Trym said. He sauntered over to Kaya.

"Why are you crying?" he murmured.

"It's so sad."

Baffled, he studied her. "I didn't think you liked the lion?"

"What...?"

"I know you, Kaya." He gently wiped away the tears on her cheeks. "You didn't care a fiddle about Levi, did you? Yet here you are, crying."

"Yes," she whispered. She sounded surprised.

They stood in silence for a long moment. Trym's face was pale, but Kaya thought he seemed oddly peaceful.

"C'mon, let's get going," he told her, putting his arm around her. "We have a Christmas brunch to go to."

IN LONGYEARBYEN ZOO, a lion roared.

FINLAND

A BIRD DOES NOT SING BECAUSE IT HAS AN ANSWER

Johanna Sinisalo

8th of May, 2042
4.55 a.m. (OA) / 11.55 a.m. (Central)

THE BOX IS now in my eye camera. I didn't jack in until the satellite announced that the avatar was in the close vicinity of the Box. A drone dropped the avatar to the border of the Observation Area, and from there it's as if it has traveled to the Box with its very own feet. That took something like three weeks.

I advance toward the Box, swaying a little. The sensors produce a genuine feel of balancing oneself on twigs and moss. I switch the dark vision off, despite the wee hours here. The sun has of course already risen because I am on the 60th latitude north. The sun is barely over the horizon, but it is light enough to see comfortably. The slanted light in the forest is magical. The sunlight streaks into the ethereal dusk under the big fir trees. Dew drops glimmer on the lowest branches of the trees and on the grasses, shreds of mist still linger in some of the damp hollows.

The sensors transmit the intoxicating smell of the green and humid forest into my olfactory nerves. The silicon-coated avatar I'm virtually inhabiting smells of nothing—not least of a human being. Even the hungriest predator wouldn't consider it any more interesting than a clump of rock. It doesn't exhale carbon dioxide, its body is cool, there are no throbbing veins, no heartbeat. The super slow proceeding and almost static presence also signals its harmlessness to the wild life forms. It doesn't make any other noise but those very faint sounds its cautious steps kick up. We are not supposed to cause any disturbance to the fauna, nothing that would affect their behavior in the slightest.

That's why the avatar approached the Box so slowly before I jacked in—just a couple of meters a day. It has stood most of the days and nights motionless, or 'frozen', as we call the state. The automatic program has steered it to the jack-in point with a minimal satellite connection; from the records, I can see there has been only one navigation correction. Well done—the less electromagnetic emissions, the better.

I have to say that the most impressive experience the sensors give me is the audio. I can hear the gentle rustling sound of my steps, the whisper of the wind in the branches of conifers, but above all, there is the overpowering choir of birds. They are singing, squawking, twittering, whistling, chirping, tweeting, hooting, cheeping, bursting into long rippling melodies, delightfully uproarious. As if every single bird of the forest would love to hear its song to rise above all others, every one of them wants their songs to be echoed at the very end of their world.

I'm now half a meter away from the Box, and ready to start completing my mission.

I am here to pick up something priceless.

Or, actually, it does have a price. The Box has been hideously expensive, and the biologists, ethologists, and ornithologists of Central have all been very nervous—we have had no way to be sure if the information that the Box has been collecting in the last years is still there or if it, for some reason, is irretrievably lost. Central people wanted a human for the task but definitely not in the flesh.

A red light blinks in my field of vision. The timer reminds me that I am not allowed to move for the next hour.

OK, I'll jack out and go to the couch and have a nap. This is going to be a long day anyway.

6.02 a.m. (OA) / 1.02 p.m. (Central)

THE SUN IS now noticeably higher in the sky. Being this close, the Box looks like an angular rock. It is the tip of an iceberg. The research AI central unit, also known as its soul, and all the most vulnerable electronics are situated deep underground, down where the winter frost never reaches. A geothermal power source keeps the soul and the sensors alive. Mics and cameras are located in the nearby trees and are hard-wired to the Box, running under thick insulation. All external elmag serving the Box must be insulated, including me. No weak spots for the elmag noise to leak out, thanks. The only exception is a small external antenna on me, for my satellite contact. Central says that in this way we'll bring about much, much less elmag noise to the Observation Area than if the Box sent all its data to them through satellite or, God forbid, cellular network. Of course, there is no field here.

I have seen lots of pictures of the Box, the location of

the hatches and so on, but now on the top of the Box, there is something I didn't expect to see.

I step closer. It's a bird's nest.

And there are eggs in it. Four of them.

Now already? It is early May. Nesting this early has to be due to climate change. This task should have been carried out weeks ago. Fuck.

On top of that, the red light blinks: freeze for an hour. Again. Could be lunchtime, I guess.

7.05 a.m. (OA) / 2.05 p.m. (Central)

I'M JACKED IN again, and hurray, the owner of the nest is not in sight. I perhaps have time to open the hatch in the side of the Box and download the data package. The distance of the nest from the hatch is about a meter and a half or so, not too close.

I walk slowly to the hatch and extend my instrument set. I pull out an opening tool. 4-2-3-3, that many rotations first to the right, then to the left. Even as OA is strictly a no-no for all humans in the flesh, you never can be sure. If some berry-picker got hideously lost and ended up here, they would immediately see that the Box is not a real rock. Better have a combination lock.

I pry the hatch open at the same second as a bird parent dashes to the nest, landing skillfully on the eggs. Female, I presume. It eyes me with caution, the rapid movements of her head signal alertness, the feathers on her neck are a bit puffed up.

I decide to freeze. *Electromagnetic noise must be kept in utter minimum during the task, especially when other life forms are in close contact.*

As I jack out and flash back to my control board, I can't avoid thinking what the avatar must look like in the eyes of that bird: a total moron. A big, motionless, stone-cold creature stands there, it has something resembling a mouth, which is wide open, and then there is something like a tongue sticking out of the jaw-thing and the tongue-thing is stuck into a hole in her nesting rock.

7.44 a.m. (OA) / 2.44 p.m. (Central)

THE MOTHER BIRD has not gone anywhere, although I tried to give it some time by jacking out for a toilet visit. Back in, I barely had time to notice that the male parent brought an insect in his beak to the mother. Oh damnation, now the mom doesn't ever have to leave the nest if the dad is bringing her takeout all the time.

I make a very cautious attempt to complete the opening of the hatch with super slow movements. The bird mom glances at me and utters a sound, a kind of low whistle. A sign of worry or perhaps even an alarm? I decide to freeze again, just in case. *Interfering with or disturbing the natural behavior of any animal species is strictly forbidden.*

That rule is very understandable. There are very few places in the whole world like this, areas that human beings haven't visited for years in the flesh.

8.08 a.m. (OA) / 3.08 p.m. (Central)

THE MOM FLEW somewhere, perhaps to a bird powder room. Now I have my chance. I open the hatch, draw the opening tool back in and choose a download plug. I succeed in inserting it just before the mom returns to her eggs. That was close.

I start to download—I can do that because the wires are insulated, there is no external elmag noise.

8.55 a.m. (OA) / 3.55 p.m. (Central)

THE DOWNLOAD LIGHT stripe was progressing like a snail, there was a tremendous amount of stuff in the Box. Downloading took the better part of an hour! But, finally, the data package is safe and sound in the belly of the avatar, accompanied by a backup copy of the soul of the Box. The original AI will remain on duty. A small blue icon lights up, indicating I now have access to the data and AI.

The mom returns to the nest. Damn, the plug is still in the hatch. She hops closer to inspect the plug and sings a short note, almost a shriek. She suspects something: am I a threat?

To be on the safe side, I freeze myself again and jack out. Back in the control room, I phone Central to ask for instructions for the procedure with the bird nest. Do they think it is a risk to the birds to reside on the Box? Of course, there is nothing one can do now, but what about autumn when the birds have left for the south? Should someone come to OA again and clean the empty nest away, just in case? They say they have to consider this. It is a possibility that the nest stays, because *interfering with or disturbing the natural behavior of any animal species is strictly forbidden*. And some bird species tend to return to the same nest every spring, and if another bird couple does not squat in it before them, they will refurnish and cushion the nest for the new family.

I say OK and jack back in, but I have to stay frozen until the mom deigns to have her next little wing-stretching exercise.

In my humble opinion, the nest is not located in the best possible place. Resting on the top of the Box it is almost like on an open tray. I find the bird species from the AI's databank: it's a flycatcher. The AI tells me they are famous for that kind of daredevil nest-building; they have been reported to nest on the handrails of bridges.

9.20 a.m. (OA) / 4.20 p.m. (Central)

THE FEMALE LEFT the nest and has, astonishingly enough, stayed away those few minutes I needed to draw the plug back into my side and close the hatch. Mission completed! Now all I have to do is to leave the Box very carefully. I have instructions to keep frozen at all times except when both parents are away from the nest. When this scarce slot to move occurs, I'm allowed to take a step or two. The plan is to walk the avatar to a distance of twenty-five meters from the Box. That may take two weeks, if I'm lucky. When I have reached that distance, I will jack out and let the avatar walk by itself to the border of the Observation Area. A drone will eventually come for it and the precious data.

10.30 a.m. (OA) / 5.30 p.m. (Central)

I HAVE TAKEN one step away from the Box.

* * *

11.45 a.m. (OA) / 6.45 p.m. (Central)

ANOTHER STEP. YAY! (Yawn.)

12.22 p.m. (OA) / 7.22 p.m. (Central)

CENTRAL WANTS ME to turn around and walk backward. The ornithologists realized that this way I can shoot material of the nest for days, to be added to the data package. Now I am allowed to jack out only when the flycatchers are away from their nest. They need me to direct the eye camera. Of course, the avatar would be able to produce footage of the nesting pair as well without my assistance, but nothing can replace the human response, Central reasoned. (And, of course, they pay me to do my job.)

1.40 p.m. (OA) / 8.40 p.m. (Central)

THE HUMAN RESPONDER is dying of boredom. It would actually be pretty entertaining to watch the flycatchers—I have hardly ever seen live birds except for city pigeons because songbirds are so scarce nowadays—but the female is mostly tightly perched on the nest. The male brings an insectoid tidbit to his spouse now and then. I wonder if female birds sitting on their eggs are like pregnant women with cravings. "I want mosquitoes, you nitwit, those wasps are too crunchy!"

This must be the most tedious avatar gig I have ever done. Or anyone has ever done. Having a single step in an hour and mostly staring at one point.

Hey. There is that small blue icon, the downloaded data package! The AI has had ample time to analyze and organize the data, and perhaps there is something fun to pass the time. If I take audio I'm able to simultaneously direct the eye camera. I ask the AI to read me some headlines. AI's pleasant, neutral voice delivers me two main audio titles: *Raw Data. Analyzed Data.*

"Analyzed one, please." The raw stuff is just plain recordings.

AI recites subtitles to my ear. When I hear *Decoding baseline vocalizations* I say, "Stop."

Whatever it is, I'm so bored that everything goes. I tell AI to give me a sample.

2.23 p.m. (OA) / 9.23 p.m. (Central)

I'M ENCHANTED.

I hear a clamorous melody by a male bird—AI tells me first it's a mated male—recorded by the Box. Then the smooth, disembodied, patient voice of AI recites an interpretation: *Do not come further. This is my territory. The insects are mine. This is the place of my nesting.*

Another melody of another mated male ensues, declaring: *I'm strong, I'm capable. I have a female, I have a nest. Retreat, stranger.*

AI classifies the next song to belong to a still unmated female. *I'm fertile, I'm cunning, I'm crafty, I'm ready.*

Perhaps that song is a direct reply to another male, whose loud trill has told all the forest, *I'm seeking a friend, I'm seeking a mate, I'm strong and beautiful and valiant, my singing is sonorous, come to me!*

Then, a short, subdued chirrup from an already-mated female: *I have a nest. I'm cunning, I'm crafty. Come to me.*

Oh my God, the already-taken birds are sleeping around! This *is* entertaining!

I ask and the AI tells me that in a mating pair of songbirds, both male and female songbirds may have affairs. That maximizes the possibility of successful fertilization and in some cases enlarges the gene pool beneficially.

At the same time, the female leaves the nest. It's time to take my step.

3.11 p.m. (OA) / 10.23 p.m. (Central)

I JACKED OUT to have a quick late dinner. I'm back just in time to hear an alarm sound sequence by my sensors. *Decoding several simultaneous vocalizations*, AI says, without asking permission.

After a rapid burst of twittering, I hear the flat, unexcited voice of the AI: *Beast on the move.* An intense chatter follows. *Beast coming this way. Beast comes from sunside to nightside.* A couple of low-key squawks—a crow, perhaps? *Small beast. Swift beast.*

I zoom my eye camera to the nest. I distinguish a nimbly moving reddish brown something on the foot of the Box.

A squirrel is on the prowl.

It leaps onto the Box in one fluid movement. A bird screeches. Another whistles a high-pitched sound. *Egg robber. Close to a nest.*

I act before thinking. I take a rapid step toward the Box and then another. I can see the shadow of the avatar falling on the squirrel, and the rodent goes stiff twenty centimeters from the unattended nest. Its nostrils palpitate, it is confused: there is something large approaching, but there's no smell to be detected. The squirrel's head turns toward me, its small pitch-black eyes gleaming: am I a real threat or only an odorless shadow?

But that split second of hesitation has been enough—I can now see the flycatcher pair rushing in, their wings spread wide, tiny talons extended, making fake attacks toward the squirrel, flapping furiously to beat the little rodent with their wings.

The squirrel turns and scurries away at lightning speed. The flycatchers pursue it like two fighter planes, uttering fierce screeches. AI decodes: *Go! Go away! Escape my fury. You do not belong here. My beak is sharp. My talons are strong. This is my territory.*

DAMN MY INSTINCTIVE reactions. The flycatcher couple was able to drive out the egg robber pretty efficiently themselves.

But only because the other birds warned them.

"AI? Do the birds have the same language?"

It is not a language in the way we understand it, AI states. *My decodings are rough and they are modified according to the human way of thinking verbally. The decoding does not consist of vocal elements only. Singing, cawing, hooting or whistling is just a part of the language, important elements are also the tone, duration, pitch, volume and rhythm of those. And body language, too. Many early human tribes, living in the woods or on a savanna, understood the language of birds: when a bird lets out an unexpected cry or takes a sudden flight, a dangerous predator is drawing close. Every chirp and trill, warble and screech, every unexpected melody, every sudden takeoff, tilting head, lashing tail, puffed crest, eager preening is a message to all the other creatures, too.*

Sitting in the Box, the AI has not only listened to the songs but also recorded thousands of repeated movements and gestures. It has combined the data from earlier knowledge of behavior patterns and mating rituals and their decoding to its new knowledge.

It has learned the language of birds.

I STARTLE AS I suddenly hear the voice of Central in my ears: "The satellite data relays that you have progressed to the opposite direction of the fixed route. Immediate navigatory correction requested."

What? Why are they using satellite connections to track me, don't they trust me?

I can see the squirrel in the distance climbing a tree, it desperately circles the trunk trying to avoid the fury of the flycatchers still hounding it, until the squirrel finds a branch and, running decisively to its outer tip, makes a giant leap to the neighboring fir tree and disappears from my sight. The mom returns to the nest straight away. The dad bird takes a stance beside the nest, the little round head making swift turns in all directions, and then I hear a series of short cheeps.

AI decodes, unasked again: *The beast is gone. Another is close.*

The female answers immediately: *Unknown creature. Big creature. Slow creature. Have caution.*

They are talking about *me*.

IN THE OBSERVATION Area humans should not interfere with anything happening. So, I shouldn't have prevented the fucking squirrel from trying to commit infanticide.

Squirrels have always stolen birds' eggs. It's their natural behavioral pattern. A flycatcher has, on the other hand, a natural behavioral pattern to protect its nest, and even if the squirrel was faster than the bird, the hair-tailed rat would perhaps only have time to steal, or break and eat, one egg before the parents interfered. That's why there are always several eggs in a bird's nest. Nature always has a wastage percentage calculated. Flycatchers do not go extinct from one egg robbery.

But I couldn't help myself. There are so few birds left, so few in the whole world.

The OA is one of the very rare places still sustaining an abundance of wild birds. When winter comes, flycatchers move to Africa, south of the Sahara. Those puny creatures fly thousands and thousands of kilometers and cross seas and enormous deserts. And how fragile the creature is, compared to a chubby, malevolent, thieving squirrel, which could just as well eat seeds from pinecones, they always have those aplenty. It should go vegetarian, damn it, like half the planet now.

And the squirrels have it good. Most of them have moved from the woods to inhabit parks and suburbs and cemeteries. People even feed the little bastards.

But the birds keep disappearing.

* * *

SHOULD I OBEY Central at once or keep watch if the egg robber dares to come back? Now the mom is sitting on the eggs, but inevitably it will sooner or later have to go to take care of some bird business.

I stay frozen. I'm a rock, I'm a snag. But I can come alive as soon as the small assassin returns.

I feel the faintest trace of external physical movement. The male flycatcher has landed on me. The female on the nest utters a short chirp.

The AI is alert: *Warning*.

The male answers with a chirrup. *Slow creature*.

The female replies: *Poison*.

I feel another minuscule pressure change, as the male gets airborne again, and then I see him landing beside the nest. Both of the birds stare at me, defiantly ruffling their feathers. Both of them enunciate short, muted tweets.

Poison.

Blinding poison.

I understand now.

I am poison. We are poison.

We thrive on information. And even though we have learned some lessons in the past, there is one Pandora's box that we cannot and don't want to close again: elmag noise.

It is our smell that follows us everywhere. It is emitted everywhere humans use electronic devices.

Of course, I also know—have always known—that migratory birds are unable to use their magnetic compass in the presence of urban elmag noise.

What I did not know is that they knew it, too. *Blinding poison*.

That perhaps now the flycatcher loses her way to Africa.

I STEER MYSELF away from the Box, running fast, fucking the regulations once again. The male has taken off and followed me, flapping its wings, driving me away like I was a giant squirrel, its beak wide open with screeching. The AI comes in with its infuriatingly indifferent voice: *Go! Go away! Escape my fury. You do not belong here. You are poison. My beak is sharp. My talons are strong. This is my territory.*

I run toward the border of the Observation Area. I hear the crackle of twigs under my feet, I reach the twenty-five-meter safe distance point.

I feel a hand on my shoulder. On my real body shoulder.

I am flashed out from the forest. For a second I feel like I am blind and deaf. Central has force-jacked me out. I really do not blame them.

I turn in my chair. Cold LED lights, dry stale air and the ugly rectangular room where everything black and white feels now, after the forest, almost like physical pain.

"I'm sorry," I say to the guy who is standing before me. "I got carried away. But the data package is safely in the avatar. I know you will take over now." I rub my eyes, feeling feverish.

The guy says: "We were just a bit worried. You have to report incorrect action, of course, but if the mission was successfully completed, I think there will be no sanctions."

I nod, relieved.

"There is some revolutionary material in the package, believe me," I say. "I had a peek."

The guy smiles. "That's wonderful to hear."

He goes away.

Exhausted, I think: now this might be a new beginning. Now we know the language of birds. One must wonder what other kinds of changes will ensue because of that knowledge?

Let me guess.

None.

ELEGY FOR A YOUNG ELK

Hannu Rajaniemi

THE NIGHT AFTER Kosonen shot the young elk, he tried to write a poem by the campfire.

It was late April and there was still snow on the ground. He had already taken to sitting outside in the evening, on a log by the fire, in the small clearing where his cabin stood. Otso was more comfortable outside, and he preferred the bear's company to being alone. It snored loudly atop its pile of fir branches.

A wet smell, that had traces of elk shit, drifted from its drying fur.

He dug a soft-cover notebook and a pencil stub from his pocket. He leafed through it: most of the pages were empty. Words had become slippery, harder to catch than elk. Although not this one: careless and young. An old elk would never have let a man and a bear so close.

He scattered words on the first empty page, gripping the pencil hard.

Antlers. Sapphire antlers. No good. *Frozen flames. Tree roots. Forked destinies.* There had to be words that

277

captured the moment when the crossbow kicked against his shoulder, the meaty sound of the arrow's impact. But it was like trying to catch snowflakes in his palm. He could barely glimpse the crystal structure, and then they melted.

He closed the notebook and almost threw it into the fire, but thought better of it and put it back into his pocket. No point in wasting good paper. Besides, his last toilet roll in the outhouse would run out soon.

"Kosonen is thinking about words again," Otso growled. "Kosonen should drink more booze. Don't need words then. Just sleep."

Kosonen looked at the bear. "You think you are smart, huh?" He tapped his crossbow. "Maybe it's you who should be shooting elk."

"Otso good at smelling. Kosonen at shooting. Both good at drinking." Otso yawned luxuriously, revealing rows of yellow teeth. Then it rolled to its side and let out a satisfied heavy sigh. "Otso will have more booze soon."

Maybe the bear was right. Maybe a drink was all he needed. No point in being a poet: they had already written all the poems in the world, up there, in the sky. They probably had poetry gardens. Or places where you could become words.

But that was not the point. The words needed to come from *him*, a dirty bearded man in the woods whose toilet was a hole in the ground. Bright words from dark matter, that's what poetry was about.

When it worked.

There were things to do. The squirrels had almost picked the lock the previous night, bloody things. The cellar door needed reinforcing. But that could wait until tomorrow.

He was about to open a vodka bottle from Otso's secret stash in the snow when Marja came down from the sky as rain.

THE RAIN WAS sudden and cold like a bucket of water poured over your head in the sauna. But the droplets did not touch the ground, they floated around Kosonen. As he watched, they changed shape, joined together and made a woman, spindle-thin bones, mist-flesh and muscle. She looked like a glass sculpture. The small breasts were perfect hemispheres, her sex an equilateral silver triangle. But the face was familiar—small nose and high cheekbones, a sharp-tongued mouth.

Marja.

Otso was up in an instant, by Kosonen's side. "Bad smell, god-smell," it growled. "Otso bites." The rain-woman looked at it curiously.

"Otso," Kosonen said sternly. He gripped the fur in the bear's rough neck tightly, feeling its huge muscles tense. "Otso is Kosonen's friend. Listen to Kosonen. Not time for biting. Time for sleeping. Kosonen will speak to god." Then he set the vodka bottle in the snow right under its nose.

Otso sniffed the bottle and scraped the half-melted snow with its forepaw.

"Otso goes," it finally said. "Kosonen shouts if the god bites. Then Otso comes." It picked up the bottle in its mouth deftly and loped into the woods with a bear's loose, shuffling gait.

"Hi," the rain-woman said.

"Hello," Kosonen said carefully. He wondered if she was real. The plague gods were crafty. One of them could have taken Marja's image from his mind. He looked at the unstrung crossbow and tried to judge the odds: a diamond goddess versus an out-of-shape woodland poet. Not good.

"Your dog does not like me very much," the Marja-thing said. She sat down on Kosonen's log and swung its shimmering legs in the air, back and forth, just like Marja always did in the sauna. It had to be her, Kosonen decided, feeling something jagged in his throat.

He coughed. "Bear, not a dog. A dog would have barked. Otso just bites. Nothing personal, that's just its nature. Paranoid and grumpy."

"Sounds like someone I used to know."

"I'm not paranoid." Kosonen hunched down and tried to get the fire going again. "You learn to be careful, in the woods."

Marja looked around. "I thought we gave you stayers more equipment. It looks a little... primitive here."

"Yeah. We had plenty of gadgets," Kosonen said. "But they weren't plague-proof. I had a smartgun before I had this"—he tapped his crossbow—"but it got infected. I killed it with a big rock and threw it into the swamp. I've got my skis and some tools, and this." Kosonen tapped his temple. "Has been enough so far. So cheers."

He piled up some kindling under a triangle of small logs, and in a moment the flames sprung up again. Three years had been enough to learn about woodcraft at least. Marja's skin looked almost human in the soft light of the fire, and he sat back on Otso's fir branches, watching her. For a moment, neither of them spoke.

"So how are you, these days?" he asked. "Keeping busy?"

Marja smiled. "Your wife grew up. She's a big girl now. You don't want to know how big."

"So... you are not her, then? Who am I talking to?"

"I am her, and I am not her. I'm a partial, but a faithful one. A translation. You wouldn't understand."

Kosonen put some snow in the coffee pot to melt. "All right, so I'm a caveman. Fair enough. But I understand you are here because you want something. So, let's get down to business, perkele," he swore.

Marja took a deep breath. "We lost something. Something important. Something new. The spark, we called it. It fell into the city."

"I thought you lot kept copies of everything."

"Quantum information. That was a part of the *new* bit. You can't copy it."

"Tough shit."

A wrinkle appeared between Marja's eyebrows. Kosonen remembered it from a thousand fights they'd had and swallowed.

"If that's the tone you want to take, fine," she said. "I thought you'd be glad to see me. I didn't have to come: they could have sent Mickey Mouse. But I wanted to see you. The big Marja wanted to see you. So, you have decided to live your life like this, as the tragic figure haunting the woods. That's fine. But you could at least listen. You owe me that much."

Kosonen said nothing.

"I see," Marja said. "You still blame me for Esa."

She was right. It had been her who got the first Santa Claus machine. The boy needs the best we can offer, she said. The world is changing. Can't have him being left behind. Let's make him into a little god, like the neighbor's kid.

"I guess I shouldn't be blaming *you*," Kosonen said. "You're just a... partial. You weren't there."

"I was there," Marja said quietly. "I remember. Better

than you, now. I also forget better, and forgive. You never could. You just... wrote poems. The rest of us moved on, and saved the world."

"Great job," Kosonen said. He poked the fire with a stick, and a cloud of sparks flew up into the air with the smoke.

Marja got up. "That's it," she said. "I'm leaving. See you in a hundred years." The air grew cold. A halo appeared around her, shimmering in the firelight.

Kosonen closed his eyes and squeezed his jaw shut tight. He waited for ten seconds. Then he opened his eyes. Marja was still there, staring at him, helpless. He could not help smiling. She could never leave without having the last word.

"I'm sorry," Kosonen said. "It's been a long time. I've been living in the woods with a bear. Doesn't improve one's temper much."

"I didn't really notice any difference."

"All right," Kosonen said. He tapped the fir branches next to him. "Sit down. Let's start over. I'll make some coffee."

Marja sat down, bare shoulder touching his. She felt strangely warm, warmer than the fire almost.

"The firewall won't let us into the city," she said. "We don't have anyone... human enough, not anymore. There was some talk about making one, but... the argument would last a century." She sighed. "We like to argue, in the sky."

Kosonen grinned. "I bet you fit right in." He checked for the wrinkle before continuing. "So you need an errand boy."

"We need help."

Kosonen looked at the fire. The flames were dying now,

licking at the blackened wood. There were always new colors in the embers. Or maybe he just always forgot.

He touched Marja's hand. It felt like a soap bubble, barely solid. But she did not pull it away.

"All right," he said. "But just so you know, it's not just for old times' sake."

"Anything we can give you?"

"I'm cheap," Kosonen said. "I just want words."

THE SUN SPARKLED on the kantohanki: snow with a frozen surface, strong enough to carry a man on skis and a bear. Kosonen breathed hard. Even going downhill, keeping pace with Otso was not easy. But in weather like this, there was something glorious about skiing, sliding over blue shadows of trees almost without friction, the snow hissing underneath.

I've sat still too long, he thought. *Should have gone somewhere just to go, not because someone asked.*

In the afternoon, when the sun was already going down, they reached the railroad, a bare gash through the forest, two metal tracks on a bed of gravel. Kosonen removed his skis and stuck them in the snow.

"I'm sorry you can't come along," he told Otso. "But the city won't let you in."

"Otso not a city bear," the bear said. "Otso waits for Kosonen. Kosonen gets sky-bug, comes back. Then we drink booze."

He scratched the rough fur of its neck clumsily. The bear poked Kosonen in the stomach with its nose, so hard that he almost fell. Then it snorted, turned and shuffled into the woods. Kosonen watched until it vanished among the snow-covered trees.

It took three painful attempts of sticking his fingers down his throat to get the nanoseed Marja gave him to come out. The gagging left a bitter taste in his mouth. Swallowing it had been the only way to protect the delicate thing from the plague. He wiped it in the snow: a transparent bauble the size of a walnut, slippery and warm. It reminded him of the toys you could get from vending machines in supermarkets when he was a child, plastic spheres with something secret inside.

He placed it on the rails carefully, wiped the remains of the vomit from his lips and rinsed his mouth with water. Then he looked at it. Marja knew he would never read instruction manuals, so she had not given him one.

"Make me a train," he said.

Nothing happened. *Maybe it can read my mind*, he thought and imagined a train, an old steam train, puffing along. Still nothing, just a reflection of the darkening sky on the seed's clear surface. *She always had to be subtle*. Marja could never give a present without thinking about its meaning for days. Standing still, he let the spring-winter chill through his wolf-pelt coat, and he hopped up and down, rubbing his hands together.

With the motion came an idea. He frowned, staring at the seed, and took the notebook from his pocket. Maybe it was time to try out Marja's other gift—or advance payment, however you wanted to look at it. He had barely written the first lines, when the words leaped in his mind like animals woken from slumber. He closed the book, cleared his throat, and spoke.

> *these rails*
> *were worn thin*
> *by wheels*

> *that wrote down*
> *the name of each passenger*
> *in steel and miles*

he said,

> *it's a good thing*
> *the years*
> *ate our flesh too*
> *made us thin and light*
> *so the rails are strong enough*
> *to carry us still*
> *to the city*
> *in our train of glass and words*

Doggerel, he thought, but it didn't matter. The joy of words filled his veins like vodka. *Too bad it didn't work—*

The seed blurred. It exploded into a white-hot sphere. The waste heat washed across Kosonen's face. Glowing tentacles squirmed past him, sucking carbon and metal from the rails and trees. They danced like a welder's electric arcs, sketching lines and surfaces in the air.

And suddenly, the train was there.

It was transparent, with paper-thin walls and delicate wheels, as if it had been blown from glass, a sketch of a cartoon steam engine with a single carriage, with spiderweb-like chairs inside, just the way he had imagined it.

He climbed in, expecting the delicate structure to sway under his weight, but it felt rock solid. The nanoseed lay on the floor innocently, as if nothing had happened. He picked it up carefully, took it outside and buried it in the snow, leaving his skis and sticks as markers. Then he picked up his backpack, boarded the train again and sat down in one of the gossamer seats. Unbidden, the train lurched into motion smoothly. To Kosonen, it sounded like the rails beneath were whispering, but he could not hear the words.

He watched the darkening forest glide past. The day's journey weighed heavily on his limbs. The memory of the snow beneath his skis melted together with the train's movement, and soon Kosonen was asleep.

When he woke, it was dark. The amber light of the firewall glowed in the horizon, like a thundercloud.

The train had sped up. The dark forest outside was a blur, and the whispering of the rails had become a quiet staccato song. Kosonen swallowed as the train covered the remaining distance in a matter of minutes. The firewall grew into a misty dome glowing with yellowish light from within. The city was an indistinct silhouette beneath it. The buildings seemed to be in motion, like a giant's shadow puppets.

Then it was a flaming curtain directly in front of the train, an impenetrable wall made from twilight and amber crossing the tracks. Kosonen gripped the delicate frame of his seat, knuckles white. "Slow down!" he shouted, but the train did not hear. It crashed directly into the firewall with a bone-jarring impact. There was a burst of light, and then Kosonen was lifted from his seat.

It was like drowning, except that he was floating in an infinite sea of amber light rather than water. Apart from the light, there was just emptiness. His skin tickled. It took him a moment to realize that he was not breathing.

And then a stern voice spoke.

This is not a place for men, it said. *Closed. Forbidden. Go back.*

"I have a mission," said Kosonen. His voice had no echo in the light. "From your makers. They command you to let me in."

He closed his eyes, and Marja's third gift floated in front of him, not words but a number. He had always been poor at memorizing things, but Marja's touch had been a pen with acid ink, burning it in his mind. He read off the endless digits, one by one.

You may enter, said the firewall. *But only that which is human will leave.*

The train and the speed came back, sharp, and real like a paper cut. The twilight glow of the firewall was still there, but instead of the forest, dark buildings loomed around the railway, blank windows staring at him.

Kosonen's hands tickled. They were clean, as were his clothes: every speck of dirt was gone. His skin felt red and tender like he had just been to the sauna.

The train slowed down at last, coming to a stop in the dark mouth of the station, and Kosonen was in the city.

THE CITY WAS a forest of metal and concrete and metal that breathed and hummed. The air smelled of ozone. The facades of the buildings around the railway station square looked almost like he remembered them, only subtly wrong. From the corner of his eye, he could glimpse them *moving*, shifting in their sleep like stone-skinned animals. There were no signs of life, apart from a cluster of pigeons, hopping back and forth on the stairs, looking at him. They had sapphire eyes.

A bus stopped, full of faceless people who looked like crash test dummies, sitting unnaturally still. Kosonen decided not to get in and started to head across the square, toward the main shopping street: he had to start the search for the spark somewhere. It will glow, Marja had said. You can't miss it.

There was what looked like a car wreck in the parking lot, lying on its side, hood crumpled like a discarded beer can, covered in white pigeon droppings. But when Kosonen walked past it, its engine roared, and the hood popped open. A hissing bundle of tentacles snapped out, reaching for him.

He managed to gain some speed before the car-beast rolled onto its four wheels. There were narrow streets on the other side of the square, too narrow for it to follow. He ran, cold weight in his stomach, legs pumping.

The crossbow beat painfully at his back in its strap, and he struggled to get it over his head.

The beast passed him arrogantly and turned around. Then it came straight at him. The tentacles spread out from its glowing engine mouth into a fan of serpents.

Kosonen fumbled with a bolt, then loosed it at the thing. The crossbow kicked, but the arrow glanced off its windshield. It seemed to confuse it enough for Kosonen to jump aside. He dove, hit the sidewalk with a painful thump, and rolled.

"Somebody help, perkele," he swore with impotent rage and got up, panting, just as the beast backed off slowly, engine growling. He smelled burning rubber, mixed with ozone. *Maybe I can wrestle it*, he thought like a madman, spreading his arms, refusing to run again. *One last poem in it—*

Something landed in front of the beast, wings

fluttering. A pigeon. Both Kosonen and the car-creature stared at it. It made a cooing sound. Then it exploded.

The blast tore at his eardrums, and the white fireball turned the world black for a second. Kosonen found himself on the ground again, ears ringing, lying painfully on top of his backpack. The car-beast was a burning wreck ten meters away, twisted beyond all recognition.

There was another pigeon next to him, picking at what looked like bits of metal. It lifted its head and looked at him, flames reflecting from the tiny sapphire eyes. Then it took flight, leaving a tiny white dropping behind.

THE MAIN SHOPPING street was empty. Kosonen moved carefully in case there were more of the car creatures around, staying close to narrow alleys and doorways. The firewall light was dimmer between the buildings, and strange lights danced in the windows.

Kosonen realized he was starving: he had not eaten since noon, and the journey and the fight had taken their toll. He found an empty cafe on a street corner that seemed safe, set up his small travel cooker on a table and boiled some water. The supplies he had been able to bring consisted mainly of canned soup and dried elk meat, but his growling stomach was not fussy. The smell of food made him careless.

"This is my place," said a voice. Kosonen leapt up, startled, reaching for the crossbow.

There was a stooped, trollish figure at the door, dressed in rags. His face shone with sweat and dirt, framed by matted hair and beard. His porous skin was full of tiny sapphire growths, like pockmarks. Kosonen had thought living in the woods had made him immune to human odors, but the stranger carried a bitter stench of sweat and stale booze that made him want to retch.

The stranger walked in and sat down at a table opposite Kosonen. "But that's all right," he said amicably. "Don't get many visitors these days. Have to be neighborly. Saatana, is that Blaband soup that you've got?"

"You're welcome to some," Kosonen said warily. He had met some of the other stayers over the years, but usually avoided them—they all had their own reasons for not going up, and not much in common.

"Thanks. That's neighborly indeed. I'm Pera, by the way." The troll held out his hand.

Kosonen shook it gingerly, feeling strange, jagged things under Pera's skin. It was like squeezing a glove filled with powdered glass. "Kosonen. So, you live here?"

"Oh, not here, not in the center. I come here to steal from the buildings. But they've become really smart, and stingy. Can't even find soup anymore. The Stockmann department store almost ate me, yesterday. It's not an easy life here." Pera shook his head. "But better than outside." There was a sly look in his eyes. *Are you staying because you want to*, wondered Kosonen, *or because the firewall won't let you out anymore?*

"Not afraid of the plague gods, then?" he asked aloud. He passed Pera one of the heated soup tins. The city stayer slurped it down with one gulp, the smell of minestrone mingling with the other odors.

"Oh, you don't have to be afraid of them anymore. They're all dead."

Kosonen looked at Pera, startled. "How do you know?"

"The pigeons told me."

"The pigeons?"

Pera took something from the pocket of his ragged coat carefully. It was a pigeon. It had a sapphire beak and eyes, and a trace of blue in its feathers. It struggled in Pera's grip, wings fluttering.

"My little buddies," Pera said. "I think you've already met them."

"Yes," Kosonen said. "Did you send the one that blew up that car thing?"

"You have to help a neighbor out, don't you? Don't mention it. The soup was good."

"What did they say about the plague gods?"

Pera grinned a gap-toothed grin. "When the gods got locked up here, they started fighting. Not enough power to go around, you see. So, one of them had to be the top dog, like in *Highlander*. The pigeons show me pictures, sometimes. Bloody stuff. Explosions. Nanites eating men. But finally, they were all gone, every last one. My playground now."

So, Esa is gone, too. Kosonen was surprised at how sharp the feeling of loss was, even now. *Better like this.* He swallowed. *Let's get the job done first. No time to mourn. Let's think about it when we get home. Write a poem about it. And tell Marja.*

"All right," Kosonen said. "I'm hunting too. Do you think your... buddies could find it? Something that glows. If you help me, I'll give you all the soup I've got. And elk meat. And I'll bring more later. How does that sound?"

"Pigeons can find anything," said Pera, licking his lips.

THE PIGEON-MAN WALKED through the city labyrinth like his living room, accompanied by a cloud of chimera birds. Now and then, one of them would land on his shoulder and touch his ear with its beak, as if to whisper.

"Better hurry," Pera said. "At night, it's not too bad, but during the day the houses get younger and start thinking."

Kosonen had lost all sense of direction. The map of the city was different from the last time he had been here, in the old human days. His best guess was that they were getting somewhere close to the cathedral in the old town, but he couldn't be sure. Navigating the changed streets felt like walking through the veins of some giant animal, convoluted and labyrinthine. Some buildings were enclosed in what looked like black film, rippling like oil. Some had grown together, organic-looking structures of brick and concrete, blocking streets and making the ground uneven.

"We're not far," Pera said. "They've seen it. Glowing like a pumpkin lantern, they say." He giggled. The amber light of the firewall grew brighter as they walked. It was hotter, too, and Kosonen was forced to discard his old Pohjanmaa sweater.

They passed an office building that had become a sleeping face, a genderless Easter Island countenance. There was more life in this part of the town too—sapphire-eyed animals, sleek cats looking at them from windowsills. Kosonen saw a fox crossing the street: it gave them one bright look and vanished down a sewer hole.

Then they turned a corner, where faceless men wearing fashion from ten years ago danced together in a shop window, and saw the cathedral.

It had grown to gargantuan size, dwarfing every other building around it. It was an anthill of dark-red brick and hexagonal doorways. It buzzed with life. Cats with sapphire claws clung to its walls like sleek gargoyles. Thick pigeon flocks fluttered around its towers. Packs of azure-tailed rats ran in and out of open, massive doors like armies on a mission. And there were insects everywhere, filling the air with a drill-like buzzing sound, moving in dense black clouds like a giant's black breath.

"Oh, jumalauta," Kosonen said. "*That's* where it fell?"

"Actually, no. I was just supposed to bring you here," Pera said.

"What?"

"Sorry. I lied. It *was* like in *Highlander*: there is one of them left. And he wants to meet you."

Kosonen stared at Pera, dumbfounded. The pigeons landed on the other man's shoulders and arms like a gray fluttering cloak. They seized his rags and hair and skin with sharp claws, wings started beating furiously. As Kosonen stared, Pera rose to the air.

"No hard feelings, I just had a better deal from him. Thanks for the soup," he shouted. In a moment, Pera was a black scrap of cloth in the sky.

The earth shook. Kosonen fell to his knees. The window eyes that lined the street lit up, full of bright, malevolent light.

He tried to run. He did not make it far before they came, the fingers of the city: the pigeons, the insects, a buzzing swarm that covered him. A dozen chimera rats clung to his skull, and he could feel the humming of their flywheel hearts. Something sharp bit through the bone. The pain grew like a forest fire, and Kosonen screamed.

The city spoke. Its voice was a thunderstorm, words made from the shaking of the earth and the sighs of buildings. Slow words, squeezed from stone.

Dad, the city said.

* * *

THE PAIN WAS gone. Kosonen heard the gentle sound of waves and felt a warm wind on his face. He opened his eyes.

"Hi, dad," Esa said.

They sat on the summerhouse pier, wrapped in towels, skin flushed from the sauna. It was evening, with a hint of chill in the air, Finnish summer's gentle reminder that things were not forever. The sun hovered above the blue-tinted treetops. The lake surface was calm, full of liquid reflections.

"I thought," Esa said, "that you'd like it here."

Esa was just like Kosonen remembered him, a pale skinny kid, ribs showing, long arms folded across his knees, stringy wet hair hanging on his forehead. But his eyes were the eyes of a city, dark orbs of metal and stone.

"I do," Kosonen said. "But I can't stay."

"Why not?"

"There is something I need to do."

"We haven't seen each other in ages. The sauna is warm. I've got some beer cooling in the lake. Why the rush?"

"I should be afraid of you," Kosonen said. "You killed people. Before they put you here."

"You don't know what it's like," Esa said. "The plague does everything you want. It gives you things you don't even know you want. It turns the world soft. And sometimes it tears it apart for you. You think a thought, and things break. You can't help it."

The boy closed his eyes. "You want things too. I know you do. That's why you are here, isn't it? You want your precious words back."

Kosonen said nothing.

"Mom's errand boy, vittu. So they fixed your brain,

flushed the booze out. So, you can write again. Does it feel good? For a moment there I thought you came here for me. But that's not the way it ever worked, was it?"

"I didn't know—"

"I can see the inside of your head, you know," Esa said. "I've got my fingers inside your skull. One thought, and my bugs will eat you, bring you here for good. Quality time forever. What do you say to that?"

And there it was, the old guilt. "We worried about you, every second after you were born," Kosonen said. "We only wanted the best for you."

It had seemed so natural. How the boy played with his machine that made other machines. How things started changing shape when you thought at them. How Esa smiled when he showed Kosonen the talking starfish that the machine had made.

"And then I had one bad day."

"I remember," Kosonen said. He had been home late, as usual. Esa had been a diamond tree, growing in his room. There were starfish everywhere, eating the walls and the floor, making more of themselves. And that was only the beginning.

"So go ahead. Bring me here. It's your turn to make me into what you want. Or end it all. I deserve it."

Esa laughed softly. "And why would I do that, to an old man?" He sighed. "You know, I'm old too now. Let me show you." He touched Kosonen's shoulder gently and

Kosonen was the city. His skin was stone and concrete, pores full of the godplague. The streets and buildings were his face, changing and shifting with every thought and emotion. His nervous system was diamond and optic fiber. His hands were chimera animals.

The firewall was all around him, in the sky and the cold

bedrock, insubstantial but adamantine, squeezing from every side, cutting off energy, making sure he could not think fast. But he could still dream, weave words and images into threads, make worlds out of the memories he had and the memories of the smaller gods he had eaten to become the city. He sang his dreams in radio waves, not caring if the firewall let them through or not, louder and louder—

"Here," Esa said from far away. "Have a beer."

Kosonen felt a chilly bottle in his hand and drank. The dream-beer was strong and real. The malt taste brought him back. He took a deep breath, letting the fake summer evening wash away the city.

"Is that why you brought me here? To show me that?" He asked.

"Well, no," Esa said, laughing. His stone eyes looked young, suddenly. "I just wanted you to meet my girlfriend."

THE QUANTUM GIRL had golden hair and eyes of light. She wore many faces at once, like a Hindu goddess. She walked to the pier with dainty steps. Esa's summerland showed its cracks around her: there were fracture lines in her skin, with otherworldly colors peeking out.

"This is Säde," Esa said.

She looked at Kosonen, and spoke, a bubble of words, a superposition, all possible greetings at once.

"Nice to meet you," Kosonen said.

"They did something right when they made her, up there," said Esa. "She lives in many worlds at once, thinks in qubits. And this is the world where she wants to be. With me." He touched her shoulder gently. "She heard my songs and ran away."

"Marja said she fell," Kosonen said. "That something was broken."

"She said what they wanted her to say. They don't like it when things don't go according to plan."

Säde made a sound, like the chime of a glass bell.

"The firewall keeps squeezing us," Esa said. "That's how it was made. Make things go slower and slower here, until we die. Säde doesn't fit in here, this place is too small. So you will take her back home before it's too late." He smiled. "I'd rather you do it than anyone else."

"That's not fair," Kosonen said. He squinted at Säde. She was too bright to look at. *But what can I do? I'm just a slab of meat. Meat and words.*

The thought was like a pinecone, rough in his grip, but with a seed of something in it.

"I think there is a poem in you two," he said.

KOSONEN SAT ON the train again, watching the city stream past. It was early morning. The sunrise gave the city new hues: purple shadows and gold, ember colors. Fatigue pulsed in his temples. His body ached. The words of a poem weighed down on his mind.

Above the dome of the firewall he could see a giant diamond starfish, a drone of the sky people, watching, like an outstretched hand.

They came to see what happened, he thought. *They'll find out.*

This time, he embraced the firewall like a friend, and its tingling brightness washed over him. And deep within, the stern-voiced watchman came again. It said nothing this time, but he could feel its presence, scrutinizing, seeking things that did not belong in the outside world.

Kosonen gave it everything.

The first moment when he knew he had put something real on paper. The disappointment when he realized that a poet was not much in a small country, piles of cheaply printed copies of his first collection, gathering dust in little bookshops. The jealousy he had felt when Marja gave birth to Esa, what a pale shadow of that giving birth to words was. The tracks of the elk in the snow and the look in its eyes when it died.

He felt the watchman step aside, satisfied.

Then he was through. The train emerged into the real, undiluted dawn. He looked back at the city and saw fire raining from the starfish. Pillars of light cut through the city in geometric patterns, too bright to look at, leaving only white-hot plasma in their wake.

Kosonen closed his eyes and held on to the poem as the city burned.

KOSONEN PLANTED THE nanoseed in the woods. He dug a deep hole in the half-frozen peat with his bare hands, under an old tree stump. He sat down, took off his cap, dug out his notebook, and started reading. The pencil-scrawled words glowed bright in his mind, and after a while, he didn't need to look at them anymore.

The poem rose from the words like a titanic creature from an ocean, first showing just a small extremity but then soaring upwards in a spray of glossolalia, mountain-like. It was a stream of hissing words and phonemes, an endless spell that tore at his throat. And with it came the quantum information from the microtubules of his neurons, where the bright-eyed girl now lived, and jagged impulses from synapses where his son was hiding.

The poem swelled into a roar. He continued until his voice was a hiss. Only the nanoseed could hear, but that was enough. Something stirred under the peat.

When the poem finally ended, it was evening. Kosonen opened his eyes. The first things he saw were the sapphire antlers, sparkling in the last rays of the sun.

Two young elk looked at him. One was smaller, more delicate, and its large brown eyes held a hint of sunlight. The other was young and skinny but wore its budding antlers with pride. It held Kosonen's gaze, and in its eyes, he saw shadows of the city. Or reflections in a summer lake, perhaps.

They turned and ran into the woods, silent, fleet-footed and free.

KOSONEN WAS OPENING the cellar door when the rain came back. It was barely a shower this time: the droplets formed Marja's face in the air. For a moment he thought he saw her wink. Then the rain became a mist, and was gone. He propped the door open.

The squirrels stared at him from the trees curiously.

"All yours, gentlemen," Kosonen said. "Should be enough for next winter. I don't need it anymore."

Otso and Kosonen left at noon, heading north. Kosonen's skis slid along easily in the thinning snow. The bear pulled a sledge loaded with equipment. When they were well away from the cabin, it stopped to sniff at a fresh trail.

"Elk," it growled. "Otso is hungry. Kosonen shoot an elk. Need meat for the journey. Kosonen did not bring enough booze."

Kosonen shook his head.

"I think I'm going to learn to fish," he said.

THE WINGS THAT SLICE THE SKY
Emmi Itäranta

THERE IS A picture in one of the halls in the South, in Kalevaland, a tapestry woven with great skill. It is as wide as the wall, and so lifelike that when you gaze at it, you can hear the wind and the waves, and feel the shine of the stars on your skin. So they say.

It pictures three men on a ship: a spell-singer, a blacksmith, and a warrior. They have travelled far to claim what they believe is theirs by right. The spell-singer's white beard beats wildly about his face in the storm, and he holds a sword ready to strike, facing a hideous thing hovering in the air.

She wears the face of an old hag; her nose is crooked, her gums bare, and her back hunched. Her thick skin folds into wrinkles, and her only visible eye bulges from her head like a serpent's egg. Her bare breasts hang withered, dry leather pouches, and her bony arms have grown a thick, black plumage—dark wings that slice the starry sky in two. The long, sharp claws on her knuckled toes grapple for the treasure in the boat. She is recognisable as a woman, yet everything a woman must not be: old, ugly, furious, greedy—and shameless enough not to hide any of this.

A monster to be slain.

Hands will arrange threads to form an image that has first been drawn by words and songs in the mind's eye. Therefore I shall now seize words: they have the power to shatter and heal, to unravel and build and make things anew.

MANY OF THE tales of Kalevalanders have carved a space for what I was, but little has been said of where I came from. If I am to be honest, there is not much to tell. I was born at Earth's end, under a low roof, on the distant shore of a cold river so far in the North that people called it Underworld. In my thin-worn memories it is a landscape veiled by dusk, where the dead were as much at home as the living. Hunger resided in every hut, and every day was scraped together around it. I see my parents as shadows in the corners, my sisters shrinking and pale on the floor like waning moons.

I still had sisters back then.

I grew up in Underworld, until I was sent to serve as a maid in the nearest village and eat from the pots of a large farmhouse, Pohjola. There the son of the master took note of my comely figure. I had no dowry, but soon the master and mistress of the house understood I did not by any means arrive without assets. I had something better than linen and silver: I knew how to turn away the frost from spring fields so the crops would be spared, and I knew how to sing to the beasts and charm them to stay away from the cattle. If the enemy approached the lands of Pohjola intending to raid and plunder, I knew how to raise mists to make them lose their way or summon the storm to thrash their ships.

Thus I became the daughter-in-law of the largest house in the North.

SOME SAY I used my sorcery to ensnare my husband. That is the talk of the envious and the fearful. I had no need. At the time my face was as beautiful as my body, and many eyes followed me as I walked in the farmhouses and across the yards. He would not look away either, yet what he loved the most was the way my mind moved, agile and sharp as a sword polished with a whetstone in a bold warrior's hand. He was good to me, and I to him. Eight moons after the wedding feast I gave birth to a daughter, bright-eyed and beautiful. The child opened her mouth to scream at the moment of sundown, and so I named her Ilta, 'evening' in my mother's tongue. A year later I pushed another child from my womb into the world; she gave her first cry at dawn, and we named her Aamu, 'morning'.

My daughters were but wee lasses when they picked up the shuttle and began to weave. Ilta threaded golden yarn into her cloth and Aamu twined silvery strands into hers, as the two of them sat on a high cliff edge from which you could see afar. As I watched them grow like beautiful birds, I thought for the first time that they could be seen too, sitting on their pedestal, like bait for any predator to approach. But I tried to cast this worry from my mind because life was good. Our house was wealthy and happy, and peace prevailed in the North. Once in a while news reached our lands of skirmishes

South in Kalevaland, but they were too far away to be any of our concern.

SONGS HAVE GRANTED me many a power and spell-lore, and most of them are true. Some I was gifted at birth; others I learnt with hard work and effort. Yet there is one thing that is beyond my knowledge. I have never known to look into the future and weave the threads of fate in different directions. I lack the skill to see the tapestry forming before it has taken its irreversible shape and the strands have knotted themselves into a noose around my neck.

When I think of everything I have lost, I imagine the tapestry that my daughters wove day in and day out, sitting on their tall seats under the bare sky, the images in which they recorded every happiness and, as time went by, every sorrow. I imagine my fingers tracing the texture of the cloth. They linger when they meet my lost loved ones: my husband, who has passed into Tuonela; my older daughter, claimed by a firebolt; and my youngest, whose hands will never weave again. My claws crook as if to maul when they come across the loathed faces: the spell-singer, the blacksmith, and the warrior. I imagine my hands finding the thread that keeps everything together, and yanking.

The pictures begin to unravel. The threads run loose, the weft and the warp, and one at a time all my miseries melt away. I can embrace my daughters and the father of my children again. Spears and swords are shrapnel in the wind, there is no need for warships or a fence of venomous vipers. A treasure locked in the mountain melts into the blacksmith's furnace and has never caught anyone's eye, including mine. The gates of Pohjola have swung open again. Look: we draw closer to the moment when everything could still have been changed, the first image.

This is where it begins.

A shipwrecked old man is crying in misery, and I—curse my soft heart—go and rescue him.

I ROWED TOWARDS the wretched weeping that carried from the mouth of a ditch lined by willows. The day was calm; the pointed leaves of the bushes hung above murky water like silver-haired rain. I pulled my boat ashore and moved the branches aside.

The man was a pitiful sight to behold. He lay in the mud with his clothes tarnished and torn, his skin covered in bruises. He was not from these lands: his shoes were a different make, there were unfamiliar patterns on his belt and his tunic was an odd shape. Large bundles of his white hair and beard had fallen out, and I saw blood on his gums. The same illness had haunted my childhood home when we had little to eat besides bark bread and bone broth. I remembered the taste of blood in my mouth, the feeling of an uprooted tooth against my tongue and the hunger gouging my insides. I remembered my younger sisters, whom my spells had been unable to keep in this world, who had withered until we eventually carried their twig-like bodies to the burial ground and piled rocks on top of them. In their memory, we cut branches off a living tree in the grove, one for each.

The man's body shook with sobs. I stepped closer and spoke to him.

"What rotten luck has befallen you to bring you to a strange land in such a state?"

He lifted his head. He only then seemed to notice me. He wiped his face and sat up. In his posture, I saw an attempt at dignity.

"Who are you, old dame?" he asked. "To speak to me like that? In my homeland, I am held in high esteem."

"Louhi is my name," I responded. "And I am the mistress of these lands. Who are you yourself," I paused before continuing, "your excellency?"

The old man lifted his chin. His eyes were bloodshot.

"You may have heard of me, or my singing. They call me Väinämöinen."

"Whoever you are," I said, "I can't leave you there. Are you able to get up?"

I offered my hand and he took it. I wrapped his arm around my shoulder as I walked him to the boat. He did not refuse my help despite it coming from a woman.

I rowed the man to Pohjola. I spent a week feeding him and bathing him in the sauna before his wounds closed and the bruises all over his body began to heal. He said little, but I managed to carve enough words out of him to know that he had been shipwrecked. He had floated waterborne for a long time, then swum from one isle to the next clinging to some paltry piece of wood in the cold sea. He had survived by eating mussels and raw fish and waterfowl eggs until he had finally managed to flounder to the shores of the North.

Then one evening as I sat fomenting his wounds with a compress of crushed plantain leaves and he sipped willow bark tea, tears began to roll down his face again.

"Why do you weep, Väinämöinen?"

He dried his eyes with a clean shirt sleeve. His dirtied rags had been useless, so I had given him new garments from my storehouse.

"What would you ask for," Väinämöinen asked, "in exchange for a horse from your stable and food for the way to see me safely return to Kalevaland? Homesickness aches in me and I long to hear familiar birdsong in my ears."

The question surprised me. I had not helped him in hope of a reward, and it had not occurred to me to ask for one. When I did not respond at once, Väinämöinen continued: "Is it gold you wish for, or silver? I can get you both."

The long stables of Pohjola were full of stallions, there was enough grain to feed more than one village, and the coin chests were so heavy it took the strength of several servants to move one.

"Your silver is of no use to me," I said, but a thought crept into my mind. "Have you heard of the Sampo?"

It was a stab in the dark, a fortunate guess. The lore was told at the hearths of the North, of a thing of mighty magic with a ciphered cover that would never stop moving. As its crank turned, the world itself revolved around the stars in the sky, and riches would fall from the Sampo's ever-grinding mill like rain. Whoever could forge this device would never lack for anything, and there would always be bread at the table of their people.

I thought again of the taste of blood on my tongue, of the bones of my sisters and other children in the burial groves that had grown in number in the long years when the crops froze in the fields.

I saw on Väinämöinen's face immediately that the same stories were also told South in Kalevaland. He stiffened and his breathing stopped for a moment.

"Are you asking me to bring you the Sampo?"

"Would you know how to make it?"

"The Sampo is far more valuable than a horse and a sleigh," Väinämöinen said slowly. "If I deliver the Sampo, what else will you offer?"

"What do you ask for?"

"Would you give me your daughter?"

That cursed tall cliff edge. His cursed, wandering man-eyes.

I knew my girls. I knew they would not agree to be traded like cattle. Ilta would only marry someone she wanted, and Aamu would not marry anyone. Together we had sent one suitor after another away. But this was the Sampo. I had to negotiate this contract wisely.

"My daughter?" I said. "The matter can be discussed. If you'll bring me the Sampo."

"I have no skill to forge the Sampo myself," Väinämöinen replied, "but there is someone in my homeland who has. The best of all blacksmiths. He forged the sky itself."

By then I had understood he tended to exaggerate. I expected little, but said nevertheless, "As I said, we can discuss the matter when I have received the Sampo."

Väinämöinen's face brightened.

"We have an agreement," he said.

In hindsight, all my troubles began there and then.

BY THE TIME the storm arrived months later, I had surmised many times that the bearded old fellow had made an empty promise. At least the horse I had given him was old and ill of temper. But when I least expected it, the winds threw a man to the yards of Pohjola who clearly would have preferred to be anywhere else. He cursed Väinämöinen and made to leave, but he had no sooner taken one look at Ilta swishing her skirts than he began to ask for a furnace. I watched him roll up his sleeves, which revealed admittedly muscular arms and realised this must be the heroic blacksmith Väinämöinen had spoken of. Ilmarinen was his name. As he spent days puffing up his biceps and banging the metal, squinting at various shapes turning up in the flames, I noted a change in Ilta's behaviour. Usually, she would not look at suitors twice, but now she began to busy herself with all kinds of errands around Ilmarinen. She went to see him working several times a day, carried beer for him from the house and returned from the blacksmith's forge, her cheeks reddened by more than the glow of the furnace.

I thought it best to have a maternal conversation with her.

"What do you know of Kalevaland, my girl?"

"Little do I know, Mother. But I suppose the same lingonberries grow there as here, and the woods echo with the song of the same birds."

"What do you know of the life of the daughter-in-law at a husband's home, my child?"

"If the husband is good, I suppose it is like tasting honey bread and sipping mead all day long."

"And suppose he is not good? What if the lot of the girl is better in her mother's house, weaving golden yarns rather than sweeping the floors of a stranger's hut?"

"Why do you ask such things?"

"The blacksmith will propose to you. Will you accept?"

A glow rose on Ilta's face and she would not meet my eyes, but she said, "I will not. Why would I?"

I wanted to believe her at the time.

* * *

IT WOULD BE easy to put the blame entirely on them, the so-called heroes of Kalevaland, but in one matter I admit my guilt: I allowed the Sampo to place a too-powerful spell on me. That is the strand I would pluck out most harshly from the tapestry of the past, tear it into tiny pieces and sow them into the sea. In that yarn, I hang myself time and again when I think of my mistakes. Wise Louhi, mighty Louhi, who wanted to secure the stability of her family and realm. Foolish Louhi, weak Louhi, who could not see beyond the shine of the ciphered cover.

The dawn came when the fire was finally extinguished, the smoke dissipated from around the furnace and the most miraculous of all things shone in the ashes. I could not tear my eyes off it. Much has been sung about the Sampo, but little said about the way it looked. If you had been there at that blood-red sunrise and cast your gaze towards the Sampo, you would have known why.

"What is it?" asked the oldest of the servants, who had stopped to watch the work of the blacksmith.

"Do you not see?" my husband asked. "It is a chest that fills itself ceaselessly with flour, salt, and coin."

"Has old age claimed your eyesight, Father?" Aamu asked. "That is a spindle, and it spins endless silver yarn from empty air."

"Smoke has swallowed the eyes of you both," Ilta said. "It's obviously a mill that grinds wealth into the world."

"Precisely," said blacksmith Ilmarinen. "I see a mill too when I look at it."

I said nothing. In my eyes, the Sampo was a tree. On its trunk and at its top the stars of the sky shone bright. Flour spilled from the branches like the yellow dust of flowers in springtime, salt like heavy rain that feeds the earth, and coins like heavy-hanging fruit that you only need to reach for and they will fall ripe into your lap. No one in my realm would ever taste blood again and spit teeth from their mouth because of hunger.

When I was finally able to tear my gaze away from the miracle, I gestured for three strong servants to carry the Sampo and I walked with them inside the mountain, to a place I had prepared. For of course, I had already understood back then that the Sampo must be protected. I ordered everyone to leave. I wished to be alone with my treasure.

For a long time, I watched it and listened to it, and it seemed to whisper to me. I could not decipher the words, but I knew it spoke my language. I recited the protective spells for the Sampo. With my mind I sought its roots and told them to grow long, push themselves into the ground and pierce it to the depth of nine fathoms. One root I knotted to the rocky hill Pohjola where my house stood; another I bound by the water. The third, longest of all, I tied to the very heart of Earth and thought, *There will be no such storm in this world that will uproot my Sampo now.*

That was the first night I stayed on the brink of its whispers.

In the morning I secured the doors with nine locks and hid the keys in a secret pocket at my skirt waist. After weaving my spells, I was exhausted. I rested inside the mountain for a day, and for another. Yet I felt no thirst or hunger. For the first time in my life, I seemed to have eaten my fill. I would open my eyes occasionally, and ceaselessly the Sampo would rain wealth from its branches.

When I finally stepped back into daylight, Ilta and Ilmarinen avoided each other. I caught her alone, and to be certain I spoke to her.

"Did the blacksmith ask you?"

"He did. I refused. In the North a woman's words have weight, and the daughter of the household carries golden yarn in her loom. I hear it is different in Kalevaland, and the lot of the daughter-in-law is the worst of all."

But when she sat down at her loom, the posture of her smooth shoulders was slumped.

I sent Ilmarinen home with his pointed hat crooked. The Sampo ground security for the North in the shelter of the rock, and I thought all was well.

But sometimes men gossip and nothing will send their words wagging like women. Apparently, the fairness of my daughters had loosened the tongues of Väinämöinen and Ilmarinen, because after that a motley crew of suitors from Kalevaland began to appear in Pohjola. As soon as we had sent one away, the next was waiting in line, each of them with ever more dumbfounding demands. A warrior called Lemminkäinen was the most impossible of all. You might imagine a wife at home would prevent a man from courting. You would suppose such subtle hints as 'ski down the Hiisi demon's elk', 'shoot down the swan of Death in Tuonela', and 'plough the field of adders' would drive the message home. You might anticipate that once a man has drifted in death's dark river, been chopped into pieces and stitched back together, he would know better than to go after the daughters of Pohjola.

Persistent and bone-headed, these great heroes.

Yet Ilta had softened to Ilmarinen as early as his first visit, and for long weeks I had listened to my daughter's sighs since then. When the blacksmith came courting again, she lacked the spirit for inventing the strenuous tasks for the suitor we used to come up with, barely able to conceal our delight as one aspiring groom after another headed for his inevitable downfall. Instead, Ilta began to help the blacksmith to survive his trials. She thought she was keeping it a secret from me; but what kind of a mother would I have been if I had not noticed?

I understood then that this was serious. I collected a stunning dowry for my daughter and organised a handsome wedding. My heart was torn off its roots as I saw to her journey towards Kalevaland, but I watched them glow at each other, Ilta and Ilmarinen, and I wanted to believe in my daughter's happiness.

Around that time, I also began to hear rumours concerning myself: about my sparse teeth, my infamous greed, my ability to send diseases to taunt people. I had my suspicions about the origins of this gossip, but I decided to turn it to my benefit. If the idea of me as a monster would scare off enough of those striving to be heroes, life in the North would be more peaceful.

I did not invite Lemminkäinen to the wedding. He had been so much trouble already that I had erected a tall fence around Pohjola, and on its sharp posts I had cast a spell to make them look like living snakes, each one hissing louder and slithering faster than the next. Images of dead, cut-off heads impaled on the fence grimaced at any strangers. I was pleased with the illusion I had conjured. I hoped it would chase away others like him.

I should have understood parasites like him would not give up so easily. But the Sampo bound my eyes from too many things, and its whispers hid other sounds from my ears.

THE MAN WHO took me for his wife, made me the mother of beautiful daughters and the mistress of vast lands, has barely been given any space in songs. He was a good man: he never spoke ill of my lowly birth, and always treated me well. I treated him well too, and each morning we greeted each other with contentment.

How he was taken from me remains one of the greatest griefs of my life. Even now I think I might have been able to prevent it. That day I was inside the mountain again, held by the chains of the Sampo's glimmer. I had forgotten myself there as soon as I had woken up, and I did not feel the passage of time as I watched the silver raining from the bright boughs, the smooth salt falling before my eyes, and the flour bins filling.

I woke to cries and knocking from behind nine doors.

"Mistress!" the servants cried. "Come quickly, terrible things are happening!"

I tore my gaze off the Sampo and started towards the sound. The images of the branches hanging low with coin vanished from my eyes when I saw what the tumult was about. I stopped and turned still as a stone before the sight.

Blood dripped onto the brown dust of the ground as Lemminkäinen lifted something to the pointed end of a fence post. A head that wore the face of my beloved and well-cherished husband.

My heart stopped beating; my breath stopped moving. My soul escaped to the sky, watching the terror from there like a bird, feather-light because my body was too weighty, the pain in my chest too much to bear. From high up, I saw Lemminkäinen pierce the head with the pole: the head I had held in my lap, whose lips I had kissed, whose hair my fingers had dug in, who had closed his eyes and lowered himself to my chest in bed hundreds and thousands of times. It wore the same face, yet it had nothing to do with my husband: it was a bloody and bruised piece of strange flesh, separate from him in every way.

I rose ever higher to be able to see further, all the way to the river of Tuonela, to catch a final glimpse of him before he placed a foot on the daughter of Tuoni's ferry and would vanish to the land of the dead. But it was too late. He was already gone; while I had sat still as a boulder inside the mountain, unseeing, sensing no hunger, hearing nothing but the swish of salt and tingling of silver.

From my height I watched Lemminkäinen turn towards my body that was rooted in the ground, look at me and smile, and that smile turned his beautiful face as ugly as plague. Still staring at me, he ordered a maid to bring water so he could wash the blood off his hands.

My spirit which had for a moment escaped the pain bursting in my chest, fell back into my body from the sky. Even before I beckoned, the song began to quicken at the roots of my heart and roll off my tongue. It filled the yards and the fields, it reached across the rocky cliffs of the North and summoned swords and spears to defend my home, to grieve for my broken family, to cast a punishment on the murderer. I wish now I had slain him there and then, ripped his chest open with nothing more than the sound of my voice and pulled his heart to wriggle in the dust of the yard like a dying fish. But everything was as slow as if a stone had swallowed my body, and unfortunately, the magical powers he had been given were not without vigour. He flew to the sky as a bird and evaded the arrows shot after him.

I sent a falcon to chase him. It came back with empty talons and told me Lemminkäinen had escaped to hide

in the skirts of his mother, moaning that the evil troops
of the North were after him, a poor lonely man.

You may cry a river, wretch, you may cry a lake.

My warriors marched far and burned villages on their
way. I spun stout spells around my warships, I sharpened
the spears with my song and charmed them to find their
aim with precision. Wider around the viper fence I raised
a wall of frost to protect the North, so my home would
be safe from then on. But the casket of misfortune that
the arrival of the Sampo had flung open, would not close.

A moon passed; a summer passed. Then another. When
the blacksmith arrived in Pohjola again the following
winter, I ordered the frost to give way and had the viper-
gates opened. I thought he might bring my daughter to
visit home or at least some news of how bright Ilta's days
were as the mistress of Ilmarinen's house and hearth.

But one side of his sledge was empty, and a great dark
cloud crouched on his brow. When I asked how my
child was faring in Kalevaland, the blacksmith looked
troubled and then managed to somehow spit out that
death had claimed my Ilta. And before I even had the
chance to understand what he was saying, he was already
demanding to have Aamu as a replacement for her sister.

My voice twisted into iron blades.

"You have some gall! I will push my girl into the rapids
before I give her to you. You were useless in looking after
my first poor child!"

The words were barely out of my mouth when my
heart cramped and coiled. My breath would not flow.
My eyes blurred, and I dropped onto my knees. Through
the mist, I sensed some caterwauling and sounds of a
brawl from the direction of the hearth. I fell. Servants
flocked about me. I almost ordered my spirit to leave

my body again, like it had done when my husband was murdered. But I understood this pain was about more than grief: my heart struggled to beat and pump blood into my veins, and if my soul were to fly to the heavens now, my body might close the gates, and freeze into stiff stone to which it would not be able to return. So I clung to my pain with claws and teeth, wanting to sense it.

Everything else disappeared. Someone screamed far away. A gull, I thought. Amidst the cries, the hooves of a horse battered the ground. My senses went out like a candle.

When I woke, the room was draped in winter shadows. I was not sure if it was a dark day or a bright night. A servant sat in the corner and jumped to attend to me.

"What happened?" I asked when I saw the expression on her face.

"Mistress, perhaps you should eat or drink something first," the servant began.

I interrupted her in a soft voice. "Tell me."

"The blacksmith took her. Aamu."

"Surely someone made a chase?"

"Yes, but his horse was too fast."

"Go," I told her.

"Would you like me to bring some food, mistress?"

"I would like to be alone," I said.

Three days and three nights I sat in my chamber. On the third night, I walked along hard-packed snow to the woods and called to every animal who would heed my call. Wolves came, and foxes, and squirrels and lynxes and falcons. I asked one favour of them: *Find out what happened to Ilta, and what happened to Aamu. When you know who took my daughters, come back and tell me.*

They went, and over the days and weeks, they began to bring me knowledge. It was said Ilta had treated the servant of the house poorly, and in revenge, he had conjured a bear to maul her. As if those mortal wounds were not enough, it was said Ukko Jumala the Highest had become so furious with my daughter that he had sent a thunderbolt to kill her.

Ilta was not without fault. Sometimes she knew her worth all too well and did not always treat kindly those she considered unworthy. But if it is true that she simply baked a stone into the servant Kullervo's bread, and this was his revenge, was the retribution reasonable in any way? An annoying but harmless taunt, punished with a painful and violent death in the claws of a bear—is that justice? And the tale about Jumala the Highest: perhaps true, but at the same time, a punishment from gods has always been a handy excuse for explaining the bloodbaths of humans.

Aamu had not been any luckier, the birds knew when they returned from their travels. Ilmarinen had transformed her into a seagull on an islet with his song when she did not wish to be taken by force to sweep the blacksmith's floors, to lie in the place of her sister.

Let a blazing swirl of the sea swallow easily vexed men who take justice into their own hands to deal too-harsh punishments to women.

After that, I was ready for anything from the flock of Kalevaland. My power had diminished, as my poor heart had wriggled in terror of the blows it had received. I went to strengthen the fences of Pohjola, I wove the spells to be denser and the snakes wriggling at the gates keener, and I made the bloody heads on the fence posts grimace twice as terribly. I had taken my husband's battered head into the burial grove under a stack of stones long ago and cut a branch off a living tree in his memory. But where the severed head had been, I conjured the most terrifying image that wore his face. I bewitched it to laugh and scorn at anyone who was not from Pohjola, and to spit blood on them.

I also strengthened the protections of the Sampo. The nine locks aside, I had a bolt made by the best blacksmith in Pohjola. Around it, I spun a spell so strong that it would have vanquished even myself if I had not known the exact pattern in which it could be unravelled.

Occasionally I would vanish for days. My people believed I sat inside the mountain at the foot of the Sampo, and often I did. But when I could garner the strength, I flew as a bird, seeking my child. I knew I would recognise her among other gulls. She was still my Aamu, and I was still her mother. She too would recognise my cry and come to me, and together we would find the magic of making her human again.

But the sea is wide, and its shores are vast and even wider is the sky for gulls to fly. I only encountered birds who carried their own bird-souls, never one in whose eyes I saw her gaze.

Then came the day I knew to expect despite the fact I was never a seer.

Väinämöinen, Ilmarinen, and Lemminkäinen sailed their vessel to the shore of Pohjola. They were not frightened by the fence of snakes or the grimacing effigies. They walked into my house as if it was their home.

"We have come to claim our share of the Sampo," Väinämöinen announced. Drizzle had caught on his beard and beer weighed on his breath.

"The Sampo is not for sharing," I said. "It belongs

to me. You promised it in exchange for my helping you return home. Have you forgotten?"

The lies slid from Väinämöinen's tongue so smoothly they dispelled my last doubts about where the rumours about me had come from.

"You held me as your prisoner," Väinämöinen replied. "I bought my freedom from you with the Sampo, because it was the only thing I could think of in my great distress. I knew you would accept nothing less."

"We had an agreement," I said.

"Agreement?" This time Lemminkäinen was speaking, handsome and far-minded, ugly and plague-tongued. "An offer made under great duress is no agreement. Lies roll from your mouth like dung, you long-toothed matriarch of Darkland."

Ilmarinen remained quiet, scowling at me from under his brows.

"If you won't give us the Sampo willingly," Väinämöinen said, "we will take it by force."

You may cry a river.

The numbers of my warriors are not small. I have not gained or retained my powers by spells alone. If the Kalevalanders had been ordinary men, or any of them had arrived alone, none would have made it further than the entrance. But they too had been granted powers of sorcery, and my own had worn thinner because of great grief.

When Väinämöinen sat down on the bench next to the window and pulled a flat instrument made from fishbone from his leather pouch, beginning to pluck its strings with his sharp claws, I had no time to recognise it as a weapon.

And while it brings bile to my mouth, I must admit

he knew how to fashion notes. From the strings of his kantele he spun music that glittered like a piece of jewellery. It turned like a handsome bird from distant lands; it extended its hand like a beautiful and desirable lover. It reached out and twined like a golden thread and turned everyone towards itself. I, too, stopped to listen, and while I was listening, sleep began to soothe my eyes, such inviting and languid rest I could not remember experiencing for many years. I lay down on the floor. The hard planks felt like a soft bed underneath my side.

Everything else faded away and I fell to sleep where nothing existed but the sweet caress of music.

THE SCREECH OF a crane woke me. At first, I did not know where I was. My entire body was stiff; my hip ached. My throat was parched and my stomach gurgled empty as if I had not eaten or drunk for days. Slowly I pushed myself up from the floor. Other folk around me were waking up from their stupor. Memories of what had happened surfaced in my mind. With stiff legs, I rushed to the rock.

When I saw the locks hanging mauled and the doors unhinged, a tall cry rose from my throat, a spell and another. But I knew I had to use every means I had.

The numbers of my warriors are not small. My rowers are swift.

See the strands settle before your eyes to form a tapestry: it is the image you already know, and yet it is not.

The spell-singer, the blacksmith, and the warrior stand aboard their ship as a three-headed monster, shooting sparkling spell-verses from their fingers. The Sampo is bound in place, reaching its branches towards me like arms, begging to be taken back home. My largest warship is protected by a powerful charm, but the three-headed monster's cry hits it as a harsh wind, driving it towards a sharp set of stones until I hear the hard bones of the rock claw the keel open. My warriors waver and fall overboard from the force of the hit. Lightning-like, the spell-singer's verse pierces the mast, which cracks, topples, and breaks. The waves vacillate like mountains around us, but can no longer carry the ship that is held in place by the reef of rocks.

Sometimes a woman has no choice but to turn into an enormous bird of prey.

I build my spell from the pieces of the ship where my own magic still lives. As I pick up the wood and iron to make my arms and legs longer, I feel my power grow. Never before have I allowed another person to see my bird-shape. I have hidden it from the world, so my people would not turn against me. Sorcery of this sort is too much for many. I see even my own warriors back down as smooth quills push out of my skin and I rise to meet the sky; my nose arches into a strong beak and my claws grow long and able. As I spread my arms, they slice the sky as wide wings. I see wonder and fear in the eyes of my war troops, but as they understand that my strength is theirs, they come to me. I can carry hundreds without effort.

How puny the thieves look in their boat, how bare the terror on their faces, how fragile their human hands that clutch my Sampo!

From the heights I make a surge for the tree: if only I could get my claws on it, I could carry it home, protect it with charmed locks that no one would ever break. The warriors under my wings scream; others cling to the feathers on my back. The blacksmith falls to his knees in fear like a miserable animal of prey, but the other two begin to sling their spells. Lemminkäinen's sword cuts the air and the waves, water droplets flashing like blood-washed pale. The blade cannot reach me. But the oar Väinämöinen has picked up is longer, and the weight of the warriors pulls me to an odd angle. I evade too late and splitting pain hits one of my feet as my claws break. Warriors slide into the sea from my back, their cries are foam on the crests. Air escapes from beneath me and I crash against the side of the ship.

Ache throbs in my claws as I reach for the radiant tree. For one moment it is mine, but then another thunderbolt of pain strikes through me, and the Sampo slips from my mangled hold into the sea. It hits a boulder jutting under the water and shatters like burnt clay. I see the spell-singer push his hand into the water as he tries to grope for the sinking shards.

I, too, search the water in despair and catch a few fragments. But the ciphered cover is gone: gone that which secured my life, gone that which chained me to the mirage inside the mountain, and turned me away from my life and loved ones.

The sharp-clawed spell-singing monster fumbles around in the water, hands meeting emptiness. The strands settle anew, the image remains, and the light falls on it from a different direction than before.

I FELT MY power wane and my body shrink. My wings diminished to the size of an ordinary eagle, and in the form of an ordinary bird, I flew back to Pohjola, clutching the shards of the Sampo in my claws. I carried them like branches of a tree cut off in memory of my murdered family. I scattered them around the shores of Pohjola, but I was not ready to resume my human form, to step into my realm and meet the devastation the people of Kalevaland had left behind. And my own greed: for at the end of the day, it was my doing that I had summoned my warriors to the battle and taken them to their death at sea. I would have to face their families, their grieving spouses and orphaned children. Nothing remained of their sacrifice but lifeless shards, a barely recognisable shadow of what had been.

Thus, I continued to fly as a bird.

I don't know how many sunrises had passed, when a cry was carried to my ears from across the water, a cry I knew at once. It gave me direction. I dressed myself as a seagull because I did not wish to frighten her. I responded to her call: *Where are you?*

My child sang to me from across the waves: *Here, here!*

And although I did not have my eagle's eyesight, I saw her from afar. Her white form was pointed, like the shuttle she'd used to pass through the shiny strands of yarn, and her yellow beak opened to a cry of joy as I approached.

My Aamu was alive.

I landed on her stony islet and rubbed my beak against hers. I groomed her feathers, and we took small sprints of flight around each other. I dove into the waves and caught her a fish with slippery sides that twitched in my beak. But while she recognised me, I could see the human in her beginning to hide deeper. Her senses were those of a bird, and her world was a bird's world, and eventually she would forget her human body altogether.

I transformed myself into a bird of prey again, picked Aamu up in my claws as gently as I could, and carried her to an island.

For weeks and months, I sought the spell in her as if it was a sickness that the cursed blacksmith had infected her with. I tried to catch it like a thread so I could unravel it, make her human again. Sometimes I would feel my fingers close around the spell, would sense the sorcery give in and unravel; but sooner or later it always turned into a tangle, and when I tugged too fiercely, the thread would break. My daughter remained a bird.

I conjured my strongest wings and flew skyward. I did not care who saw me. The sun and the moon were easy to pluck from their places. I carried them to Pohjola and captured them inside the mountain, the stony scar of a pit the Sampo had left in the guts of the rock.

Weeks passed; months rolled by. Trees dropped their leaves, crops collapsed on the fields and the pale grass withered. I flew as a bird across Kalevaland, watching how cold and hunger began to put their strain on the people. I expected them to march to the spell-singer and demand that he atone for the crimes that made him responsible for their devastation. But he had prepared a story about the witch of the North, a smooth lie, easy to swallow.

The folks in Kalevaland were faring worse and worse. I flew to the blacksmith's forgery and made my claim.

"Tell me how to make my child human again," I said, "and I will give you back the moon and the sun."

I watched understanding unfold slowly in his blacksmith's eyes. For a moment I saw him wearing and holding a great sorrow, a grief that had changed him. For a moment I thought: *You could have been my son. The death of Ilta was not your doing. Whatever else you may have done, you were good to her. Together we might have met the grief, and it did not need to separate us, but it could have united us.*

But then the moment was over. He laughed and was a stranger and all wrong, and he said, "Do you know what I'm forging here? These are the chains that will capture the hag-dame of Pohjola inside the mountain, and she will never again come out to use her sorcery. And even without these, you would be too late, old woman. I put a spell on your child that cannot be unravelled, because its words are inscribed to the sky. She will fly as a gull to the end of her days."

And with that, I had to take wing. From the sky, I saw the people struggling in the darkness, how they ground the bark of the dying trees into their bread, lay by fading fires, and carried stones to cover the bones of their unmoving children. The taste of blood rose to my mouth again.

I returned to Pohjola and made my decision.

The years of birds are briefer than those of humans. My child calls to me from the islets, and there is nothing else in the North I will miss now. My human body is worn, strained by sorrow; in a bird's skin, I will fly lighter. Perhaps my soul has always been more bird than human.

You know the image made of me.

Take now these words, let them demolish and build and make anew.

Under my wrinkled skin, there has always been a figure you will see if you look closely enough. Another has always lived in songs, whispering between the lines. I am that song, hidden inside a louder one. I am the wings that grow from your arms: strong enough to cross all skies, even if you do not know that yet.

This morning I let the moon and the sun out of their prison of stone, because why should the whole world suffer for the deeds of a few men? As I see the lights climb back to the sky for the first time in ages, as I see the trees and grass wake again and their growth beginning deep inside the Earth, I turn towards the sea and the sky. Quills push from my skin, and each one shines in the sun like a dagger. My beak arches strong, ready to surge for prey and feed me. My sharp claws are ready to clutch, to keep me alive and defend everything I love. I no longer need the Sampo to shelter me, and I no longer hide my strength inside a mountain.

I spread my wings to slice the sky, soar higher and fly out of the bounds of the story that was always too narrow to hold me.

Author's note:
There are several English translations of the Finnish national epic Kalevala. *A few expressions used in this short story come from Eino Friberg's translation, which I have mainly relied on here. (*Kalevala – The Epic of the Finnish People, *Penguin Random House 2021.)*

CONTRIBUTOR BIOGRAPHIES

Alexander Dan Vilhjálmsson is an Icelandic novelist who lives in Reykjavík, Iceland. He explores the weird in all its multitudes, usually in fantastical novels and black metal lyrics. His Hrímland duology, starting with *Shadows of the Short Days* in 2019, merges Icelandic history and folklore with fantasy literature. Its sequel, *The Storm Beneath a Midnight Sun*, was released in 2022. These days Alexander is very occupied with infusing the mundane with the fantastical. He works in both Icelandic and English, translating back and forth as necessary. The language he chooses to write in is dictated by the work itself—a convenient excuse. Some people try to call him a musician, which he disagrees with for some reason. More details can be found on his website at alexanderdan.net

Emmi Itäranta is a Finnish author who writes fiction in Finnish and English. Her debut novel *Memory of Water* from 2014 has won numerous awards, including a James Tiptree Jr. Award honours list mention and the Kalevi Jäntti Prize for young writers in Finland. She has also published two other award-winning novels: *The Weaver* and *The Moonday Letters*. Emmi's work has been translated into more than twenty languages. She returned to her native Finland in 2021 after 14 years in the UK. Find out more at her website: www.emmiitaranta.com

Hannu Rajaniemi was born in Finland. At the age of eight, he approached the European Space Agency with a fusion-powered spaceship design, which was received with a polite 'thank you' note. Hannu is a co-founder and CEO of HelixNano, a venture- and Y Combinator-backed synthetic biology startup building the world's most advanced mRNA platform to enable previously impossible applications across human and non-human biology, including COVID-19, climate and cancer. Hannu studied mathematics and theoretical physics at the University of Oulu and Cambridge and holds a PhD in string theory from the University of Edinburgh. He co-founded a mathematics consultancy whose clients included the UK Ministry of Defence and the European Space Agency. He is the author of four novels including *The Quantum Thief* (winner of the 2012 Tähtivaeltaja Award for the best science fiction novel published in Finland and translated into more than twenty languages). His most recent book is *Summerland*, an alternate-history spy thriller in a world where the afterlife is real. His short fiction has been featured in *Slate*, *MIT Technology Review* and *The New York Times*.

Jakob Drud is a Danish author who currently lives in Aarhus, Denmark, with his two children. He's been writing for the last twenty years and loves fiction that surprises, brings new insights, and makes him laugh— something that the fantastic genres are perfect for. His first novel for children, titled *The Man from Sombra*, was published in 2022. Many of his stories can be read online, the links can be found at http://jakobdrud.com. On Twitter Jakob is @jakobdrud, if tweets about writing and life are your thing.

Johann Thorsson is an Icelandic author whose short stories have appeared in publications both in Icelandic and English, such as *Fireside Fiction* and *The Apex Book of World SF* series. His first novel, *Whitesands* from 2021, set in the United States, blends Nordic noir with the supernatural. He grew up partly in the Middle East and eastern Europe but now lives in Reykjavik with his wife, two kids and ever-decreasing space on his bookshelves. He can most often be found wasting time on Twitter as @johannthors

Johanna Sinisalo is a Finnish author and screenwriter who has won, among others, the Finlandia Prize and the James Tiptree, Jr. Award. Johanna has been called 'the queen of Finnish speculative fiction'. Much of her work deals with societal topics, such as equality and environmental issues. Johanna's writing has been translated into around twenty languages, of which four novels in English, all praised by readers and critics alike: the Tiptree-winner *Not Before Sundown* (U.S. edition *Troll–A Love Story*), *Birdbrain*, *The Blood of Angels*, and her latest novel from 2016, *The Core of the Sun*, which made the Tiptree honour list. Her novelette *Baby Doll* was shortlisted for the Theodore Sturgeon Memorial Award in 2008 and the Nebula in 2009. You can find several of Johanna's short stories in English in many anthologies such as *Year's Best Weird Fiction, Volume Four* (2017), and she has also edited *The Dedalus Book of Finnish Fantasy*, an anthology of Finnish speculative fiction. As a screenwriter, Johanna's most known work is the original story for the 2012 cult SF comedy movie *Iron Sky*.

John Ajvide Lindqvist is a Swedish author with a background as both a magician and a stand-up comedian. Today he's a well-known author with several acclaimed novels and short stories, several within horror and fantasy. His debut novel was *Låt den rätte komma in (Let the Right One In)*, in 2004, and his works include novel titles such as *Hanteringen av odöda (Handling the Undead)*, *Människohamn (Harbour)*, *Lilla stjärna (Little Star)*, and also the short story collection *Pappersväggar (Let the Old Dreams Die)*. 'Border', one of the short stories in this collection, was made into a feature film in 2019. Lindqvist was also a writer for the television series *Reuter & Skoog* (1999) and wrote the screenplays for Swedish Television's drama series *Kommissionen* (2005) and for the film *Let the Right One In*, based on his novel. His work has been awarded several times, especially in connection with the script for the film *Let the Right One In*, but also the Selma Lagerlöf Prize. His work has also been nominated for awards such as Tiptree, Hugo, BFA and Stoker. John is married to the author Mia Ajvide and lives in the archipelago of Roslagen, Sweden. Find out more on his website: www.johnajvidelindqvist.com

Karin Tidbeck is a Swedish author who lives and works in Malmö as a freelance writer and translator and writes speculative fiction in Swedish and English. They debuted in 2010 with the Swedish collection *Vem är Arvid Pekon?* Their English debut, the 2012 collection *Jagannath*, received the Crawford Award and was shortlisted for the World Fantasy Award. The novel *Amatka* was shortlisted for the Locus Award in 2018. Their 2021 novel, *The Memory Theater*, was named one of the best speculative fiction books of the year by *The New York Times*. Karin's short fiction is published at Tor.com, *Uncanny Magazine*, *Lightspeed* and more. They dedicate their free time to games, historical fencing and Forteana. Find them online at karintidbeck.com and on Instagram as @ktidbeck

Kaspar Colling Nielsen is a Danish author who debuted with *Mount København (Mount Copenhagen)* in 2010. The sequel was published in 2013—a futuristic narrative called *Den Danske Borgerkrig 2018-24 (The Danish Civil War 2018-24)*. Both works are on the borderline of novel and short story collection, where the grotesque, tragicomic, and social satirical intertwine in a unique form of narrative art. The topical *Det europæiske forår (The European Spring)* came out in 2017 and was shortlisted as the best foreign novel for the Prix du Livre Inter in France in 2019. His short story collection *Dengang dinosaurene var små (When the Dinosaurs Were Small)* was published in 2019, and the novel *Frelsen fra Hvidovre (Salvation from Hvidovre)* in 2021. Kaspar's books have been translated into twenty-one languages.

Lene Kaaberbøl is a Danish writer whose work primarily consists of children's fantasy series and crime fiction for adults. She's the author of the book series *The Shamer Chronicles, Katriona, W.I.T.C.H., Nina Borg* (with Agnete Friis), *Madelein Karno*, and *Wild Witch*. Several of her books have been made into movies (such as *The Shamer's Daughter*), and her *Wild Witch* book series provided the basis for a Danish children's fantasy film of the same name. Lene received the Nordic Children's Book Prize in 2004. In 2009 Lene, and her co-author Agnete Friis, were awarded the Harald Mogensen Prize by the Danish Criminal Academy (Det danske Kriminalakademi, DKA) for the novel *The Boy in the Suitcase*.

Margrét Helgadóttir is a Norwegian-Icelandic author and anthologist living in Oslo, Norway. Her short fiction appears in many venues, such as *Slate*, *Luna Station Quarterly*, *Girl at the End of the World*, and *Sunspot Jungle*, to name a few. Her debut book—*The Stars Seem So Far Away*—was a finalist at the British Fantasy Awards 2016, and is an apocalyptic road tale set in a far-future Arctic world. Margrét is the editor of the anthology *Winter Tales* (2016) and the anthology series *Fox Spirit Books of Monsters*, seven volumes published between 2014 and 2020. Three volumes were shortlisted for the British Fantasy Awards as Best Anthology (2016, 2017 and 2018), and Margrét was also awarded *Starburst Magazine*'s Brave New Words Award in 2018 for her editorial work on *Pacific Monsters*. Read more on her website: https://margrethelgadottir.wordpress.com

Maria Haskins is a Swedish-Canadian writer and reviewer of speculative fiction, who currently lives just outside Vancouver, Canada, with a husband, two kids, a snake, several birds, and a very large black dog. Maria's work has appeared in *The Best Horror of the Year Volume 13*, *Strange Horizons*, *Black Static*, *Interzone*, *Fireside*, *Beneath Ceaseless Skies*, *Flash Fiction Online*, *Mythic Delirium*, *Shimmer*, *Cast of Wonders*, and elsewhere. Her short story collection *Six Dreams About* *the Train* was published by Trepidatio Publishing in 2021. Find out more on Maria's website: mariahaskins.com, or follow her on Twitter, where she is @mariahaskins.

Rakel Helmsdal is a Faroese multi-artist. She has so far published twenty-five books (novels, short story collections and picture books), as well as plays, short stories, and poems. Rakel sees herself as a storyteller for all age groups, and she chooses the medium—texts, plays, poems, pictures, sculptures—depending on what she feels that the story requires. Rakel is the co-author of the book series *Little Monster and Big Monster*, together with Icelandic author and illustrator Áslaug Jónsdóttir and Swedish author Kalle Güettler. The books have so far been published in nineteen languages. Rakel's works have been nominated five times for the Nordic Council of Ministers' Children and Youth Literature Prize. Her novel *Hon, sum róði eftir ælaboganum (She Rowed After the Rainbow)*, from 2014, received the West Nordic Children and Youth Literature Prize 2016. She has also been nominated for the ALMA Award (Astrid Lindgren Memorial Award) on four occasions.

Tone Almhjell is a Norwegian author who writes fantasy in both English and Norwegian. She has a master's degree in English Literature from the University of Oslo. She was working as a journalist when, in a fit of bravery and/or madness, she decided to quit her job, sell her flat, and write fiction full-time. Her debut novel, *The Twistrose Key*, was first published in the U.S. in 2013 by Penguin but has since been published all over the world.

The novel, a middle-grade portal fantasy, was very well received. Among other accolades, it was named a Kirkus Best Book of the Year as well as one of the best debuts for young readers in 2013 by the American Booksellers Association. The companion book, *Thornghost*, also received great reviews and was nominated to ARK's award for children's books in 2016. Tone currently lives in Oslo, Norway, with her husband, two sweet kids, and two stubborn cats. Her story in this anthology, 'The Cormorant', is inspired by a fairy tale from Northern Norway by Regine Normann. It's Tone's first story for adults.

Thore Hansen is a Norwegian author, illustrator, and cartoonist. Hansen debuted with the short story collection *Grimaser (Grimaces)* in 1975 and has since published many books for children and adults—almost fifty in total. He is known for his characteristic illustrations, and in addition to his own publications, he has also illustrated several books written by other authors. He is particularly well-known for his collaboration with Tor Åge Bringsværd on the tales of Ruffen and *Det blå folket (The Blue People)*, among others. Hansen has won several prizes for his work, including The Norwegian Ministry of Church and Education's Cartoon Prize (1980), and the Norwegian Ministry of Culture and Church's Prize for Children's and Young Adult Literature—a total of five times, the Nordic School Librarian Association's Children's Book Prize (2002), and the Book Art Prize (2004). In 2020, he won the Norwegian Cartoonist Forum's honorary prize, 'Sproing'.

Tor Åge Bringsværd is a Norwegian author who writes both for children and adults. He is the recipient of several awards as an author and playwright, including the Norwegian Critics Prize for Literature, the Ibsen Prize, and the Arts Council Norway Honorary Award. He has been translated into several languages (despite his name having two impossible Norwegian letters that almost no one outside Norway knows how to pronounce). He lives with his wife in a small village in southern Norway, where a river occasionally flows through their garden. While there are few fish in the river, there are, on the other hand, ducks and beavers. Beneath a big apple tree at one end of the garden, Tor Åge spends most of the year writing in his office cabin, complete with a weather pig (Nasse Nøff, a.k.a. Piglet) on the roof and a lively badger family beneath the floor. When the cold comes and ice freezes on the sidewalks, he prefers to escape south to Lanzarote, that blessed pile of rocks off the coast of Africa. His life motto is: Coincidences are our friends.

CONTRIBUTORS' COPYRIGHT NOTICES

FIND US ONLINE!

www.rebellionpublishing.com

/solarisbooks   /solarisbks   /solarisbooks

SIGN UP TO OUR NEWSLETTER!

rebellionpublishing.com/newsletter

YOUR REVIEWS MATTER!

Enjoy this book? Got something to say?

Leave a review on Amazon, GoodReads or with your favourite bookseller and let the world know!

NEW SUNS

ORIGINAL SPECULATIVE FICTION BY
PEOPLE OF COLOR EDITED BY NISI SHAWL

INTRODUCTION BY LEVAR BURTON
INCLUDING STORIES BY INDRAPRAMIT DAS
E LILY YU, REBECCA ROANHORSE, ANIL MENON,
JAYMEE GOH AND MANY OTHERS

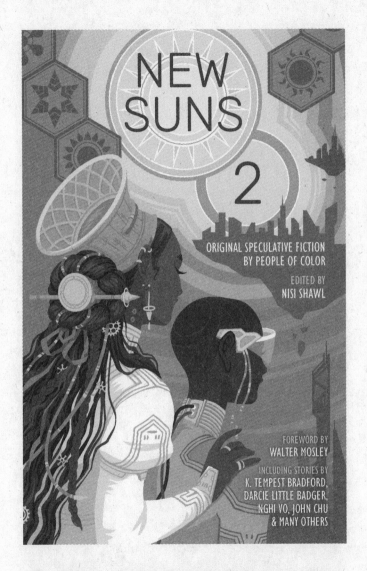

NEW SUNS

2

ORIGINAL SPECULATIVE FICTION
BY PEOPLE OF COLOR

EDITED BY
NISI SHAWL

FOREWORD BY
WALTER MOSLEY

INCLUDING STORIES BY
K. TEMPEST BRADFORD,
DARCIE LITTLE BADGER,
NGHI VO, JOHN CHU
& MANY OTHERS

☉ SOLARISBOOKS.COM

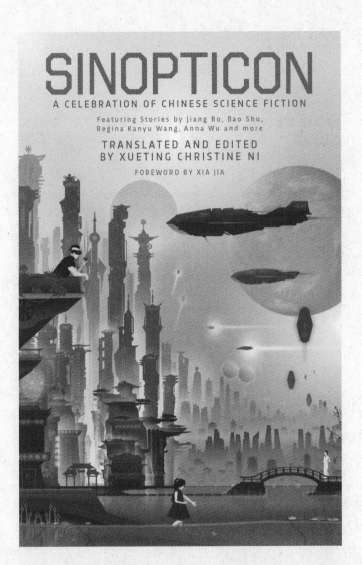

SINOPTICON

A CELEBRATION OF CHINESE SCIENCE FICTION

Featuring Stories by Jiang Bo, Bao Shu,
Regina Kanyu Wang, Anna Wu and more

TRANSLATED AND EDITED
BY XUETING CHRISTINE NI

FOREWORD BY XIA JIA

◐ SOLARISBOOKS.COM